The Fortunicity of Birdie Dalal

The Fortunicity of Birdie Dalal

CLAIRE DUENDE

TRYPHENA PRESS

www.tryphenapress.com

All characters and events in this publication, other than those clearly in the public domain, are fictitious and any resemblance to real persons, living or dead, is purely coincidental

ISBN: 978-1-9162728-1-1

A CIP catalogue record for this book is available from the British Library

To Philip, Charlie and Emma

and James - *forever in our hearts*

PROLOGUE

This is the story of how I came to England and the events that made me who I am today. People say I am Indian and in a way that is true. They also say I'm from India and I tell them they are mistaken. I was born near the source of the Nile and I grew up in the lush hills of my father's tea plantation in Uganda. So, I suppose you could call me Ugandan and that's what I called myself, until I realised that people aren't really interested in what you call yourself. They will call you what they wish, and the best thing is not to call yourself anything. Just be.

CHAPTER 1

How do we know? How do we ever know who we will meet and the part they will play in our lives? Walking along a busy street and a soft waft of air from a passing stranger tickles the skin on your forearm. Perhaps, within moments, that stranger will reach out and pull you out of the way of a passing car - or in years to come, that very same being will be complicit in bringing an end to your existence. Or you to theirs. How do any of us know where the strands of our lives are interwoven?

It was June 1971 when I first met Sabu.

The sun seemed painfully bright that day and the colours of the saris and local African dress especially dazzling. It was the first time I had ventured out of the house after weeks of crippling sickness. Nanda assured me that I was only extra sensitive to the light because I had been shut away in my bedroom for so long. According to my cousin what I needed was an outing to take my mind off my condition, to enjoy some fresh air and wipe the cobwebs away. At first this sounded appealing, but then I realised that our opinions of fresh air were very different. Whereas I would have enjoyed a slow walk around the Makerere Botanical Gardens, Nanda's idea was a visit to downtown Kampala where we could do some 'serious shopping' as she put it. Since I had moved to the city following my recent marriage, Nanda had enveloped me in her world of shopping sprees, cocktails and swimming parties with her numerous girlfriends. It was not the sort of life I was comfortable with, not only because of the expense, but also because female frivolities had never been part of my life, until now. And at this moment, after weeks of lying on my bed in a darkened room, overwhelmed by sickness and demons, watching the ceiling fan go round and round, the thought of her whirlwind life left me feeling as lank as a dried out mango leaf.

'You need to get out,' Nanda assured me as she bundled me into her chauffeur-driven car that morning. My cousin had been extremely attentive ever since she had learned of my condition and, as usual, was an expert on the subject, even though she had never experienced the joys of morning sickness and was not even married yet.

'What you need is a good piece of retail therapy,' she advised.

I donned my sunglasses and looked out over the hills of Kampala as the driver set the Mercedes into gear and we headed down towards the commercial centre. It had rained during the night and the air that streamed through the open window was fresh and clear. Nanda was right. It was good to get out.

After spending nearly an hour in the commercial centre, we headed on to the Indian quarter where the smell of pungent cooking spices greeted us, growing more intense as we entered the melee of shoppers and stall holders. The buzz of voices became louder and louder, until it was as if a swarm of bees resided within my skull. By the time we had reached Asita's Sari Shop I was swimming at the bottom of a cauldron of colour and noise and smell, and terrible overwhelming heat. I grabbed Nanda's arm and led her down a small shaded alley between the sari shop and Mr Kamar's hardware store, my sole aim being to find a quiet spot where I could either surrender to nature or, at least to sit and drink in some air until the feeling passed.

I sat down on an old wooden crate then draped my head between my legs, rhythmically taking in long deep breaths. Nanda stood by my side, patiently stroking my shoulder until, after a while, her attention was caught by something further around the corner to the rear of the shop. Still keeping within my sight, she tiptoed to the far corner of the outbuildings, seemingly intrigued by what she saw. With her arms folded across her stomach, she stood watching a display of some kind; then looking back at me briefly she took a couple of steps further on, as if she was straining to listen, her head cocked to one side and a smile on her lips.

After several minutes I started to feel normal again and, giving in to my curiosity, I joined Nanda to see what she was watching so intently.

On a large patch of flat ground immediately behind Mr Kamar's hardware store stood several people under a cotton awning, all engrossed as they watched a small boy standing on a stool set in front of a large colourful rug. He looked familiar but I couldn't think where I had seen him before. Wearing a sky blue turban, with a large fake jewel in the centre, his smooth brown torso was exposed but on his legs he wore a pair of voluminous trousers in a light muslin fabric. Altogether he looked like a character from the story he was recounting. His outfit was even topped off with an elaborate belt and what looked like a curved sword in the holder attached to his side.

The boy was midway through telling an elaborate tale in perfect English involving a wicked genie, flying carpets and a beautiful girl who needed rescuing.

Although my people have a built-in weakness for a good story, it was remarkable to see just how this little boy kept the audience spellbound with his sheer magnetism and beauty. His arms swooped, his eyes grew as big as saucers and the whole timing of his rendition was impeccable. Unusually, for a boy so young, his voice had a rich timbre which seemed to come, not just from his lungs, but somewhere deeper - from the belly of his talent.

Nanda and I approached the makeshift tent so we could hear the tale better and stood just under the sharp square of shade. Within moments, a sly-looking youth came up to us and shook a wooden dish, inferring we were to add to the few coins already lying at the bottom. I fumbled in my purse and added a fifty cent coin. Obviously unsatisfied, the boy looked me directly in the eye and raised the dish higher, shaking it slightly, just below my chin. Nanda, irritated, waved him away.

It wasn't difficult to fall into the thread of the story and soon we were caught up in the carefully crafted suspense. Not once did the boy falter or hesitate. Finally he built the tale to a crescendo so that at the end everyone sighed and laughed, some clapping with satisfaction and relief. At this point many looked at their watches, shook their heads, and set off on their way as the boy scooped and bowed elaborately.

The boy appeared to be satisfied with his act and bowing again to the few remaining onlookers, he went to a large jug of water that was set at the side and drank in long gulps. Finally, he tilted his head back and poured the remaining water over his face.

Nanda and I watched in fascination until once again I felt a sour taste in my mouth and, swaying slightly, reached out to my cousin's arm.

'That was a wonderful story,' Nanda called out to the boy. 'Please, would it be possible for my cousin to sit down on your little stage? She's not feeling well and needs to rest.'

In a moment the boy had leaped forward and led me to his stool which he brushed down before guiding me to sit.

'You are not well?' he asked, a concerned look upon his face. 'Do you feel the urgent need to vomit?'

I nodded weakly.

'Wait here,' he said and darted down the alley leaving a cloud of dust behind him as he headed towards the main street. After only a few minutes he returned with a bottle that he held aloft as a prize. The glass glistened with cool condensation and there was an amber liquid inside.

'Ginger soda,' he announced. 'The absolute genuine best drink to squash the vomit feeling.' He deftly removed the top and handed me the bottle with the panache of a bartender.

Slowly I sipped the contents until my nausea passed.

'See,' he said proudly. 'It works.'

'Indeed it does, yes. Thank you. What's your name?'

'I am Sabu.'

'Sabu?'

'Yes, Sabu. Of the great Sabu.'

'You mean Sabu is your father?'

'No, I am Sabu, born again of the great Sabu.'

'And who is Sabu?'

'You do not know Sabu! You have not seen the greatest films of all time? You have not seen Elephant Boy? Or The Thief of Bagdad or The Arabian Nights?'

'The films? Yes, I think I have. They are old films.'

'Yes, great Hollywood films. It was a long time ago when I did those films.'

'Oh, I think I see. You are saying that you believe you are Sabu reborn here. Now?'

The boy nodded proudly, his back straight, his bearing regal.

'Nani said the minute the great Sabu died, I was delivered, plop, onto the blanket of my dearly beloved mother. Sadly, she never held me in her arms and never knew that I was the great Sabu reborn through her. A wonderful miracle indeed.'

'Your mother?'

'Oh no, my mother was not the miracle part. My mother was very sad, or I should say it was very sad about my mother. But my nani would always rock me to sleep and tell me tales of my big adventures in my life before and promise me that this life will be even greater.'

'And you think that is true?'

'Oh yes indeed I do. What I do here,' he made a large swooping motion with his arm. 'Here is just the beginning.' He leaned forward in a conspiratorial fashion and spoke close to my ear. 'Here is where I learn my craft.'

I nodded and took a last sip of the ginger drink.

'And what of your father?'

'My father? Oh, my father is not of importance,' and he waved his hand as if shooing a fly.

'So you live with your grandmother?'

His head rocked from side to side as he considered his answer.

'Well, yes… And no.'

'Meaning?'

'My grandmother has joined my dear departed mother, not long ago. But she has been a very dear person to me, and she has made me strong.'

'So where do you live?' asked Nanda.

'I have friends. Sometimes I stay here, sometimes there. But I am happy. I am fine.' He shot us a dazzling smile.

We learned that on market days he would set up his awning behind Mr Kamar's shop where many of his regular audience would visit, always expecting a different story and never being disappointed. Some evenings he would tell his tales at the railway station, although the sound of the engines and piercing whistles would often drown his voice, which he didn't like at all. Not one bit.

He told us that the youth who collected the money was called Kartik and he was as sly as a hyena, although this piece of information was delivered with a smile and a shrug.

I looked around to see if Kartik was close enough to hear this comment, but he was nowhere in sight.

'He's supposed to keep only one quarter of the money he collects but sometimes I see him slip some more coins into his pocket when he thinks that I'm not looking.'

'And don't you think that is dishonest?'

Another shrug.

'Better to have a snake in your hand and know he is a snake - that way there are no surprising surprises! I always watch him from the side of my eye. I need him and he needs me, and we watch. We are always watching.'

Nanda agreed that this was wise as she looked at her wrist and gave a start.

'We must go. Kenzi will be waiting with the car. Are you well enough to go now?'

'Perfectly well, thank you,' I said smiling at the boy. 'Thank you for your magical remedy.'

Sabu gave a sweeping bow and his turban nearly brushed the dusty ground.

We had said our farewells and Nanda and I had just turned the corner onto the main street when I remembered that I had never offered to pay for the drink. I hesitated, wondering if we should return but then no, something gave me the impression that he would have refused payment and I didn't want to offend him. So we continued on our way.

Over the following weeks it became the highlight of our regular shopping trips to visit Sabu's makeshift tent and listen to his elaborate tales of tragedy, love and triumph. Every time we made our visits the story was different, and the boy would deliver his rendition with such talent and passion that sometimes I wondered if he really was the reincarnation of the great actor, Sabu.

Upon our arrival we would be acknowledged with a slight nod and the mildest of smiles, but his voice would not falter, and the fable would continue without the least form of hesitation.

After Sabu's story telling we would sit and chat on his colourful rug. I would take some delicacies that we would share - sometimes small spiced honey cakes that my housemaid Mirembe would bake, or fresh mangos and papayas that I would bring from the farm. And I would always bring drink, usually ginger soda in full honour of his first kindness.

When the last of the cakes was consumed and we were tired from the heat of the day, Nanda's old chauffeur Kenzi would come to collect us from the nearby street. We would sink into the soft leather seats and let the breeze through the windows gently pummel our faces as we headed towards the outskirts of the city. From the oppressive dusty streets of Kampala we would glide seamlessly to the compound where I lived with Jack. He would be away at the university for the day so I would kick off my shoes by the front door and pad along the cool tiles to our bedroom, closing the shutters, before I flopped onto our marital bed for my afternoon rest.

As my body changed so did the pressure in the country. The new president, Idi Amin Dada, now had an iron grip on the land. There were more soldiers on the streets and increasing tales of the brutal torture and murder of native Ugandans, especially those from the Acholi and Lango tribes. The locals would often just call him Dada, a seemingly affectionate name for such a harsh and vicious leader.

There were rumours of grumblings in the presidential

palace. Amin resented the Asians for their supreme role in business. He said we had too much power and controlled too much of the wealth of his country. Asians whispered quietly in corners saying this was how Hitler had felt about the Jews before the war. Some were already making plans to leave Uganda.

Over the weeks I became aware that often, when we visited Sabu's shelter, there would be two or three soldiers standing on the edge of the back alley, listening intently to the boy's tales. Their dark faces would mirror the emotions of the story, looking genuinely anxious when it seemed that all was lost, their shoulders relaxing when the intricate fables were satisfyingly resolved. Although their presence overshadowed the events, being a visible reminder of Amin's tentacles threading through our everyday lives, usually the soldiers stood back and observed in good humour. Apart from one. He would stand rigid and unsmiling, watching Sabu's every move. Through all the highs and lows of the stories, this man's face would remain expressionless and he would never take his heavily lidded eyes off the boy, his only action being the occasional reptilian lick of his tight dark lips.

As the date of my child's birth approached, and the country became more volatile, I grew nervous for Sabu and pleaded with him to come and stay at Rutubasana.

'I won't be visiting for a while, Sabu and I want to know that you're safe. Why don't you come and stay on my father's farm? You could help a bit and you could go to school in Jinja. Don't you want to go to school?'

'Oh no, indeed not,' he insisted. 'School work is too boring. I know all my reading and writing. My nani was very good to me. Every day I went to school, every day with my board and chalk. Very good writing I have. But it's all much better in my head.' He patted his temple and grinned.

'But I'm not happy with these soldiers who watch you all the time, Sabu. Things are changing in Uganda.'

'Don't worry about me, Miss Bulbul. You never need to worry about me. I am the great Sabu and look here, I have my magic carpet. I can just fly away!'

He looked up at me with his large dark eyes framed by thick lashes and shot me a radiant smile.

Sabu had a way of being so completely sure of everything that his certainty became infectious and I convinced myself that I was over-reacting. But I should never have listened to Sabu. He was only a child and he couldn't see the dark cloud moving slowly across Uganda.

Chapter 2

The narrow bed has squeaky springs and the horsehair mattress feels lumpy under my back. If I move my foot more than an inch, the sheet that greets it is icy cold, so I stay rigid and look up at the ceiling which is illuminated by the yellow light filtering through the curtains. My nose is numb so I pull the sheet half over my face for warmth but then it gets damp with my breath, so I pull it down again. Everything is cold and hard. The linoleum floor, the metal windows, row upon row of black framed beds.

Moh sleeps soundly in the cot by my bed and I can just make out the lump of my sleeping mother-in-law, Ashika, a few feet away.

How can she sleep? How can any of these women sleep? Perhaps it's because many of them have been here for a while already. To them it's just another routine in their new lives, but to me it's my first night in this strange, foreign land. I try to shield my thoughts from the vast, barren future that lies ahead.

Strange to think that only yesterday we were still in our old world, the sun shining as usual at Entebbe airport, the heat baking our skin as we walked across the bright runway. For a moment I hesitated at the top of the airplane steps and turned towards the glistening waters of Lake Victoria in the distance. Flashing images of happy sailing trips with Nanda and her parents, dangling our feet in the cool waters as we sat on the edge of her father's boat, the time I lost my front tooth when I bit into a passion fruit, my Uncle Deepak losing his temper when he discovered we had fed most of the chapatis to the fish. For the last minute I drank in the warm air of my country until Jack took my arm and gently led me into the dark interior of the plane.

One of the women mumbles something in her sleep but I can't make out the words. She turns over and the bed creaks.

I wonder how Jack is in the men's dormitory. This is a very different England to the one he knew in Cambridge. He would have led a privileged life as a student in one of the best universities in the country with his grand rooms and his society dinners. It's like a game of snakes and ladders - hit the snake and slither right to the bottom. This is our lives.

It seems like a lifetime ago since Idi Amin made his announcement and Dicken, our dear American friend, calmly explained the scenario.

'You've got to appreciate, Birdie, that politics is just grown children playing in a large playground. What you've got here is Idi Amin, the big bully boy in the schoolyard who comes along to the teeter-totter, or "see-saw" as you call it. All you little Asians are sitting on the end but what does he see that's so tempting at the other end? A great big expanse of air. So he gets his great fat backside and plonks it down on the plank. Wham! All of you Asians go flying in the air like ants and he ends up free to do what he likes with your businesses and money.'

For a split second the idea of Amin's trousers stretched over his ample posterior was a comical vision.

'But I can't understand it. Why?'

'Because he can,' he replied. 'Because he's resented you all for a long time. It's smash and grab. Of course he's got it all wrong. He thinks that he can just give your businesses to unskilled Ugandans and they'll be able to succeed but they won't have your experience and they won't have your nous.'

'What's nous?'

'Know-how, cleverness. It's not just about a business being worth a certain amount of money. It's the years of management that's at the heart of each one of them. And he's planning on cutting out the hearts.'

'And us? What will happen to all of us? We have to leave everything behind! One suitcase. That's all we can take. One suitcase and fifty pounds. How long will that last us!'

'I know, Birdie. It's not fair but it's a fact and you're going to have to get your head around it.'

'We could always refuse to go. We're Ugandans. My passport says I am Ugandan. Pappa's passport says he's Ugandan. He was born here. He's getting old. He refuses to go.'

'None of you has a choice, you'll have to leave. If you want to live, you must go. As Jack's got a British passport, you'll probably go to England. Your brother, Sanjay, will most likely stay in the States with his job. I'm not sure what your father will do. You'll need to see if you can get him a British passport so he can go with you. Or Sanjay will have to arrange something. You can't stay here. Amin's got a blood lust and there are rumours that he's building concentration camps for you lot. You should get out. Follow the rules, get out and start a new life.'

It was easy for Dicken to say with his white skin and his Texan drawl. Americans can go anywhere with their Coca Cola and Elvis Presley. My people are insignificant in the world's eyes. We may as well be buried in the red dust of Uganda.

Everything about our arrival at Heathrow today was stripes of grey. The dark grey of the drizzling clouds, the glistening grey of the wet concrete runway. Slotted between these lay the cold damp air. So cold.

Inside the terminal the airport officials and security staff herded us methodically into areas cordoned off with thick rope. Some of them wore uniforms and the same blank faces as the soldiers from Uganda. But there was something different. For a while I couldn't work out what it was. It wasn't their white skin, it was something else. Then it came to me. Not one of them was carrying a weapon. Strange, when we seem to have been looking down rifle barrels for the past ten months. Perhaps we are safe after all. If the English guards walk around without weapons it must be a peaceful country and that, in itself, must be good.

We progressed from one queue to another. Passport control, x-rays, vaccination certificates. Anything to declare?

'We've just been expelled from our country and brought the only possessions we have in the world. You want to know if we have anything to declare?' Jack retorted.

'Those are the rules,' the guard responded, his face expressionless.

'Haven't they loosened those rules slightly for refugees?'

'Sorry sir, rules are rules.'

Luckily Jack was oblivious to the gold bangles that both his mother and I had pushed to the top of our forearms and tucked under long sleeves. We were given the stamp of approval and sent through to an area in the Arrivals zone. There we waited for transport to take us to our new lodgings.

The family waiting next to us were heading north to Yorkshire; the mother told me it was the nearest place to Leicester they could choose.

'Why Leicester?'

'Well, it was very lucky,' she explained. 'We saw an advertisement in a local newspaper in Kampala. It said,

"Don't come to Leicester, we have too many Asians already." So we thought, well, we've never heard of Leicester before but if there are a lot of Asians there already, that is a good sign and it would feel good to be among our own people. So we've decided to live in Leicester. It's agreed. It may take a bit of time to find our way in with work and such but we have decided, so that is it.'

It must be comforting to nurse a plan.

It's the first morning of our new lives in England.

Moh wakes happy and chirpy. He is fascinated by the morning ritual of the other inhabitants of our dormitory. His large dark eyes follow every movement and for a while it seems to take his mind off his stomach, but not for long and soon he starts to whimper. Ashika takes him from me muttering something about finding where we can heat some baby food. As usual, when it comes to my son, I let her take control, and I stay behind to tidy our belongings, storing a few clothes in the small chest of drawers beside my bed.

Among the occupants of the room are two young women who welcome me warmly. They ask to hear my story. After a brief summary, I learn that they are sisters from Kampala and arrived with their parents six weeks ago. The older one, Shai, seems to be about my age. She stands tall and boney with a slow and easy manner, Her younger sister, Padma, is shorter with quicker movements and speech. They say their father, who is housed in the men's quarters, used to own a small shop on the outskirts of the city and their mother was a seamstress. But that was in the past. Nowadays their mother, Neha, spends most of her time working in the camp kitchen.

I learn that this building is usually used as student accommodation and that there are around 250 of us being housed here. It's supposed to be a transitory camp but some residents have already been here for several weeks; few have moved on to other camps. They explain that we are not all treated equally. Some of the residents don't possess papers and are called 'stateless'. They are known as detainees and don't have the same freedom as other residents, only being allowed to go out of the camp for one hour a day. They also have to work for their keep. They are the ones, the girls say, who we will see doing the menial jobs - always keen to please in case they're sent back to Uganda.

There are set times for meals and strict rules to adhere to. Two kitchens function and we are to eat in separate dining areas - one for those who eat meat (although beef and pork are never produced) and another for those who are vegetarian. The problem is, they say, that up until recently the vegetarian meals have mainly consisted of rice, bread and potatoes with hardly any fresh fruit or vegetables. Residents were becoming sick and complaints were made. These complaints irritated the camp administrator who accused the refugees of being ungrateful but, eventually, a committee was formed to ensure adequately nutritious meals are being served.

'The British do like their committees,' says Shai.

'So, committees as well as queues!' I remark.

'Oh yes,' they giggle. 'They love their queues. Everything has to be orderly. Even a shower rota - you are only allowed a full shower every other day because they say that they don't have enough water. It's a strange thing to say, when all it seems to do here is rain!'

'And then we have to queue in the dining rooms for every meal. And of course we need to queue to see any of the officials who are able to help us in any way, so we can get somewhere to live, or find jobs.'

I ask why they've already been here for six weeks when, even now, we haven't yet reached the compulsory deadline for evacuation.

'Pappa was worried that soon England would say "We're full up, no more Asians can come in." That's why he booked our tickets very quickly. We are lucky he managed to sell the goods from his shop to one of his Ugandan friends, before the soldiers came to take it over. Then he went very quickly to the travel agent and booked our tickets. Quick as a flash, or "Bob's your uncle," as they say in England.'

I'm tired and overwhelmed and lack the energy to ask why the English say their uncles are called Bob.

I find Jack waiting for me at the bottom of the stairs and we go through to the dining room where Ashika is feeding Moh. After breakfast we're herded into the gloomy common room where a tall, lank man stands on the stage at the end of the room. His hair is mostly grey with only a few streaks of blond remaining and his skin is pallid and dry. After a good deal of throat clearing and fumbling with sheets of paper, he eventually places his notes on the wooden stand at the front of the stage. It reminds me of our school assemblies. Should we sit? Are his shoulders bowed by his concerns of what he can possibly do with so many foreigners invading his country?

'First of all, I would like to say a big welcome to all our newcomers.'

I look around and see there are only a handful of us.

'I know this is all very strange to you and I hope you are all able to understand my English. If not, well, I'm afraid we don't have a translator today but I'm sure your fellow residents will help you later and will explain what I've just said.'

He then goes on to tell us that we are situated in the district of Kensington, West London, an affluent area with a combination of residential homes as well as shops. In fact, he informs us, we are extremely lucky to have found ourselves in London rather than some remote airfield as have so many of our kinsmen. This way we will be close to where everything happens and we will be well set up to find ourselves jobs.

'I've heard, and I know it to be true, that you are all good workers and I'm sure you would like to get settled as soon as possible so you can start earning an income for your families. Remember, we're here to help you. Please raise any concerns you may have with the Resettlement Board and we will look into it forthwith.'

I try to remind myself that we are free people, that somewhere, out there, beyond the metal windows and the grey buildings, there will be a life for us. Maybe even sunlight. Shai and Padma's explanation of the camp was much more fun and human than this man's voice that rattles like dry stones in my head.

When we leave the common room we are shown around the camp grounds. The precinct consists of two large concrete buildings surrounded by a high brick wall, with a pair of large black wrought iron gates at the entrance. I notice how close we are to the normal London street beyond. An old lady passes by, leading a small fluffy haired dog; they both have blue tinted hair and the dog wears a tartan coat. Following shortly behind her is a long-haired youth with a shaggy coat and then two businessmen wearing suits and carrying briefcases. They carry black umbrellas but it's disappointing to see that they don't wear bowler hats like Mr Banks in Mary Poppins.

CHAPTER 3

Rutubasana. She is the song of my soul. With her undulating hills verdant and lush, capped by translucent blue skies above. She is the flashing white smiles of my father's workers, the deep rhythmic songs as we pluck the tea tips and wend our way down to the sorting sheds. She's the earthy smell of the evening air as the birds come back to roost. The cries of the galagos and rasp of the cicadas during the warm velvet nights, the polished dark floorboards of our high-ceilinged bungalow, the veranda, with clear wide vistas across my father's land. The laughter, the warmth, the breath deep in my lungs.

She is home. She is lost.

My grandfather bought the first five acres of this promising farmland when he was in his thirties. At the time he had a trading business in Jinja, but it is said that Rutubasana caught at his heartstrings and after he purchased it he barely left the land throughout his life. Initially he built a small single storey building in a dip at the end of the red scar track that now runs down to the sorting sheds. Over time, the farm prospered, he married and bought more land, every few years increasing the acreage and employing more workers. The farm grew and so did the activity in the processing buildings. One day my grandfather looked up at a quiet plateau further up on the hill where the evening sun reflected off the glossy leaves of the mango trees, and that is when he saw a Great Blue Turaco sitting on a lone branch. Taking the sighting of this lucky bird to be a good omen, my grandfather then announced to his wife that this was where that he would create their new home, up on the ledge where the evening breezes could be harnessed as he looked over his land at the end of every day.

And so it was that our family home was built with nothing spared in the attention to detail. It was to be airy and cool without sacrificing light or views with all five bedrooms leading onto verandas or balconies and each equipped with large ceiling fans that whirred and creaked as they grew older. The two bathrooms were installed with the best that Ugandan plumbing would allow and even the kitchen, which was rarely used by the family, was fully fitted with the best ovens and two large sinks sunk into the stone worktop.

My grandfather planned for a large family, but it was a sadness that only two fully formed children came to see the light of Rutubasana. Twelve years passed between my father and his younger sister. On each of those years, at least one floral offering would be placed in front of the little shrine under the jacaranda tree.

My father married late and also was only to have two children, our family life being cut short by the death of my mother. Two children only. My brother who took no interest in the farm and me, the daydreamer. Too impulsive, too independent, too wayward.

Dicken came into our lives shortly after my mother's death when I was around seven years old. I'm not sure how my father and he first met but, despite the gap in their ages, they had an easy friendship based on their love of nature and a shared sense of humour. I imagine my father was lonely. Not only had he recently lost his wife, but he now shied away from his usual social contacts and visitors seldom came to our farm. We all enjoyed Dicken's company and I know that Sanjay and I grew to love him as we would an uncle.

In the warm evenings the two men would sit out on the veranda for hours, sipping their scotch and sodas discussing world politics, music, wildlife and literature. At night I would hear the mumble of their conversations as I lay in bed, but I could rarely make out the individual words. Their low voices, mixed with the rhythm of the cicadas and the purr of the ceiling fan, was the lullaby of my childhood and I felt safe and secure. I was where I belonged.

Our American friend worked as a guide on wildlife tours, sometimes taking tourists through the rain forests and out onto the savannah to see the larger wildlife such as elephants and lions, at other times leading them out on to the marshes to survey the huge array of richly coloured birds. Although Dicken would take a rifle as protection, he would refuse to take any individual who wished to do harm to a living creature. He would insist that only cameras were allowed, turning away in disgust from wads of banknotes offered by drooling trophy hunters.

Sometimes he would take tourists as far as the mountains near Rwanda to see the gorillas in the forest where they would stay in huts built into the trees and trek through virgin territory. One day, he said, he would take me there but for the time being the Mabira rainforest would have to do. Often, when we were young, my father would let Dicken take Sanjay and me out for the day. We would sit in the back of his old jeep, with its stars and stripes painted on the rear door, bouncing around on the seat as the basic suspension of the vehicle tried to compensate for the rough ground.

Sanjay would always be more interested in the mechanics of the jeep, giving little attention to the wildlife, but Dicken could see my excitement when we witnessed such creatures as cheetahs, rhinoceros or swathes of multi-coloured birds. Eventually it was just me and Dicken, and I would sit in the front passenger seat where at times I would close my eyes and hold my fingertips out to the breeze, drinking in the deep green smells of the jungle - the earth, roots and leaves of my beloved Uganda.

As well as the connection through our love of wildlife, it was Dicken who fed my passion for books and film, often taking me and Sanjay to the cinema in Jinja to see the latest Hollywood movies. There we saw films such as 20,000 Leagues under the Sea, High Society, African Queen and Casablanca. We would always stop at the kiosk outside the building first to buy a bag of salted popcorn and a drink of soda before entering the gloom of the interior, blinking madly to help our eyes adjust to the dark.

After trips away Dicken would often give me books left by the tourists and although he tried to censor them before passing them on, he was not very diligent. Some novels were quite explicit for a growing girl. At least it helped me learn some of the facts of life, a subject that was never mentioned by the teachers at school and was certainly avoided by my father.

From time to time we would ask our friend where he came from and what had brought him to Uganda but he would always come up with a different story until we came to learn that we should just sit back and listen to the tale without giving it any credence. Despite his woven untruths I knew he was a good and loyal friend, and this he would prove further in the years to come.

Chapter 4

'You need some socks or warm tights,' says Jack when he sees the goose pimples on my legs.

'I'm fine. In any case Shai and Padma tell me that there's a charity that comes around with donated clothes. I think they come on Friday mornings. That's only two days away.'

Jack grunts his disapproval.

'Maybe a coat or a jumper but who wants to wear second-hand underwear? Anyway,' he adds, 'we've been stuck here for three days and it's about time we had a look at our surroundings - the big world of London.' There's a new tone to his voice, prickly and resentful.

I relent and it's agreed we will leave the next morning after breakfast. Jack's mother doesn't want to face the cold and says she'll stay behind with Moh. As usual, she acts as our son's main carer and is concerned about his routine. The outing will disturb his morning sleep, and in any case, we don't have a pushchair and he's too heavy to carry very far.

I can't decide how to dress in the morning. Although I would usually wear western clothes in Uganda, the clothes I've brought are too lightweight and flimsy for this London winter. Finally, I select a pair of cotton trousers, two shirts, a cardigan and then, just as I'm leaving our dormitory, I dart back to grab a dupatta scarf for extra warmth. On my feet I wear my plimsolls with some short white socks.

We set out from the black wrought iron gates of the residency and walk down the hill towards Kensington High Street where in front of us we can see two enormous department stores that make Kampala's Drapers look like a pimple on the bottom of a hippopotamus.

The tarmac is jammed with tall red buses and black London cabs and the pavements are awash with well-dressed pedestrians dodging each other as they clasp crisp shopping bags to their sides, an unblinking purpose to their stride. On the traffic islands that sit in the middle of the broad road, crowds of people wait for the signals to dictate when they can cross. As soon as the lights change, they swarm on their way. The smell of diesel exhaust fumes hangs in the air.

After a short walk along the street to explore the smaller shops, we go into one of the department stores through heavy mahogany doors that gleam with polished brass and sparkling clear glass. A uniformed door man assesses us as we look at the large printed board in the main foyer. There are six floors selling everything from chinaware to sofas, children's toys to dress fabric. Where do we find socks in such a place as this? The guard is still watching us and I realise how incongruous we must look. Eventually I gather up my courage.

'Please,' I ask, 'do you know where we can buy socks?'

He continues to assess us and at first I don't believe he will speak. Finally, he clears his throat.

'Would that be ladies' socks or gents' socks, madam?'

He says that if we are requiring ladies' socks we should proceed to the Hosiery department on the second floor, past the Haberdashery department, next to the Lingerie department. However, if we are in need of men's socks, we should look for the Underwear section within the Menswear department on the third floor. Jack understands perfectly well but I realise that my English vocabulary is not as wide as I had always thought. Perhaps my education was not so well rounded after all, having never discussed the subjects of lingerie and hosiery at school.

The store twinkles inside. Glass chandeliers hang from

high ceilings. Display cabinets exhibit piles of beautiful bone china and crystal glasses that bounce light back into the room. We walk through the Perfumes and Cosmetics department where elegantly designed bottles and boxes are tantalisingly displayed on polished shelves. High heels click gently on the pale marble floor as the staff calmly go about their business.

A black lady, bearing a similarity to the singer Diana Ross, is being lavishly served by an attendant who arranges a selection of perfume phials on the countertop in front of her. The customer wears tight trousers tucked into high leather boots and a purple coat trimmed with fur draped across her shoulders. Her hair is cut in a sharp bob and her nails, painted the same colour as her coat, sparkle with light as she conducts the scene to her liking, pouting and spraying the scents extravagantly in the air as the shop assistant flounces around her.

We walk on past through a heady scent of jasmine and further on I catch a trace of lime and perhaps a hint of bergamot which slowly fades as we progress through to the centre of the store. The escalators rise up like metal beasts.

When we reach the second floor, our footsteps are muffled by the thick luxurious carpet and softly piped music filters through the speakers in the ceiling. Row upon row of socks, stockings and undergarments are on display, some hanging from carousels, others in wooden trays or glass cabinets.

I select three pairs of plain dark socks along with some thick black tights - dull items from a store overflowing with choice but they are the cheapest I can find and will serve the purpose.

Two shop assistants stand behind the counter, talking earnestly and looking at the hands of one of them. They glance up briefly, see me then return to their conversation.

I wait patiently until Jack joins me at the end of the

counter and adds a pair of tan leather gloves to the little pile, giving me one of his lopsided smiles as he does so. I pick them up. They are beautifully soft. The label says they are from Italy.

I put the gloves aside.

'Take them,' he said. 'They'll keep your hands warm.'

I answer him in English.

'No, Jack, thank you. I don't want them.'

I know that Jack hasn't even looked at the price. Sometimes I think he lives in a different world. He can quote Keats, Shakespeare and Rudyard Kipling but he's incapable of deciphering a grocery bill. Thank goodness he has Ashika and me to watch out for him.

The shop assistants eventually finish their conversation and one puts a consoling hand on the other as she leaves, announcing to all of us that she is going to take her tea break. The remaining attendant, now unable to delay any longer, eyes the socks and tights suspiciously, her pursed scarlet lips resembling a monkey's bottom.

'You…want…these?' She asks slowly.

'Yes please' I say.

'The gloves?' She holds them high in front of us, pinched between her manicured thumb and forefinger.

'No thank you.'

She looks enquiringly at Jack. She has bright blonde hair like Marilyn Monroe. Perhaps she aspires to be in films. Maybe her disappointment has soured her.

'Do…you…pay…money?' she asks Jack, having discarded the gloves and rubbing her thumb on her fingers to indicate cash.

Jack merely looks at her as if struck dumb.

'Money?' she asks again, rubbing her fingers, her gaudy rings catching the light.

Jack blinks several times but doesn't answer.

I bang my purse down on the counter and start to count

out the money.

'He understands you perfectly well.'

She looks surprised. I see a faint blush creep up under her thick powder.

'I think you should know that my husband has a Master's degree in English from Cambridge. That's Cambridge University. He also teaches 18th century English literature at Kampala University. He understands you perfectly well.'

Jack raises his hands and looks to the heavens as he walks away, while I wait for my change before joining him at the escalators. We descend in silence and make our way out onto the street where we stand outside the main door, looking at the stream of pedestrians walking along the pavement. It's raining slightly now, and as dark as dusk.

'I can't believe you said that!'

'She was treating us like imbeciles. Just because we're foreign doesn't mean that we're ignorant.'

We stand, not speaking, watching the train of bustling shoppers with umbrellas marching across our path.

'Actually it's 19th century not 18th,' he says.

'What do you mean?'

'English Literature. 19th century. I teach 19th century, not 18th.'

'19th century or 18th - what's the difference? At the moment you don't teach anything anyway!' We both laugh bitterly as we set off to return to the camp.

As we walk past the large plate glass windows, I catch a glimpse of two strangers walking under the overhang of the shop frontage as they avoid the rain. The man is tall and upright with a tweed jacket and a confident air; the woman wears a shawl over her head which is tilted at a dejected angle. An incongruous pair - a distinguished foreign gentleman with a poor refugee by his side. I will not succumb to this. I will change. I will blend. I will succeed. I will plan.

On our return I see that we have three new lodgers in our dormitory – two older women and a very pretty girl, nearly a woman, the daughter of one of them. The two ladies cluck away and say every thought that comes into their heads, a constant stream of words taking the long way round. Ashika seems pleased to have met the women and is more animated than I have seen her for several days. My mother-in-law likes to talk of trivialities, they are like little bubbles of joy in her life. I'm not a good companion for her.

The new girl is silent. She sits on her bed and takes out a few things from her suitcase, unfolds them, strokes them, then refolds them, packing them away again. Then she sits quietly with her hands on her lap, looking blankly at the floor.

Is she entirely normal? Possibly a little simple-minded.

Chapter 5

Four years ago I had never even heard of my husband, Jack Dalal.

I had just been out on the western peak with Okello and a handful of pickers when I returned to see Aunt Latika's Mercedes parked in the drive. Kenzi was in the kitchen with Kuki, sitting on a high stool with a long glass of nimbu pani in front of him. They were laughing about something as I entered, and the chauffeur greeted me with an extra chuckle.

'And how is my Miss Bulbul today?'

'Very well thank you Kenzi, and I hope you are too.'

The large man conceded and chuckled.

'Why is my Aunt Latika here?'

He shrugged.

'And Nanda?'

'She's at home. I only bring your aunt.'

My aunt's visits were rare. Despite my father being older than her by a good twelve years, she usually had the upper hand when it came to organising family events, but I couldn't think of any notable occasions coming up.

The door to the living room was ajar and my bare feet were silent on the dark wooden floor.

'But you can't escape the fact Ravi, she's twenty-three years old! I had been married for six years by the time I was her age. It's all very well and good you thinking that she can keep you company in your old age, but what about her? Doesn't she need a husband, a family? Doesn't she want children?'

'She's never shown any interest.'

'All young girls are interested. I realise it's nice for you to have the company and I'm aware that she's brilliant on the farm. In fact I think she's made some wonderful improvements here, but she needs her own life. And you won't live forever. You have to face facts Ravi – she needs her own life.'

'That may be but I can't imagine any man would be able to cope with her. She's too outspoken. She wouldn't make a good wife. In any case, there's the problem of her mother. I doubt any man would be prepared to take on the tainted blood.'

'I know, I know, but it doesn't mean that all is lost. There are other avenues.'

'And what would they be, may I ask?'

'Remember Ravi, we are in the 20th century. We are modern people and Bulbul's generation are more broad-minded. Not every man would be concerned by her family's history.'

'That's nonsense, Latika, just conjecture. I can't think of any young man from a good family who lives in Uganda who would be prepared to marry her mother's daughter.'

'Ah, well, that's because you live like a hermit here. As well as keeping your daughter living like a hermit. But I'll put that matter aside for the moment. As you know we lead a very sociable life and I, my dear brother, have come across the perfect candidate.'

I couldn't see my Aunt Latika's face through the crack in the door, but I could visualise her expression, similar to one of our hens when they have laid a large egg.

'And who would this perfect candidate be?'

'He's a very nice man. Gentle. A bit older. And good looking, in his way. Very well educated. Cambridge in England. His father was Doctor Dalal, do you remember him? He was friends with Gupta.'

'I'm not sure I do. And if he is such a perfect candidate

why isn't he married already?'

'I don't know. Some little dalliance with an English girl, I believe. But that's all history. What I do know is that he came back when his father was ill, just as any good son would. However, unfortunately Dr Dalal didn't survive, bless his soul. So Jamal stayed and took on a post at the university. He only has his mother, no brothers or sisters, so he stayed. He has an important job and a good salary. And his family is respectable.'

My father mumbled a reply.

'It's true she can be tricky at times, but she'll have to learn to comply. She'll need to bend like a sapling. If you leave it any longer, she'll be as brittle as an old tree and it will all be too late. Then you'll die. I know, I know, one day you will die. We all do my lovely brother, even you, whether you like it or not. What will happen to her then? Sanjay isn't interested in running the farm, he's got his life in America.'

My father had moved position, but I still couldn't hear his response, only that of my aunt.

'I doubt it. He's got a good job and he's following his dream. He's always had a passion for engineering and with his qualifications he can go wherever he likes in the world. He has no interest in the farm. You can't change him. A leopard doesn't change his spots. Just let Bulbul and Jamal meet then we can take it from there. They may not like each other, but I have a feeling that they probably will.'

An objection.

'You can't do this Ravi, you've blocked her life all the way. You know she wanted to go to university and she would have done well. You know that. But no, you wanted her here.'

The jewels on my aunt's hand glinted as she gave a dismissive wave to my father's question.

'Nanda, my darling Nanda. She has no interest in studies. Even though she was very good at her schoolwork she has never aspired to university. She loves being at home with us. She leads a very comfortable life and has so many friends. She's always busy.'

Another rumbling from my father's direction. Again another wave of Aunt Latika's hand.

'Nanda's younger than Bulbul. We still have time.'

'No, no, I tell you Jamal is the perfect match for Bulbul, I feel it in my bones.'

I walked on silently to the bathroom where I took a shower in scalding water. I scrubbed my body vigorously and all the time I thought: this is my body, this is my skin, these are my breasts, my thighs, my neck, my hair, mine, mine, mine. They are not someone else's to give, not someone else's to take. The words rang in my head loud and clear, but somewhere, deep down, mingled with the stubbornness in my heart, there were tiny whirlpools of excitement in the pit of my stomach. Maybe all this would not just be mine, maybe my skin would slip against another's, like satin and silk, two bodies entwined, and the secret yearning that would settle on me in the hush of the night would finally be fulfilled.

CHAPTER 6

It is Friday and the Women's Voluntary Service holds the donated clothes stall this morning. The tables are set out in one of the side rooms with the first choice being given to the new arrivals.

Shai and Padma brief me beforehand.

'We get some good quality clothes donated, especially because we're in a rich area. I don't know how the others get on when they're stuck on an old airfield, but here it's fine. Check the jumpers first - some of them can be itchy, but if it says "Cashmere" on the label grab it fast - they're always the first to go. Then trousers, you need warm trousers. And boots, get some boots if they have your size. You'll be really glad you did.'

Jack holds back as we approach the door.

'You need some warmer clothes Jack.'

'No, I don't, I'm fine.'

For once Ashika and I agree.

'Come on Jack, you know your tweed jacket isn't warm enough. Just come in and see what they have.'

His mouth is pressed tight.

'No, I won't take charity. I refuse. Give me Moh and I'll meet you in the common room afterwards.'

Ashika shrugs as he walks away and we stay in the line. This is not the time or place for pride.

There are two middle-aged women in the room and in front of them is a line of trestle tables piled with clothes. One of the volunteers is unpacking a large cardboard box, the other one greets us as we enter and looks me up and down.

'Now you look like you must be a size 10, that's the size here in England which is more like an 8 in American sizes. I'm not sure what you go by in your country. Some of your people seem to understand English sizes, some American. See here, I've got a wonderful camelhair coat, and it's from Harrods. Harrods is a very smart shop that we have here in Knightsbridge which actually isn't very far from here at all.' She emphasises these names so I can ingrain these important symbols of London life into my mind.

I try on the coat and Ashika comments on how lovely it is.

'Here, you take it,' and I pass it to her.

There is another box being unpacked, and a jacket catches my eye as it's laid on the trestle table.

'Can I try that on please?'

'This one?'

It's grey and black with subtle diagonal stripes and large lapels.

'Ah yes,' she looks at the label. 'Very smart indeed although wouldn't you like something a bit quieter?'

'I'm sorry?'

'Something that will blend in a bit more easily?'

'No thank you, this will do very well.'

There's a long mirror propped up near the back of the room and I wait until I can view how it looks when I put it on. I like the fit. It sits well around my shoulders and waist but my cotton trousers and plimsolls let it down. That's too bad, I think, but at least it's smart and warm. A start.

As I turn back to the table, I catch sight of a piece of clothing in a similar fabric. A pair of trousers. I realise they are the completion of a trouser suit. They fit perfectly and I swing gently at my reflection in the mirror.

After half an hour we come away laden with a pair of dungarees, an anorak, and two thick jumpers for Moh, as well as Ashika's coat, a cardigan, my trouser suit, and a pair of patent leather boots. We did ask about some men's clothes for Jack but were informed that he would need to go himself if he required any items. They will be open again next week so perhaps he could drop by then. When we return to our dormitory Shai and Padma are just on their way downstairs but quickly dart back when they see us arrive with the clothes.

'Show us what you've got,' says Padma.

She holds up my jacket and checks its label.

'Biba!' she exclaims. 'Very smart! You're so lucky finding something from Biba!'

I ask if it's a good make and am informed it's the very best, and the shop is only within walking distance.

'Of course it's too expensive for us to buy anything but we like to go and visit, just to to see the beautiful clothes. That doesn't cost anything. We'll take you.'

They check the boots, notice the Russell & Bromley sticker and announce their approval. They are turning into London consumers at a rapid rate.

I find Jack in the common room. He's sitting on one of the old leather sofas reading a newspaper while Moh sits at his feet, chewing a wooden building block.

'It's unbelievable that the world just stands by while that bloodthirsty monster destroys our country. Why don't they do something!' he explodes as I approach.

'What can they do? They don't want to start a war.'

'Africa's one big war already. Better to get rid of the murdering bastard before there are no Ugandans left. They say he drinks the blood of his victims. It wouldn't surprise me it was actually true - he's such an evil creature! I'm grateful we managed to get out when we did.'

A volunteer comes over and asks us if we would like a nice cup of tea as if it will solve all the problems of the universe. How lovely it would be to believe that it could.

The tea tastes different to tea back home, but it's warm

and comforting.

'Guess what,' exclaims Jack. 'On a happier note I've had a letter from Buster.'

'Buster? From your old university? Does he know you're here?'

'Not here exactly, but in England, in London. The Resettlement Board redirected his letter. He's invited us to come and stay for a weekend. Won't that be nice? Something to look forward to.'

'When?'

'In three weeks' time.'

He tells me that Buster lives in a part of the country called Wiltshire. The suggestion is that we take the train from London on the Friday afternoon and he'll meet us at the station. Some other friends will be staying and Jack knows the husband from many years ago. Buster and his wife don't have children. Unsuccessful, Jack says, so he thinks it best that we leave Moh with Ashika. We'll only be away for two nights.

What can I wear to a country weekend with smart friends from Jack's academic years? He doesn't ask if I would like to go, just assumes I'm as pleased as he is with the invitation. But he has a new light in his eyes so I don't mention my fears. He'll say that any reservations I may have are trivial. Men don't understand these things.

Lying on my hard bed in the dark, I think through my dilemma and mentally visualise some of the women I saw on our shopping trip. It's hard to pinpoint any definitive style. Some younger women wore short skirts, some trousers. The dark woman in the perfumery wore tight trousers and high boots. Was it her clothes that made her look so right, so powerful? Was it how she was dressed that had the assistant fussing around her, pulling out more bottles and laughing along with her? No, it was more than that. It was her confident air - the way she sprayed the scents in the air without a care, the way she carried herself. It was more than her clothes; it was her demeanour.

I think back to the lurch in my stomach as I caught sight of my reflection in the shop window, my head covered by my shawl, bowed against… the rain? No, we were sheltered from the rain at that point. But, there on the busy street, with the backdrop reflection of Londoners busily on their way, I was set apart, not even by the colour of my skin. I was dressed as a refugee and I carried myself as a refugee.

I remember Mrs Patel, our schoolmistress, who would make us walk along the gym with books on our head saying, 'Carry the books upon your head like a lady and you will carry the world.' We would laugh off this ridiculous phrase, but it's only now that I understand what she meant.

My mind is whirling. I only have three weeks to shake off the shackles of being a refugee, to turn myself into a wife who Jack will be proud to present to his friends.

I realise I'll need help with my plan. I'll consult Shai and Padma. They're intelligent girls, modern girls, who seem to know a good deal about England already. I'm sure they will be able to help me.

In the morning I have my allocated time to have a shower. Strange how such a simple ritual in the past has turned into a highlight of our existence. The washroom has a high ceiling and a row of seven shower cubicles, all with peach coloured plastic curtains. At the far end there's a large frosted window with thickly painted metal bars. Below this window there's a chunky grey radiator that does little to warm the area. It takes courage to remove my clothes and dive into the shower. The only place to leave towels is either on the wet floor or the hooks above the bench that runs along the wall. This is located seven paces from the outer edge of the nearest cubicle. I know this because I've counted. Getting to and from the shower cubicles needs to be done with lightning speed.

This morning it sounds like there's only one other person in the shower next to me, otherwise the washroom is empty.

At first the spray of water is like fine pins of ice but finally the heat filters through and I let the warm water cascade over me. We have our restrictions on the days we can shower and the times we can shower, but so far there are no rules on how long these showers should be, so I stand in warm bliss and lose myself in my thoughts. After a while I become aware of a scratching sound coming from the next-door cubicle. Scratching or is it scrubbing? It sounds as harsh as Kuki scrubbing the floors at home. And between the sounds of scratching, I hear a sob and a moan and then another sob and some muttering. Cleanliness taken to the extreme.

We come out of the cubicles at precisely the same time and quickly head towards the bench for our skimpy towels. She's the pretty new arrival from our dormitory. Her skin is rubbed raw and her eyes are red from soap or weeping. She seems embarrassed when she sees me and avoids catching my eye, her hands fumbling as she tries to gather the towel around her. I see her skin is grazed and sore, most probably from the scouring brush she holds in her hand.

'Are you all right my good friend?' I ask.

She doesn't answer and turns away.

'Why do you scrub so hard? You are cruel to your skin.'

A sob erupts from her throat, but she smothers any more sounds as she quickly gets dressed and leaves the washroom, her clothes sticking to her damp and raw skin.

Later I find Shai and Padma and ask them about the new girl in our dormitory. They are scantily informed.

'She's with her mother and aunt, and they're from Mbarara. We think they are just the women. There are no men, but we don't know why. I think my mother knows something about them. Or maybe Ashika knows more? She seems to be friendly with the mother.'

'What's the girl's name?' I ask, ashamed that I haven't asked her myself.

'Hana' is the reply. Hana means happiness.

CHAPTER 7

When I was young, I would think of Aunt Latika's house as a palace. Maybe it was the tall columns that held up the portico over the front terrace, or perhaps it was the way it gleamed like gold in the evening sun before the great orb dipped behind the seventh hill of Kampala.

The lawn of the garden was as smooth as a billiard table and sweetly scented roses grew around the foot of the veranda. My aunt had told us these special roses were from Damascus - a rare breed used by French perfumers. And so our evenings were scented by the subtle aroma of cumin and ginger emanating from her well-equipped kitchen, gently mixed with the sweet smells of soft pink flowers that made me think of distant lands.

Aunt Latika was just seventeen when she married, unaware that the life ahead of her would be as comfortable and affluent as it proceeded to be. Uncle Deepak was only working as a clerk in an office when they first wed but he had a quick wit and it transpired that he could play the stock market as a gifted musician would play a sitar. His business acumen, together with his easy-going and friendly manner with people, gained trust and a wide social group of friends which, in turn, led to attaining further business clients. Before long he had a thriving business in downtown Kampala as well as an office in Nairobi and an association with a large corporation in New York, where he would visit several times a year.

Over time, as my uncle's wealth increased, the house became grander and Nanda, their only child, became more cherished and indulged. It was lucky she had a sweet nature as otherwise she could have become spoilt and selfish, but this was not the case. As well as being cousins, we were good friends despite the very different lives we led. Whereas I spent my childhood years dressed in shorts and tee shirts, helping on the farm when I wasn't at school, Nanda was preoccupied by clothes and the finer, more feminine elements of life.

But we would laugh about our differences and I would often watch, fascinated, when we were out shopping as she would try on outfit after outfit. She would tilt her head this way and that, as she viewed herself in the mirror, smoothing the fabric of the costume with her manicured fingers before making a purchase, often to find a duplicate already hanging in her extensive closet.

Two weeks after my aunt's visit to Rutubasana, I was sitting on her perfumed terrace eating mango kulfi as I looked into the eyes of my future husband and listened to the dark timbre of his voice. Was it his looks? His thick hair which my father would say needed a good cut despite it barely touching his collar? His mouth, his hands? No, I just sat back and listened to the music of his voice.

He called himself Jack.

'Jack?' I said, 'I thought your name was Jamal.'

He grinned and blinked charmingly.

'I changed it when I went to England. My parents blessed me with a name that sounds like a nursery rhyme, Jamal Dalal.'

'Better than Jamala Dalala.'

We laughed.

'Does your mother mind?'

'About my name?'

'Yes. Doesn't she mind that you changed the name they gave you at birth?'

He shrugged.

'Old traditions,' he said. 'I'm a modern man.'

He laughed when he heard I was usually called Birdie despite my aunt insisting on calling me by my birth name, Bulbul. He said I was a modern girl too. Was there a note of complicity in his tone? Were we a modern pair together? That was too intimate to consider.

He had driven to the suburbs in his old blue Ford and I remember how, at the end of the afternoon, he sauntered easily back to the car with his linen jacket hooked over his shoulder by one finger, his chinos loose on his tall frame. I also remember how I was slightly indignant that he was equally polite and attentive to each and every one of us without the mildest hint that I could be more important than the others.

It was undoubtedly a disaster. Jamal – Jack Dalal, would have tasted the mango kulfi, looked out over my aunt's perfectly tended garden, and decided that he rather liked the bachelor life where his mother waited for him at home, where he could drink and play with his academic friends. And he would have thought that he wouldn't want to be hitched to a tricky country girl with no city graces, raised on a farm surrounded by men. A young woman who was tainted by the sordid death of her mother.

But it appeared that Jack Dalal found me amusing and so our courtship loped along, not in any regular form, not in any conventional sense. Sometimes I wouldn't hear from Jack for days; once there was silence for a full two weeks. Was he tired of me? Bored? I never voiced any fears and was nonchalant when he rang me to explain he had been suffocated by an overload of work.

Aunt Latika was getting impatient.

'He can't go on like this, stringing you along.'

'He's not "stringing me along". He hasn't promised anything. We're just getting to know each other.'

'How long does it take to get to know each other?'

'I'm not sure, aunt. A lifetime?'

'Exactly. If we all took a lifetime to get to know each other then none of us would get married at all.'

'Are we talking about a time machine here?'

'No, no, you know what I mean. You can get to know each other but then you can get to know each other *too much*. The mystery disappears. It all becomes mundane. You need to nip it in the bud.'

'And how do you suggest I do that?'

'He needs a prod. A good prod with a pitchfork.'

And sure enough Jack proposed to me within a few weeks and I wondered quietly whether Jack had come to the conclusion himself or whether there had been machinations in the background by my very clever and very calculating aunt.

CHAPTER 8

'The first thing we need is a plan,' says Padma who is always quick and enthusiastic with her ideas. Was I like that once? I can't remember.

We are sitting in the common room and Padma has a pile of magazines on her lap. They are thick and glossy with perfect images of beautiful women and impossibly expensive outfits, modelled in front of mansions and luxury cars. The magazines have been donated by the rich women of Kensington - a strange gift to penniless refugees but useful for our research.

'We need to see what the fashion is now.'

We flick through the pages but there's so much variety, it's hard to decipher a particular style. Sometimes there are vast prices written in a discreet corner and I see that whole project is doomed. How am I ever going to dress stylishly if all the fashionable clothes are so expensive?

'Don't worry,' says Padma, 'these are just to show us what sort of clothes are being worn at the moment. Not everything is as expensive as this. Let's look at the hairstyles. It all starts with the hair.'

The crisp pages show models with sharp cuts shaped around their heads. The sisters say that the most famous cut is the Sassoon cut by Vidal Sassoon. Shai says he cuts the hair of royalty and stars and I wave that idea away, accidentally knocking some magazines to the floor.

As I gather up the magazines my eye catches a small advertisement near the back of one of the glossy publications. There's a line drawing of a woman with a short bob. It reads "Models wanted for Designer Hair Salon. Knightsbridge." It gives a phone number.

'Yes, yes,' says Shai 'I've heard about this. All the hairdressers want models to practice on, even the smart ones.'

'Do you have to be very pretty?' I ask.

'No, no, nothing like that. They just want you to have good quality hair so they can practice. Just think, if their trainees practice on their rich clients and they make a mess of it, they will be in such trouble. Big trouble. So they get models so they can learn on them.'

'Do you have to pay?'

'I don't think so. If you do, it's not very much.'

'And I would get a stylish cut like this? Then that's where I must start.'

Things are moving in the right direction.

I see an image of my mother's hair. It was not straight as mine but curled voluptuously around her face and lay like a shawl on her shoulders. Sometimes she would let me brush it for her and she would sit back on the sofa as I played with various hairstyles. Her eyes would glaze over deliciously, just as a cat being stroked. I loved those times when she was all mine, when I wielded the power in my hands and the room rang out with my chatter.

I remember how, at night, she would come into my bedroom to kiss me goodnight and the edge of her curls would tickle my face. I especially recall the nights when she had spent time preparing herself to go to a party or dinner with my father. She would smell of fresh perfume, honeysuckle with some richer musky undertones. As she walked around the room, rearranging objects on my shelves and tweaking the shutters, she would leave behind a trail of warm scented air, her bracelets jingling as she moved.

After my seventh birthday she didn't come so often to tuck me into bed at night and I couldn't understand why. She would spend days lying in her room with the shutters closed and I would notice a musty odour if I ventured in. Soon her waist began to thicken, and I overheard Kuki and Okello's mother talking of the new addition to our family. I realised there was soon to be a baby. But my mother was not happy. As her belly grew, she became more and more detached. Inch by inch the house felt enveloped by a thick clawing fog of depression, obliterating the wide skies beyond and in the gloom, my mother descended into a dark place.

I can't remember a definite point of shock when I heard the news, it was more a gradual dawning of what had happened. The first morning there were several unknown adults moving in all directions and hushed mutterings which ceased as soon as Sanjay or I passed by. The big clock in the hall ticked on but there was no news and still they searched.

My father, who had been away on business in Nairobi at the time, returned in the afternoon, at first oblivious to any concerns about his wife. I heard afterwards that he was thoroughly grilled by the police and it was only on checking his rail ticket that the police put aside their suspicions and Pappa was allowed to join in the search. Of course, I wasn't aware of this at the time, but I gleaned these details bit by bit as I became older and more resilient.

Eventually the car was found a couple of miles southwest of Kasowa, parked up on a dusty mound overlooking the turbulent rapids of the White Nile. There was no note, no apology, just the silence of the hot leather seats and an old sweet wrapper left in the seat well.

They never found her body, but that was no surprise. The crocodiles would have made sure that not a morsel was left.

Although questions were asked, I remained wicked in my

silence for I never confessed how I had seen her leave the night before, how I had stood on the lowest step of our veranda, wearing my pyjamas, asking where she was going, pleading that she take me with her. I never told them how, earlier that same day, she had been constantly irritated with me for squabbling with Sanjay, how I could do nothing right and how, eventually she shut herself in her bedroom and relinquished our care to the capable hands of Kuki. I couldn't find the words. I didn't have the courage.

How could I confess to them it was all my fault?

CHAPTER 9

What was this feeling I had running down the back of my neck? Almost like a vibration, a silent ringing in my ears. This shopping trip with Nanda did not feel the same as our excursions the previous year.

My baby son was now four months old and memories of the pain, the blood, the hours in the operating theatre afterwards were starting to soften. Every day I was regaining my strength. I had spent these past months in our house in Kampala with the support of Jack's capable mother. Now I longed to return to Rutubasana to spend time with my father so he could get to know his grandson. But first I had arranged with Nanda that we would have another outing to Kampala, just as we used to. We would take our time wandering through Drapers department store, maybe purchase some new shoes and then visit Sabu, once again to listen to his enchanting tales.

Nanda arrived in her Mercedes earlier than usual to pick me up, her loyal Kenzi in the driving seat.

'I had to sneak out,' she whispered. 'Mama was complaining, saying it wasn't safe. I don't know what's got into her head. I can't see why anything is different.'

'So why is that? You still see your friends in Kampala don't you? Jael and Pavani and the others?'

'Well, yes, we still meet but not in the centre of Kampala. None of their parents like it. So we go to the country club. It's comfortable there.'

It was true that the political temperature was changing. Even Jack, who was relaxed about most things, had said he didn't like the idea of my shopping trip. But I had promised to leave Moh in the safe hands of his mother and said we wouldn't be long. Just a quick trip to make me feel normal again. My first outing since the birth of our son.

It was market day, and everything appeared as normal - the usual shops, the same stall holders, the routine calling and banter between the locals. But there was something else. Perhaps it was me. Maybe now, having had a child, I was more sensitive to my surroundings. A primeval mother's instinct to sniff out potential danger, note any shift in the landscape.

Nanda held my arm as we walked in the blistering heat down Kampala Road.

'Come,' she said, 'let's take some masala chai at Madam Bakshi's'.

We walked on and turned the corner of the street anticipating the usual bustle around our favourite tearoom. Madame Bakshi's was closed. Firmly closed. There were planks of wood nailed across the door and front window and the yellow striped awning hung torn and dejected over the facade. I squinted between the slatted boards to see the shop was empty inside apart from one overturned table and a few pieces of crockery set on the side shelves.

'She's left!' called out another shop keeper. 'Gone to Bombay.'

'She read the tea leaves!' added his wife, laughing.

There was dust on the window ledge and the threshold of the entrance. It looked like the shop had been closed for some time.

We made our way towards Mr Kamar's hardware store and I realised that I had forgotten to bring any treats to eat, or any ginger soda to rekindle our bond with Sabu after all these months.

We passed Asita's sari shop and slipped down the side alley to the open area behind the stores expecting to see the large colourful rug laid out with the poles at the four corners and the wide sheet of cloth tied across. The area was empty - only dry red dust and a pile of wooden crates.

My heart lurched as if the path had been sliced away from under our feet.

We stood, lost and hesitant for a few moments before I led my cousin to the front of Mr Kamar's shop and we entered through the beaded doorway. An old woman sat on a high stool and looked at us through thick glasses.

Mr Kamar? He was recovering. His sister was looking after him following his time in hospital. What was wrong? A broken skull, ribs, and his hands, many broken fingers. Why? The soldiers. They didn't like what he said, or maybe he wouldn't pay them the money. The boy? Who? The boy, Sabu? Nothing. The boy, Sabu who used to tell the stories? A shrug. I grappled for any other leads. Kartik? There was a flicker of recognition. Where is Kartik? There was a slight wobble of her head, then she pointed diagonally across the street to a small grocery store. There, she replied. There is Kartik.

The interior of the shop seemed pitch black after the brightness of the street, and it appeared to be empty apart from some scant arrangements of jackfruit, sweet potatoes and papayas. We could hear sounds of boxes being scraped on the floor in the back room.

'Hello!' I called out and slow footsteps approached.

The lad had grown taller in the last six months, but he recognised us and his face took on a defensive, almost belligerent look.

'Yes?'

'You remember us, don't you Kartik?' He gave a slight nod and glanced out at the street.

'You're a friend of Sabu's, aren't you? Do you know where he is?'

A shrug.

'Don't you know where Sabu has gone? You used to be friends.'

Again, he lifted his shoulders. 'He gone.'

'Where?'

'He go, when the soldiers come. After Mr Kamar go to hospital Sabu don't come back.'

'Do you have any idea where?'

'No.'

'Is he still telling his stories?'

'Don't know.'

We stood in silence and Kartik shifted his weight from foot to foot.

'Are you sure you don't have any idea where he is?' Then, remembering the boy's avarice, I added 'I could pay you for any information.'

A gleam came into Kartik's eye.

'How much?'

'Let me see.' I checked my purse. 'I have a hundred shillings. You can have that if you tell me where Sabu is.'

'I don't know, surely.'

'Well, where do you *think* he might be?'

Kartik pulled at his eyebrow, thought for a moment, then shrugged again.

'What if I give you fifty shillings now, Kartik? Then, you can ask people where Sabu is. Can you do that? If you find out where he is, you can come and tell me. Then I'll give you the other fifty shillings. A hundred shillings, just to tell me where Sabu is. How about that?'

Kartik gave a perfunctory nod, his eyes fixed on the notes.

'Here's my address in case you learn anything else about Sabu's whereabouts. Anything at all. Here,' I said as I scribbled my address and telephone number on a piece of paper. 'Let me know if you learn anything else about where he is. There'll be more of this if you do.'

He nodded and put the money and my scribbled note in his back pocket.

We were on the threshold of the door when Kartik mumbled something.

'What was that?'

'The soldiers. They like Sabu. They like his stories. Maybe they find him before you.'

As I looked back into the dark shop, I wasn't sure if the look I detected was a smirk, or a grimace.

On the way home I asked Nanda if we could drive past the railway station to see if he was there, but Nanda said we should just go home now. She didn't feel comfortable. There was little chance of us finding him.

We should ask around. We should ask if anyone had seen a little boy with a blue turban decorated with a gaudy jewel and a curved sword tucked into his belt.

Chapter 10

The day is bright and I have an urge to walk in this rare sunshine. At lunch I suggest to Jack and Ashika that we visit Kensington Park Gardens.

'I'm told the gardens are pretty and we can walk there easily from here.'

Jack and Ashika agree that it would be good to leave the camp, but my mother-in-law laments the lack of a pushchair as Moh is growing heavy.

A plump hand touches my arm. I recognise the lady, but I've never spoken with her before.

'Excuse me, my dear, but I overheard your conversation. Did they not tell you? You can borrow pushchairs from the caretaker.'

'Is that so? Where do we go?'

'His office is around the back of the building, a shed really. He's not a particularly nice man but all you have to do is sign for a pushchair and then return it when you've finished.'

I thank her deeply. Just think of the amount of freedom we can now have. Our lives will change.

So far we've seen little of Mr Caxton, the caretaker. He doesn't appear to do much maintenance and until now we haven't had any need to cross paths with him.

The long shed, which serves as his office, is sandwiched between the high perimeter wall and the side of the building housing the women's quarters.

I knock on the door of the shed and there's a gruff call

from within. As I enter, I'm hit by fumes from a paraffin heater which puffs and crackles in the corner. The warmth in the room is damp and oppressive.

Alfred Caxton is a large man with grey stubble hair and a flabby double chin. He's eating a thick sandwich and looks up from reading a comic, a trail of grease around his mouth.

At first I don't understand what he says.

'Excuse me?'

'So, what's a pretty young Paki like you doing venturing into my lion's den?'

I hesitate.

'We would like to take a walk in the park. I was told I can borrow a pushchair here.'

'Only if I've got one.'

'Well, yes. Obviously.'

'That's right. Now I would have to check if I've got one.'

He continues to eat his sandwich leisurely, chewing in a circular motion observing me insolently.

I wait, my cheeks growing warmer as each second passes.

'Well? Have you?'

'Patience, patience my little Paki.'

'You're not even bothering to look!'

'All in good time. Can't you see it's my lunch break. Can't interrupt a man's lunch break.'

'It won't take you a minute. And anyway, what is this word 'Paki'? My name is Mrs Dalal.'

'Now, now, don't get all uppity. It's only an endearment. You'll have to learn not to take things too seriously if you're going to survive in this country.'

'Oh I understand, so you think I should laugh, "Ha Ha Ha" when I hear someone call me a little Paki. And that is the way I will *survive* in this country?'

'Well, yes, I suppose, if you put it like that, yes. There's a lot to be said for having a sense of humour.'

'Ha. Ha. Ha!'

Mr Caxton stops chewing and looks at my hand on my hip. My father would always admonish me for standing like this.

A raised eyebrow, and he starts chewing again, returning to read his cheap newspaper.

'Have a seat,' he mumbles through a mouth stuffed with white bread. He doesn't look up.

For a moment I nearly sit down, then turn back. As I move, I catch sight of a folded pushchair propped up against the rear door.

'There, you see, there's a pushchair. So you do have one after all.'

He looks up at me, looks at the pushchair, then very slowly one by one he sucks the tips of his fat fingers.

'Mr Caxton, are you going to let me use this one or not?'

'Calm down, don't get on your high horse.'

'And what horse is that?'

'A saying, only a saying. You'll learn. I can tell you've got a lot to learn.'

There's a hard light in his eye as he finally wipes his hands on his trousers and pulls down a chunky blue book from a shelf next to his desk. He inspects the pages closely.

'What are you doing now?'

'Just checking to see that the pushchair hasn't been booked out already. Or maybe it's the faulty one that needs to be repaired.'

'Well? How long does it take to check a book?'

'Just checking,' he replies, his tongue poking around the inside of his cheeks.

'Oh yes, it seems we do have one after all. And there it is.' He has a sly smile on his face as he slowly points towards the back of the shed.

'Thank you. Can I take it now?'

'Very well. Help yourself.'

The pushchair is light, and I start towards the entrance door.

'Of course, there's the small matter of the fee.'

'Fee?'

He holds up his finger.

'There's a small charge for using it. A nominal fee, that's all.'

'Which is?'

'One shilling. Or, if we're talking new money, five pence.'

'But I was told it was free. We can borrow the pushchair and we don't have to pay anything.'

'Not sure who told you that.'

'I know for a fact that it's free. Let me sign where I need to, but I will not pay.'

'Just a token charge towards wear and tear.'

'Towards your pocket you mean.'

'Not at all. These things need upkeep.'

I can barely catch my breath.

'In that case, Mr Caxton, let me sign your book and I will check with the administrator about this charge later. If there is a charge, then I'll return and pay it. I will take it now though.'

'No need to check with the administrator. He doesn't involve himself with all the nitty gritty of what goes on with maintenance.'

'So he lets you fill your pocket from the poor misfortunate people who barely have a penny to their name?'

'Not my fault you're all in this sticky situation. I try to help where I can.'

'Mr Caxton. I've seen your type before. The only kind of help you know is the "help yourself" kind. So, I won't pay you your money. I'm not an ignorant "little Paki". Good day!'

I'm panting hard and my hands are clammy and shaking as I push the chair ahead of me. I realise I may have made an enemy, but I'm proud that I held myself strong.

My family are waiting near the wrought iron gate and I

embrace each of them on my return. Ashika can't suppress her surprise at my uncharacteristic affection towards her. She's wearing her smart camelhair coat from Harrods and looks elegant with her hair in a bun which helps to accentuate her fine bone structure. Moh kicks with delight when we lower him into his chariot, and he manages to continually kick off his soft shoes as we walk on the wide pavement towards the gardens.

'What's that shrine?' I ask Jack as we stroll eastwards along a path.

'Oh that. It's the Royal Albert Memorial. Queen Victoria built it in memory of her husband Albert. She loved him very much.'

'How sad. Was he young when he died?'

'Not much older than me.'

'How did he die?'

'They said it was typhoid, but they didn't know so much about illnesses in those days. It could have been cancer. Anyway, Queen Victoria always loved him and she wore black for the rest of her life.'

We walk up to the shrine which rises up high on wide steps. The golden Albert sits in a relaxed position on a solid plinth under an elaborate turreted canopy. In one hand he's holding a book and one of his feet rests on some sort of box. Below, at the base of the shrine is a continuous row of carved figures. Jack says this frieze shows famous poets and musicians. Prince Albert was an extremely cultured man.

On each outer corner stand carved marble statues. We point out the elephant and camel to Moh but he's too young to understand. Each group represents the four corners of the globe and I realise how lost and rootless we are - first from Asia, then Africa and now, homeless in Europe. My brother is in the final quarter - the Americas.

Jack senses my dip in mood.

'Come,' he says. 'Let's find Peter Pan's statue.'

'Who?'

'Peter Pan. Didn't you ever read Peter Pan as a child?'

He seems surprised by my response.

'Didn't you ever see the film? A cartoon.'

'No.'

'Surprising for you. The book's much better.'

'Why'

'It's the real story. How the writer wrote it. Moh will read Peter Pan. He'll enjoy it when he's older.'

We walk along the paths as white clouds scud overhead. Three times we pass elegant women wearing camelhair coats and each time Ashika nudges me with her elbow and gives me a little tilt of her eyebrows. Is it my imagination or does her back straighten slightly on every sighting?

Moh starts to kick and cry with frustration so we stop and set him down on the grass. He stands, his legs askance, as if he feels the world moving under him. Jack lets go. He sways and falls back on his padded bottom. Holding onto Jack's hand he lifts himself to a standing position, just as an old man would.

Firmly pulling his hand out from his father's clasp, Moh manages a few steps, wobbles, corrects himself, balances, and then totters forward until he starts going too fast and trips over his feet, tumbling to the ground. The turf is not hard, and he cries only for a few seconds, more out of frustration than pain. There follow several more attempts at walking, until we are all weary and there are tears of protest as we put him back in the pushchair.

Moh is asleep by the time we find the statue of Peter Pan - a little bronze boy playing some sort of pipe, standing on what looks like a tall stump of a tree. Below his feet, interwoven into the base, are rabbits and other animals as well as figures that Jack says are fairies.

'I can't tell which one is Tinkerbell though.'

'Who's Tinkerbell?' I ask.

'A fairy. Not a very good fairy. You could say she's a bit tricky.'

'The English are so strange. So serious, yet they believe in fairies.'

'It's a child's tale, Birdie. Written for children. It's about a little boy who never grew up. It's said that J M Barrie, the author, was inspired to write Peter Pan by the death of his brother when he was a child. The boy died in a skating accident and his mother was heartbroken. So Barrie wrote about a little boy who would never grow up, who would stay a child forever. I think he felt it would comfort his mother.'

I look at our sleeping son, the crescents of his long lashes crowning his cheeks, a stubborn curl of hair pointing skywards. A slice of fear, the vertigo of loss. How does a mother ever recover from losing a child.

The skies are darkening overhead. I take Jack's arm.

'Let's go…' I nearly say the word 'home'.

CHAPTER 11

I've heard it said that what you learn by eavesdropping is stolen information. But as a child I was unaware of this. What I have learned since, is that you can never give those words back.

It was the quiet time. Only days had passed since my mother's death. Sanjay and I crept around the house, hiding away from my father and speaking in whispers, sometimes forgetting our sorrow and smothering our mouths with our hands, guilty as we gulped back our laughter.

The house continued to function well and meals arrived on time as Kuki took control, sometimes with the help of Jama, Okello's mother, her presence probably more for company than particular need.

They were in the kitchen, talking as Kuki stood near the sink and Jama sat close by on one of the high stools. That was when I became a thief, as I sat on the bench near the back door and their voices floated through the green fly mesh at the open window.

'No, no, it be in her blood. You can't fight the blood.'

'No, you wrong. She always good, missie. No bad bone in her body. She kind, so kind.'

'Without the baby. Maybe. Yes. No baby ok but some woman change with baby inside them.'

'Don't be silly Jama. It normal to change.'

'No, it change the head!'

'What you mean?'

'It turn good blood bad - like black mamba in the blood.'

'Black mamba!'

'I tell you, Kuki. It do strange things. It be lucky, very lucky that only the baby die with her.'

'Why lucky?'

'I hear bad stories. Bad!'

'Oh yes?'

'Like cousin of Hasani. Her belly big and fat, ready for her time. Everybody happy and waiting for the baby. Already she have two little ones. Little girl who wants to help mama with the baby. And baby boy, not walking.'

'And?'

'Bad juju in the air. One day husband have to take a cow to market in Masaka. He not want to leave his wife. Wife not normal, very strange.'

'How?'

'Crying. Different. Talking to baby inside her. Very quiet, like this.'

'"I don't leave you," he say to his wife, but she get cross with him. "Don't be so silly. Cow must go to market. Go. Go!" And so he go to market. But it a bad choice. Bad!'

'So what happen?'

'The first thing he see when he come back is blood. Blood everywhere! She kill her two babies first and then she kill herself.'

There was the sound of metal hitting metal.

'No! Killed her children?'

'Yes, my dear. Kill her own babies. So believe me. It a good thing that missie drown herself and not kill the kiddies too.'

'She never do that!'

'I tell you Kuki, it a madness. It take a woman, like bad juju.'

'I never hear nothing of a mama murdering her babies!'

'It not so strange. Not so strange. Doctors have name for it. Sometimes it when baby inside. Sometimes madness comes after baby born.'

I heard Kuki agree that she knew of this. Her aunt had suffered from it and so had her cousin.

'You see,' replied Jama, 'It be in the blood of families. It be in the blood of Miss Bulbul.'

'No, no, she be fine.'

'We hope Kuki. We hope. But we only know when a baby growing inside her. Then the bad juju come. Remember what they say. The more you love them, the more you hurt them.'

I remember the words and I particularly recall my toes and the formation of my feet. All the time I was listening to their words I was looking at my dark feet, scuffed and dirty from playing barefoot around the grounds. I thought how my mother used to scold me for not wearing my plimsolls and would warn me of the scorpions and snakes that lurked in the undergrowth. And I thought of a black mamba slithering through my veins.

Chapter 12

I've seen little of the caretaker, Alfred Caxton, since the incident with the pushchair but when I do see him, I notice how silently he pads around the grounds; soft and quiet for such a large man. As he walks, he angles his neck forward and tilts his head slightly from side to side. He reminds me of a fat lizard. Always watching. For what?

I ask the plump lady who first told me about the pushchair.

'You want to stay away from him,' she warns. 'He's not a good man. Have you seen the scales he has in his shed?'

'What type of scales?'

'Those little scales they have in the jewellers. For weighing silver and gold.'

'No, I haven't seen them. Why would he have those?'

'Why do you think? He's got a little business going on. The residents here need money, and the only thing of any value they have with them is gold. He's clever.'

'Have you seen him do it?'

'I've heard rumours. But do you think he's paying the market price for the gold? Of course not! He's a bad one. He's got a room at the rear of the shed as well. Goodness knows what goes on there. I saw some boxes of cigarettes last time I went in. They were stacked up in the back. Now what would a caretaker need with so many cigarettes?'

I'm sickened that the man is profiting from our situation and wonder if I should report it to the authorities.

'Leave it alone,' says Jack. 'If the residents are silly enough to feed the man's greed then that's their problem.'

'But he's taking advantage of them. He won't be giving them a fair price!'

'Probably not, but they'll be getting something. They probably don't know where to go to sell their gold and they wouldn't want to ask the administrator as technically they weren't supposed to have brought it into the country in the first place.'

'But it's not right, Jack.'

'There will always be a million things that aren't right, Birdie. You can't mend the world.'

It's announced that the administrator has arranged for a group of us to visit some council flats in East London. Five apartments are becoming available but any residents who are interested are to visit the housing estate before putting in a formal application.

'They probably want to be sure applicants won't back out as soon as they see how ghastly they are,' warns Jack.

I feel I should do something to move us forward as there doesn't seem to be much hope of anything else at the moment.

Ashika refuses to come.

'Why would I want to go to Hackney? Isn't that the name of a horse cart? I want to be with people like me. My old friend, Vada, has gone to live in Hounslow. Why can't we go to Hounslow like her, or Leicester? Mrs Ramada has moved to Leicester to live with her nephew.'

I pass her Moh and board the minibus with Shai, who takes me to the back of the bus away from the driver's cigarette smoke. It's raining throughout the journey and the smell of diesel harnessed within the prickly fabric of the seats is nauseating.

The young girl, Hana, is on the bus. She sits behind her mother and her aunt and seems oblivious to the constant stream of words that spill out of their mouths. Never once do they glance back at her or throw her a comment, but she is lost in thoughts, seemingly unconcerned. Her profile reminds me of a beautiful statue I've seen in a book. Greek possibly.

The bus eventually comes to a halt, and the driver flips down the mounting step. An official looking woman stands in the light drizzle holding a flip board and a poised pen. She wears bright blue eyeshadow and encasing her curled and set hair is a pleated piece of transparent plastic, neatly tied under her chin.

'I'm afraid we will only be able to see three of the properties as two of them are still occupied. However, hopefully the ones we can see will give you an idea of the accommodation becoming available.'

Eleven of us follow in line behind our guide as the watery daylight is stolen by the dark brick buildings towering overhead.

There are eyes watching us. Three young boys stop their game of football and their heads turn as one as their gaze follows our trail. An old woman eyes us suspiciously as she passes by with her shopping bags, walking gingerly in her flat plastic shoes. Faces peer over the edge of solid brick balconies, each balcony facing other balconies across the narrow gorge. The stares seem to drill into my head, and we look around nervously.

As the lift is broken, we take the exterior stairs that cleave to the side of the building. A stench of urine greets us as we pass the shadowy area where rubbish bins sit. All the flats are approached from exterior corridors and the front doors are chipped and scratched. It's a squeeze getting us all into the first flat's entrance hall, but we soon disperse and none of us comment on the stale smell or the dripping tap. Our guide extols the virtues of the coats' cupboard and the electric heating that works by coins slotted into the machine in the kitchen. She stands on a stool and demonstrates how you feed the metal box and two dim lights come on. The floor is red linoleum and there's only enough room for a small table that would barely fit four people around it.

We're told there's a good community in the area. For the white people maybe, but even then, I don't feel sure.

In the living room Shai wrinkles her nose and raises her eyes to the heavens. I look out of the grimy window and see there's now a patch of blue sky high above the tower block beyond. Down below, the ground is devoid of any greenery. No grass, not one bush or tree. It is all hard, grey and dark red brick. Looking up again, there's a flash of a bird soaring in the expanse of the London sky. Freedom. I sit down sharply on a stained orange sofa as my knees give way and I fall into a chasm of despair.

No one speaks as we travel back to the centre. Even Hana's relatives are subdued. I gaze out at the traffic as everyone goes from place to place, from work to home, from friends to shops, then back to their kitchens to have nice cups of tea. They weave their lives, busy and belonging while we sit useless and idle. Waiting, always waiting.

CHAPTER 13

It was nearly three weeks since the shopping trip to Kampala with Nanda and I had given up hope of ever finding Sabu.

Jack was unsympathetic and couldn't understand my attachment to a street urchin, saying I should pay more attention to my own son rather than a low caste ruffian.

'He's not a ruffian. He's the sweetest boy. You've never even met him.'

He waved the matter aside as a trivial distraction. There were more pressing concerns - his work at the university and, only recently, the disappearance of his lawyer friend, Anil.

I had begun to feel like a caged animal in our house and I hankered for the freedom of Rutubatsana.

'Perhaps it would be best if you went to stay with your father. You can leave Moh here. Maata will look after him.'

'But I want Pappa to get to know him.'

'It's better that he stays here. Safer.'

Jack was probably right. In any case, I had never looked after Moh on my own. Ashika was a better mother than I was.

The day was set, and it was arranged that Dicken would drive me home once he had delivered his latest group of tourists to Entebbe airport. He would stay in his usual hotel overnight and we would leave the following morning.

I spent the day half-heartedly organising the house before my departure. Ashika would probably re-arrange everything once I had left but I was used to that. At least she would leave our bedroom alone.

Among the papers I was tidying was a copy of the

Kampala Gazette. Jack sometimes bought it when he went into town and I would usually read it afterwards to keep abreast of local affairs. On the front page was a picture of President Amin standing big and proud in an open jeep, a jolly, friendly smile upon his face, cheering crowds surrounding him. 'You are as sly as a hyena,' I thought with loathing, and flicked through the paper nonchalantly.

Towards the back my eyes rested on the Entertainment and Events page. A jolt as sharp as lightning ran through me.

Why hadn't I thought of that? The Drive-In Cinema!

Where would a child who loved stories and film be drawn to? Where would a child who believed he was the reincarnation of one of the great Hollywood actors want to be? The cinema, of course. It was obvious. I had been a fool not to have thought of this earlier.

Lawrence of Arabia was showing at 7 pm that evening.

I checked my watch. Dicken should have arrived back in the hotel by now. There was still time. I picked up the phone.

A deep, drawling voice answered.

'How about a trip to the Drive-In for old times' sake?' I asked, straight to the point.

'What, tonight? We're heading to Rutubasana tomorrow morning. Isn't that enough?'

'Of course that's *enough*. But this will be even more. Something we can do *as well*. For old times' sake.'

'Jeeze, Birdie, I'm exhausted. It's been one hell of a trip.'

'Please, Dicken, please?'

'So, what's on?'

'Lawrence of Arabia.'

'Haven't we seen that already?'

'Yes, but I can't remember it.'

'I find that hard to believe. What else?'

'What do you mean, what else?'

'There's something else. I've known you nearly all your life, Birdie. I can tell when there's something else.'

'Well, only a little *something else.* I'll let you know when we're there.'

'Anyways, Jack won't want you to go out at night. Not with the way things are at the moment.'

'He won't know. He has an emergency meeting at the university tonight.'

'But you know he won't approve.'

'He doesn't have to approve. He won't know. Anyway, don't you remember how much I love Lawrence of Arabia? It's a drive-in, Dicken. I won't be noticed. I'll dress discreetly.'

Dicken could be a soft touch, maybe because I was the nearest thing he had to a daughter.

The music of Lawrence of Arabia sweeps you across the vast terrain of undulating sand dunes and the photography makes you almost smell the dry desert air.

A long film, it seemed an age before it paused to let the advertisements roll across the screen. I wanted to get out of the jeep, but Dicken insisted I stay inside. It was only towards the end of the interval that I noticed the small figure in khaki shorts and a white tee shirt carrying an ice cream tray. He was weaving his way between the cars and I easily recognised his lithe gait.

'Sabu!' I hissed in a loud whisper when I saw him only two cars away. 'Sabu!'

The boy continued his transaction with the occupants of the car, counting out their change and pulling at the white cap that had replaced his turban. He looked inquisitively in our direction and walked towards the jeep with his head cocked to one side.

Finally the recognition showed in his face, his shoulders relaxed and he gave a beaming smile.

'Miss Bulbul, Miss Bulbul. I can't believe I'm seeing you. Here with my own eyes. It is good news. Good news!'

'It's good seeing you too, Sabu. How are you? I've been worried about you.'

'Oh yes, thank you, I'm very fine, very fine.'

'Are you still telling your stories? We tried to find you. Nanda and I looked everywhere, but no one knew where you were, not even Kartik.'

The boy gave an ironic snigger.

'Kartik always knows everything. He's a cobra.'

'But you're not telling your stories any more?'

'No, to be sure, I'm having a little break. I am resting, like the actors. All actors have to rest sometimes.'

'I see. And what are you going to do?'

'Do?'

'Things are getting tricky in Uganda.'

'Oh, yes, I see. Tricky, yes. Choc ice? Raspberry ripple?'

'Seriously Sabu. Kampala isn't safe. Why don't you come to Rutubasana?'

'Your father's place? And go to school? No thank you.'

'No Sabu, don't worry, no school.'

'Oh good, school is not my favourite thing.'

'So you'll come.'

'No thank you, I'm very fine here.'

'Don't you miss your story telling?'

'Well, yes, and no.'

'Wouldn't you like to see some wild animals? There are lots of wild animals near my father's home. We could show you. Just come and stay for a bit, for a few days.'

Sabu bit his lower lip.

'Wouldn't you like to go into the rainforest? There's a wonderful rainforest near my father's farm. Mabira. Wouldn't you like to see Mabira? It's filled with huge trees and wild animals. Hundreds of wild animals. You don't have wild animals here in Kampala, do you?'

The boy readjusted his cap.

'And you could see how we pick the tea from the plants

on the hills, how we dry it. Okello, our manager, could teach you how you can go from one plant all the way through to how you make tea ready to drink. You could learn how to help him. And we have mangoes and papaya. You can just pick them off the trees and eat them straight away. How about that? We're going tomorrow. Just come with us for two days and see how you like it.'

'Only two days?'

'Yes, of course. Or more if you like. Just come and visit our farm in the country and see how you like it.'

Sabu paused, pulling at his mouth as he thought. Suddenly his face brightened.

'You know, Miss Bulbul, I have a certain feeling, just here,' he touched his chest, 'that you would like me to come to your father's farm.'

'That's right, Sabu, I would. Just to see how you would like it.'

'In that case, if you are really wanting it so much, yes, I will comply.'

And his smile was just as white and dazzling as always.

Where did he find that word? Such a young boy saying he would comply with my wishes. But then Sabu was unique in every way.

CHAPTER 14

Shai and Padma are determined to show me the clothes shop Biba, so the next afternoon we set off in the drizzle armed with two umbrellas that we've borrowed from the camp.

It's not a long walk and we stay close to the shopfronts to avoid being splashed by the passing cars and buses.

Above the dark glass windows of the store it reads BIBA and we walk through the door labelled 'Empire'. I feel the anticipation of entering another land.

The lighting is dim and there is the scent of musk. Sultry music is playing and the interior is enveloped in an air of warmth, comfort and luxury. Dark painted furniture and mirrored counters reflect an abundance of ostrich plumes and peacock feathers. On the black marbled floor sit several richly coloured pots holding large palm fronds and pampa grass. It all has a feeling of some hidden harem. Although only a couple of men are meandering around the shop, there are several women of different nationalities and colour. No one takes any notice. Everything seems easy and natural.

'Come,' says Shai pulling me over to the makeup counter. 'See this nail varnish? Can you see the little glittering gold bits inside? Look over there, the shopgirl's wearing the same.'

I see the nail varnish is black with gold glitter and the shop assistant has model looks with thin arched eyebrows and dark shadow on her eyelids. She wears glossy purple lipstick on her beautifully curved and pouting mouth.

'They call the style Art Nouveau,' explains Padma, 'sort of from the 1900s, but now it's modern again.'

I only nod as the music is loud and my attention is focused on all the assorted garments lined up – simple dresses, velvet coats and feather boas. It's like the most luxurious dressing up box and we skid the hangers across the rails as we admire the clothes. From time to time we inspect the price tags and glance at each other, shrugging and pulling faces.

'The people in London say the prices are good, that's one of the reasons Biba's so popular. But it's all too expensive for us,' says Padma.

'Anything's too expensive for us.'

'But look, some dresses aren't that difficult to copy,' says Shai. 'It would be easy to do if you had a sewing machine and some fabric.'

'I've got a sewing machine,' I say.

They stare at me in astonishment. Padma laughs.

'You mean you just happen to have a sewing machine! Where? In your pocket?' She pretends to search my pockets and pats my clothes.

'No, I'm serious. I've got a sewing machine. It's back at the camp.'

'Why didn't you tell us?'

'You didn't ask.'

'Well, why didn't you say you know how to sew?'

'I don't. Well, not properly. We had sewing lessons at school, that's all.'

'You don't sew, but you've brought a sewing machine all the way from Uganda to England. Why would you do that?'

'It was my mother's. And Dicken, an old friend of ours, persuaded me to bring it.'

'Well, I know how to sew,' says Shai. 'So does Padma. We can help you. All we need is some fabric and we can copy one of the dresses. Which one is your favourite?'

I pick out a simple dark blue dress, quite short with thick velvet cuffs in lime green. I think it will look good with a feather boa, but even those cost too much.

'Easy,' said Shai. 'Now you have to follow us. We're going to Kensington Market. I'm sure we'll find some good fabric there and it won't be too expensive.'

We head out into the cold air and the rain, which has grown heavier while we've been in the shop. The sisters are determined, and we walk fast, sharing the two umbrellas between us. We walk past the large department store that Jack and I visited a few days ago. The pavements are less crowded this afternoon.

Kensington Market smells of patchouli oil and I hear sitar music playing on the speakers.

'They're playing Indian music. It almost feels like home.'

'That's Ravi Shankar. Some concert that he played with George Harrison from the Beatles. They play it all the time here. I don't think the English like us Asians very much but as soon as one of the Beatles says we are okay, well then, we're okay.'

'The only problem is they have short memories,' adds Padma.

Although it's called a market, I don't see any food stalls, only row upon row of small stands with clothing, shoes and jewellery. People from all races mingle quietly, but it lacks the noise and bustle of a market back home. The sisters lead me to the back where there are a few fabric stands and before long we've chosen a material similar to that of the dress I liked. After adding some velvet for the cuffs and the cotton thread, the price is more than I'm comfortable with. A reduction is made, so finally I pay without complaint. Shai says she doesn't need a pattern, newspaper will do. My purchases are put in a bag and we head back to the camp as the day starts to close in and the London rush hour is under way.

CHAPTER 15

My father seemed unperturbed when Sabu hopped out of the back of the jeep on our arrival.

'This is my young friend, Sabu. He's come to stay for a few days. I thought he could help Okello.'

Sabu received a mild salute from my father who then took my arm and together we walked up to the bungalow as he recounted the problem he was having with tea weevils on the western slopes.

'Come Sabu, follow me.' I called behind me. 'Kuki will give us some nimbu pani. Dicken?'

Pappa continued elaborating on his preoccupation with the pests. He paused and looked around.

'Where's the baby?'

'Moh? He stayed home with Jack and Ashika.'

A slight nod and the oration continued, only mildly lulling when I hugged Kuki and accepted a cool glass of her special drink. Sabu sipped from his glass thoughtfully. Dicken helped himself to a beer from the fridge.

We went out onto the veranda and three of us sat under the shade as Sabu went to stand at the balustrade where the decking jutted out over the steep slope below. His arms stretched out either side of him and his hands rested on the top rail. I could see the back of his head turning slowly to the left, then slowly to the right as he surveyed the blue hills in the distance, then he looked down towards the sorting sheds. Slowly again his head turned, to the left, the right, the left again.

Eventually my father finished his monologue and Sabu turned back to me with a beaming smile.

'This is all very good. All very fine.'

'You like it Sabu?'

'It is like…' even Sabu was lost for words. 'It is like Paradise.'

Dicken grunted sardonically.

'Enjoy it while you can, boy.'

'Dicken!'

'Not just Sabu. All of us. We have to enjoy it while we can.'

After two days at Rutubasana, Sabu had bonded with Okello. I could see that our manager approved of the boy's quick mind and soon had him running errands and helping with the grading of the tea.

I asked Sabu if he would like to stay for a while. He would receive a small wage and could learn everything about tea production from Okello.

'Very well,' he agreed. 'I will stay for a while. But this is not my real job.'

'Your real job?'

'Yes, my true path!'

'What is your true path?'

'I am an actor. I will only do this for a little bit.'

He held his finger and thumb up, showing a small gap of half an inch - the amount of time he would allocate to deviating from his true path.

Okello agreed that, if Sabu was willing, he could stay in the annexe of his bungalow and he and his family would keep an eye on him and give him meals. Nothing was certain. Sabu was a free spirit.

Meanwhile, I would be returning to Kampala soon and I longed to visit the Mabira rainforest again. Dicken didn't need much persuading, and agreed to the trip, provided we left at dawn and kept off the main highway where possible. My father, as usual, said he would stay on the farm, but Sabu was keen to join us.

Would events have taken another turn if we had not had a puncture that morning? Each individual incident, on its own wasn't of great importance, but put together… how can one tell?

It was still dawn when we set off from the plantation and the air lay quiet, cool and moist. A buffalo bellowed in the distance and monkeys were starting their morning chatter. Kuki had packed a lunch for us in my father's old canvas rucksack and I could see some mangoes and anarsas tucked in at the side, my favourite treats from when I was a child. I hugged her, noticing how thin and fragile she had become. Kuki had worked for my family from before my birth and had been as a mother to me, since my own mother's death. I missed her when I was in Kampala.

We heard the noise and felt the thump of the puncture just before we reached the outer perimeter of the plantation. Dicken pulled the jeep over and Sabu immediately jumped up to help. Always keen, always quick.

The two of them became totally absorbed by the process of changing the tyre, Sabu standing by and handing Dicken the required tools as they bonded in their manly duties.

It was another half an hour before we set off again. Now there would be more cars and trucks on the road, something Dicken had wanted to avoid. He looked at his watch, then at me. My face was set, so he raised his eyes and shifted the gear.

We only passed a few cars as we skirted around Jinja and headed west towards the Mabira Forest. I was being lulled by the motion of the vehicle and at first didn't pay attention to the three figures on the side of the road. It seemed like a full minute before I shouted out to Dicken.

'Stop! Stop Dicken. Stop! We have to go back!'

'What do you mean? Back where?'

'Didn't you see? Those youths. Back there with the old lady.'

'Can't say I noticed, but no point in getting involved.'

'What do you mean no point in getting involved? Didn't you see? They're tormenting her!'

The jeep pulled up.

I looked back along the road. She was a small figure now, standing motionless in the distance as the two young Ugandans stretched out a sari and elaborately attempted to wrap each other in it, sashaying their hips like Indian dancers. Other objects lay scattered around their feet but the woman remained motionless.

'Go back Dicken. Go back. They're only young. There's three of us and you've got your rifle. Just drive back up, please. We can't just leave her.'

'Forget it, Birdie. I'm sure she'll be fine.'

'How can you be sure? What if we drive back later and see a hump on the edge of the road? Her dead body! How would you feel then?'

Dicken grimaced, revved the engine and swung the vehicle around.

The youths were absorbed by their sport. One of them pulled the thin fabric across his face and fluttered his eyes, the other roared with laughter. They seemed surprised to see us, puzzled by the sight of a Western man with a young Asian woman and boy.

'Ah, Auntie' I cried as I jumped down onto the side of the road. 'We've been looking for you everywhere. Quickly, gather your things and get in.'

The woman looked blankly at me. Her face lined and dusty, a look of submissive resignation.

'Quick Auntie, come on, we're in a hurry.'

The youths looked from the woman to me and then at Dicken. Both pairs of eyes rested on the rifle that sat between the front seats. Dicken lightly touched the stock. I started gathering up the discarded garments and belongings scattered on the verge. Still the woman didn't move. I grabbed her hand and pulled her towards the jeep.

'Get in Auntie' I hissed, wondering why she was so slow and why I had been stupid enough to get involved in this situation. It seemed she was totally unconcerned about her own fate.

Another tug and she appeared to wake from her stupor, slowly moving one sandalled foot after another until she was next to the step of the rear door.

'Sabu, pull her. You pull, I'll push.'

She was surprisingly light and landed in a tangle on the back seat. I threw the carpet bag after her, objects spilling out onto the seat and floor. The youths barely had time to swallow a second time when I had jumped into the front seat and we swooped back onto the other side of the road, returning on our journey towards Mabira.

We were silent for a few moments, when I started to laugh. Dicken looked puzzled. I laughed even more. A smile started to creep into the corners of his mouth and Sabu joined in.

'They didn't know what to do. Whoosh! We came so quickly and whoosh we went off again. Just like we came on a magic carpet,' Sabu added. He leaned across from the back, his hands clasping the edge of our front seats and his gruff laugh was like a trigger until the three of us were cackling like chimpanzees.

The woman sat motionless behind us, her hands folded meekly on her lap, the carpet bag still half open.

Eventually our mirth subsided.

'Now what?' demanded Dicken.

'I don't know!'

'No plan?' There was a sarcastic edge to his voice.

I shrugged.

'What are we going to do with her now?'

'How should I know?'

'Well, you should have thought about that before you told me to stop!'

'We couldn't just drive by.'

'Where were you heading?' Dicken called to the woman, over the noise of the engine.

No reply. I looked back and the woman's face was blank.

'Where are you going?' I asked.

'Jinja.'

'Where in Jinja?'

'Station.'

'Do you need to catch a train?'

She gave a slight nod.

'What time's your train?'

She handed me her train ticket which was already looking dog-eared. A third-class ticket from Jinja to Nairobi and then on to Mombasa. The train was due to leave Jinja at six o'clock that evening.

'Were you going to walk all the way to the station?'

'Yes. I must get the train.'

I turned to Dicken.

'Did you hear that? She says she's catching a train to Nairobi. It leaves from Jinja this evening.'

'Is that where she was heading?'

'Yes. But you can see it's not safe for her to walk all the way to Jinja on her own. Anyway, it's miles.'

'Well, I'm not going to drive her there now. It's totally in the opposite direction.'

'I know, but we can't just dump her back where she was. Who knows what would happen!'

'I guess we could take her there this afternoon, in time to catch her train. But what the heck do we do with her until then?'

'She'll have to come with us to Mabira.'

'What? Traipse around with an old lady through the rain forest. Are you crazy?'

'Do you have any better idea?'

'No, but I certainly don't relish the idea of having an old woman hobbling around behind us all day.'

'I don't think we have a choice. We can take her to the station this evening. Agreed?'

Dicken gave a grunt, and I studied his sharp profile. I, too, was not keen on having our new companion for the day but realised that we could hardly dump her back on the side of the road. I twisted around in my seat.

'We can take you to the station in Jinja, but we can't do it now,' I explained. 'We're going into the forest, Mabira Nakalanga. It's not safe for you on the roadside. Do you want to come with us and then we can drive you to the train station later today?'

She reached out for the ticket. 'I must not miss the train. Six o'clock.' Her leathery finger pointed at the figure *18.00 hours* and she looked at me anxiously.'

'You'll get the train. Easily. We can drive you to Jinja this afternoon. It will give you a lot of time.'

She gave a nod, without any sign of gratitude.

I tried to suppress my irritation that we had to bring her. It was a rare and special day for us, visiting my favourite nature spot for the first time in more than a year, but it seemed like there was no choice.

After a while, I looked back at her as she sat watching the scenery, calm and withdrawn. Perhaps her presence wouldn't affect the day. She didn't seem like she would be much bother.

Before long we were heading into the green shaded depths of the forest. The temperature dropped, and the energy sharpened as I could sense the exhilarating rush of oxygen to my head. The forest was always a busy place, full of noise and activity. The animals and insects had their daily tasks to survive; beetles burrowing, frogs declaring themselves but most of all the birds and monkeys competing as the loudest under the green canopy. They all screeched and called, they seemed to argue and discuss. How like the monkeys we humans were.

Eventually Dicken parked the jeep in a small clearing where we convinced the woman to change from her sandals to some old plimsolls she had in her bag. They were not ideal footwear for the jungle paths, but they were the best she had, and so we set off on our way.

Sabu looked around in awe of the beauty and I could sense that he could feel the primeval force of nature. It was rare for the boy to be quiet, but it was as if he sensed the spirituality of this natural world.

The forest was alive with birds. Sunbirds, white-spotted fluff-tails, and even a flash of a Hornbill. Iridescent butterflies wove their way through the tunnels of sunlight that pummelled their way towards the undergrowth.

After two or three hours, damp with sweat, our throats parched, we finally reached the waterfall within the heart of the forest. It was time for lunch, so we set down a blanket and sat where we could feel the moist vapour of the air as the water thundered past.

The woman had been silent all morning, watching everything with an eagle eye as she walked behind us with a remarkably firm stride.

We ate Kuki's delicacies with relish and drank cool lime water from earthenware bottles.

After eating, Dicken took Sabu to find a Mukuzanume tree to show him how he could pick off the gum and chew it to cure various ailments.

The old woman and I stayed in the shade, lulled by the sounds of flowing water and animal calls deep in the forest. Lying back on the blanket, replete and languid, something overhead caught my eye. A striped spider was spinning a large golden web in the tree above our heads and although I dislike spiders, I watched with fascination as she worked methodically, weaving and pulling, tying and fastening.

A small sound, like a puff of air came from the woman's wizened mouth.

'She weaves her web as we weave our lives,' she said in perfect English.

'But how does she know where to tie the next strand? I've always wondered about that. Spiders weave busily and the result is this amazing pattern. How do they know?'

'It's in them, it's their dharma. Like our lives. Like our dharma. See how she weaves? She creates the lines going out, like spokes on a wheel, and then she weaves round and round, connecting the thread to the spokes, round and round so it becomes like a spiral.'

'Are our lives spirals?'

'Sometimes.'

'Yes, but people don't weave webs.'

She held up her finger.

'We do. We weave the webs of our lives. You see the golden thread?'

'Yes.'

'It is like our lives. Every person has their own golden thread in their life. We can't see it. We can feel it, but most people don't listen to the feel.'

'So the golden thread that runs through our lives takes us to where we should go?'

'Our true way.'

'To our fate?'

'Our dharma,' she said. 'We are like the spider. We do what we must.'

'Is that our lucky way?'

'It can come to us as luck. Not always happy luck. But there are messages of luck in our lives. They show us our path of fortunicity. They guide us where to go.'

'But we don't have a choice?'

'Everyone has a choice. Some people listen, some people won't listen. They put their fingers in their ears like this.'

She pulled a comical face as she stuck her fingers in her ears and I laughed.

'So how do I know where the golden thread is going in my life?'

'You don't know yet. You are too young. Your life is only starting now. It will change.'

'How will it change?'

'It will change for all of us.'

'But how do I know what is my true way? How do I know what is my golden thread?'

'I think you know that already.'

'I don't. I have no idea at all.'

'Your true way is to help people.'

'Help people? I've never helped anyone in my life.'

'That is not true. You helped me today.'

'That was different.'

'Why different?'

'I had no choice.'

'You think you had no choice. But you did have a choice. You could just drive on.'

'Well, no, I couldn't have carried on.'

'No young lady, you couldn't. Because you listened, here.' She put her hand to her chest and held my gaze with her amber eyes. I realised she must have been a beautiful woman once, when she was young.

'So, have you followed your own golden thread?' I asked.

'Me? Oh no, no, no. I don't follow my thread. Look at me now, a poor woman, old, sad, sad times.'

'I'm sorry to hear that.'

'But I follow it now.'

'How is that?'

'I leave Uganda.'

'To Kenya?'

'First to Kenya, then to India.'

'Why?'

'It is time. I just go early.'

'Early?'

At that moment Dicken returned with Sabu who was grumbling loudly about the bitterness of the gum from the Mukuzanume tree.

Above their heads I spied three monkeys sitting in a line on a strong branch. They looked like Bapu, Ketan and Bandar.

'Look Sabu,' I said to distract him, 'there are the wise monkeys. But when will you ever learn?' I shook my forefinger at him mockingly and Sabu laughed. He always had a ready laugh, and the moment was past.

When we continued our trek through the jungle, Dicken sensed my mood and walked beside me when the path widened.

'What is it Birdie?'

'It just doesn't seem the same.'

'You've changed. You're no longer a child. You're a mother now. Your priorities are different.'

'No, it's something else.'

We were heading back to the clearing where Dicken had parked the jeep.

'The old woman is going to India. She says she's just going early.'

'Early?'

'Do you think there will be a war?'

'I doubt it. Amin's just got into power. He's popular.'

'I don't like Amin!'

'Like him or not, he's here to stay, for a while at least. He's got an iron grip on the country. But maybe that's the problem.'

'What's that?'

'Maybe his grip is too tight.'

Later that afternoon Dicken pulled the jeep into the parking area outside the railway station. The old lady gathered her things silently and gave a little bow to each of us in turn. As she was turning to leave, I called her back.

'Sorry, but I never asked you your name.'

'Me?'

'Yes, what is your name?'

'My name is Shreya,' and she walked away.

'Shreya,' I said to Dicken quietly. 'I've heard that name before. It was in a storybook that I read as a child. Shreya. It means *the auspicious one*.'

The jeep's engine had just started, and Sabu had settled back onto the rear seat when he let out an exclamation.

'Stop! She left something. She left this!'

He held out a slim gold chain.

'I take it to her,' he said as Dicken let the engine idle along.

With lightning speed Sabu set up the station steps, and we saw his lithe figure dip into the shadows of the cavernous building.

To the side of the main entrance an army truck was parked. Two soldiers stood, talking and sharing a cigarette. We waited.

Dicken looked at his watch and turned the engine off.

Still no Sabu.

'What's taking him so long?' I commented.

The soldiers had finished their cigarette and one leaned against the truck while the other one paced up and down.

I was just about to get out of the jeep to see what had happened when Sabu came running down the steps two at a time, yanked open the rear door and flung himself into the seat well behind me.

'Drive!' he said. 'Go!'

He pulled his cap down over his eyes and cowered on the floor. It was the first time I had seen Sabu show any form of fear.

'What happened?'
'Nothing. Nothing. Just go!'
'Did you find her?'
'Who?'
'The old lady? Did you find her?'
'No lady. No train. Go!'

As Dicken started the engine, my eye caught a movement outside the main entrance. Four uniformed figures stepped out through the wide doors and one walked forward, the gaze from his hooded eyes glued to Dicken's jeep as we sped away.

CHAPTER 16

It's the eleventh letter of rejection that Jack's received, and he still hasn't even been invited for an interview.

'It's the worst time of year to apply for a job in the academic world,' Jack says. 'Any posts would have been organised last summer to start in September. In any case, holding a masters from Cambridge was something special back in Uganda, but they're not exactly rare here in England.'

'Maybe after Christmas something will come up. It will be a new term then.'

'We can't hang around here just in case. We need to get on with our lives!'

I glance out of the window towards the high brick wall that surrounds us. A prison or a safe haven?

Over the days we've been here we've listened to the tales from our fellow inmates. Many are uneducated but have worked hard over the years and put by savings for their old age. All that has been swept away and their eyes are dull and their futures bleak.

And the cold. Everyone complains about the cold. It doesn't cost much to live in Uganda - you only need a roof over your head and some food, but here there's so much that must be spent on heating homes. But how can they tell what proportion of a month's wages their heating bills would be? In truth, no one has any idea of earnings or the cost of living, or even what employment they could possibly get.

Tilak was a dentist's technician in Kampala; he has five

children and his wife's expecting another. He doubts he'll find employment in the same line of work as his English is poor. His brother wants him to set up a grocery store in Leicester, but they have no capital and no way of borrowing from a bank. His left eye twitches intermittently and he cracks his knuckles as he talks.

'First, I need to find some type of job, but it's hard and none of us can afford to live in this area. It's for rich people here. But where do we go? I need to look for work in other parts of London but if I take the public transport to try to find work, it costs me money and then I have nothing.'

The Uganda Resettlement Board has been set up by the British government and they try to help but they are like great rusty cogs in a large machine. Many of the residents say it would be quicker for them to go out and find their own employment, but they just need to know where to look. And it's always those who speak poor English who are in the weakest position.

Jack is tired of being idle and decides to start English lessons.

The administrator has agreed that the classes may take place in one of the dining rooms every morning, from ten to eleven o'clock for the beginners and eleven to twelve for the intermediate students. This is not before checking Jack's credentials. I only wish I had been present to witness the mild flush taint Mr Johnson's pallid cheeks when he saw Jack's qualifications far outweighed his own.

Teaching equipment is limited. There's a blackboard and chalk and some thick lined paper and pencils but there are no English language books to work from. Jack must use his knowledge and creative skills to make the lessons interesting.

Meanwhile, I continue with my plan to lift myself out of this shadow world and become a modern woman.

We have already contacted the hairdresser from the advertisement and were told that the practice modelling sessions take place on Sundays when the salon is closed to the public. We are to arrive at 9.30 am.

We don't need to book in? No, just turn up. Does it cost anything? There's a very small charge, but we can't choose what hairstyle we are given.

Padma says she will come with me, but Shai says she's happy with her hair just the way it is.

If you look at a large map of London it seems to go on forever. Open out a folded map of the Greater City of London and it will cover the width of nearly two of the tables in the dining room. But if you look at the map book – the A-Z, as they call it, all the areas are sectioned, and it starts to make sense. I look at where we are based, and I run my finger along to Knightsbridge and see it's not far at all. We can walk the distance easily.

Sunday morning arrives bright and sunny but it's cold and we have dragon's breath as we walk along to the end of Kensington High Street and alongside Kensington Gardens.

Beyond lies Hyde Park and Padma tells me that she's even seen horses being ridden on the sandy track that surrounds the grass.

We veer away from the road that runs alongside the park and, following the A-Z book, we zigzag down through the side streets where the houses are high and grand with expensive cars parked outside. I catch glimpses of thick lined curtains at the windows and chandeliers hanging from lofty ceilings. Then on to the mews with smaller pastel coloured houses with boxes of greenery on their window ledges and potted plants near the doors. At one point it looks like we have come to a dead end but there's a small opening in a wall and soon we find ourselves in another elegant street leading down to Knightsbridge.

As it's Sunday, all the shops are closed, but across the Brompton Road stands a large palatial building called Harrods. We cross the road to look in the shop windows. Each window is elaborately designed with lifelike mannequins wearing beautifully tailored outfits, displays of furniture, bone china and crystal. One window even has a small car on display with smart leather luggage and tartan rugs for warmth on journeys.

'It's the best shop in the whole of England,' says Padma.

How remarkable it is that we have ended up in the centre of London when so many of our people are staying in desolate buildings in the middle of the cold countryside.

The salon shop front is minimally stylish with black framed glass windows and simple black lettering on the white fascia above. Lights are being turned on inside and three women are already waiting outside when we arrive. They assess us silently. Nobody talks.

After several minutes a young woman wearing a skimpy dress unbolts the double doors and ushers us in, asking each of us to take a seat in the front section of the salon.

In the rear are a group of seven or eight hairdressers, all dressed in black, watching a demonstration. Most of them are men, apart from one young blonde woman with a stylish bob cut.

I'm allocated to a tall thin man who has straight dark hair that still reaches his jaw line despite being tucked behind his ears. I wonder when he last had his own hair cut. Padma is allocated to the woman and is taken to another part of the salon. Sitting high in the leather seat, my hair is assessed. Without saying a word, the trainee picks up tresses and lets them drop, stands behind me and plumps up the top section of my hair, looking over my shoulder at my reflection in the mirror. He doesn't seem pleased. Maybe my hair isn't right for his design. He goes to talk to the trainer.

On a low table I spy a magazine that appears to show the latest hairstyles. I quickly tiptoe over to get it. I know we're supposed to accept any cut they give us, but maybe they are not totally fixed. I find a style I've seen before in one of the glossy magazines and, when the trainee comes back, I point to the style and ask him if he could copy it. He pouts, takes the magazine and holds it close up to his face, studying it intently.

He gives a sharp nod.

'Okay, we do.' I realise he's not English.

My hairdresser takes me over to the washbasins and puts me in another leather seat that tips back, my neck nestling into a dip formed in the side of the basin. I lie back revelling in the luxury of the apple scented shampoo being massaged into my hair. What would it be like to come here as a wealthy customer and take it all for granted? To walk down from your house in Montpelier Walk and have a cut and blow dry here on a regular basis, dropping into Harrods to do a bit of shopping on your way home? We were not poor in Uganda, but never have I seen such luxury as this.

Throughout the session the hairdresser doesn't talk to me but merely directs me by tilting my head in the direction he requires. The silence is not awkward as he seems lost in his concentration and I relax into a sensuous stupor.

Padma's hair is finished before mine which is surprising as there is a lot more cut off. In fact, at first I hardly recognise her, it's such a shock. She sits in the next chair to me as my hair is being dried and styled.

'Just like Mia Farrow' she shouts above the noise of the hairdryer, rocking the leather chair from side to side.

I smile and shrug. I don't know who Mia Farrow is; all I know is her cut is as short as a boy's and I wonder what her parents will say. What will Jack's reaction to my haircut be? Too late - it's done now.

There's little that changes a woman more than a haircut.

Padma and I went in as two young refugees, but we come out feeling as if we belong in this place, in this year, in London.

Jack is amused when we get back to the centre.

'So, what's this then?' He walks around me closely inspecting my head from all angles.

'You like it?'

'Different.'

My hair is in a sharp, angled bob with one side hanging slightly longer, just clearing my right eye. There's a stylish curl pointing forwards but the rest curves in towards my lower neck.

'And what caused all this to happen?'

'Jack, this is a new life and I'm determined to fit in. I refuse to visit your friends looking like a poor little refugee.'

'We *are* poor little refugees.'

'Not for long. I refuse! I look at the people staying here, and I can see the light dimming in their eyes. They're resigned. They think "we are poor ignorant refugees and we have to take what is given to us. We will just do what we can to survive". Well, I can tell you that I'm not just going to survive. I see what is around us and I will not just survive. I will succeed!'

'And how do you think you're going to do that?'

'I don't know. But I will. I'll find a way.'

CHAPTER 17

Three weeks after our visit to the rainforest came Idi Amin's announcement. Our ruler had dreamed that all Asians should leave the country. He said we were bloodsuckers who were milking the economy, and we had ninety days to leave. Pack our things and go. One suitcase and a few shillings was all we could take. All our businesses, our houses, boats, cars, land, everything we owned was to be taken from us. Mr Kamar's hardware store, Amal's fruit stall, Uncle Deepak's Mercedes Benz.

Rutubasana.

I was in Kampala when the news came over the wireless. My mother-in-law was dismissive.

'He's just blowing out hot air. He's like a buffalo pushing his chest out and pawing at the ground.'

But every hour the announcement was repeated until it started to feel like a reality.

I tried to phone my father, but Kuki said he was in the sorting shed. Did he know yet? Had he heard?

When Jack came home, he confirmed our fears.

'Amin's a madman. He wants to slice us out of his country like we're a bit of rotten fruit, but we're the ones who keep the country going. We employ hundreds of local Ugandans. What would they do without us!'

He helped himself to a scotch from the drinks tray and shouted to Mirembe to bring some ice.

How did Mirembe feel about us going? Would she secretly be pleased or concerned about losing her wages? Who would live in our house? Where would we go? Our future was like flashing images from a slide show, all going too fast to even focus.

'Jack, my father. I have to go and see Pappa. I can't imagine how he'll cope with losing Rutubasana.'

My husband sat back deep into the sofa, drank some more scotch and studied the ceiling as if searching for answers.

'Jack, I must go and see Pappa!'

'I know, I know, but we can't go now. Everything's too unsettled. We'll have to wait until things calm down a bit.'

Eventually I managed to talk to my father on the phone and his voice was flat and resigned, a tone I had never heard before.

'We'll come and see you soon, Pappa. Jack says it's not safe for me to come at the moment but we'll come in a few days. He'll take some time off from the university.'

I tried phoning Dicken, but he was on tour in the northern district with a group of Australians.

Everything became a waiting game.

Three days later my father ate a solitary supper and sipped his customary nightcap on the veranda before retiring to bed. He would have closed the bedroom shutters, wound up the clock on his bedside chest as usual, rearranged the mosquito net and settled his head back on his feather pillow. Just the same as any other night. The ceiling fan would have been spinning slowly and he would have reached out his hand to switch off the bedside lamp. Would he have lain there for some time before drifting off to sleep? What were his thoughts as he closed his eyes?

Kuki found him the next morning, cool to the touch with a look on his face as though he had discovered the answer to a very important question. I asked her what she meant by that. She hesitated slightly.

'It was just like he knew,' she said.

'Knew what?'

'Everything,' and she carried on peeling the cassava as if there would now be anyone to eat it.

Dicken took my father's death badly. Kuki told me he had sat beside my father for the whole morning after his death until Aunt Latika arrived - the first of us to get there. As soon as she entered the bedroom, Dicken put on his safari hat, stamped his feet and walked out of the house. He never came to the funeral. We didn't see him for a full ten days.

There was an emptiness in the warm breeze. My father was not dead; death was too final a word, a sharp machete slicing its way through our lives. No, Pappa was not dead, he had merely left the room mid-sentence to go and find his reading glasses, just as he always would do in his absent-minded way. Perpetually, half his mind on the conversation and the other half on some elaborate preoccupation concerning the planting of tea. Death, a voice in my head declared. Death is just a word. Death is silence.

The doctor said it was his heart, but my aunt said my father had died of sorrow.

'He couldn't bear the thought of leaving his Rutubasana. And now he doesn't have to. Now his soul will stay here forever.'

My brother Sanjay told me he wouldn't be flying back from LA for the funeral.

'I can't get a flight in time,' he shouted in the distance.

The phone line crackled with static and there were long pauses as our words burrowed their way under the vast oceans.

'So, when will you get here?'

'I'm not coming back.'

'What do you mean you're not coming back?'

'Look, Bulbul, I'm not going to get there in time for his

funeral and there's little point in coming back just so I can be chucked out again.'

'I can't believe you're saying that Sanjay. What about your things? What about your inheritance? You'll have to sign some documents. You know that Rutubasana is being left to you.'

'What's the use in me coming back to sign documents for a supposed inheritance that will never actually happen? And even out here I've heard gruesome stories of what Amin's men are doing to us Asians. Sorry, but you'll have to deal with it yourself, Bulbul. Close up the farm. Whatever you need to do. The only thing now is to walk away. And Bulbul?

'Yes?'

'Make sure you get out soon. Go as quickly as you can.'

CHAPTER 18

Shai leans over the sewing machine with her head at an angle as she attempts to thread the needle. She's oiled the moving parts from the little container found within the base of the Singer and so far, it seems to be co-operating. The bobbin has been loaded with blue cotton to match the fabric and now for the important test - to see if it will really stitch a garment without rucking or snagging.

I remember my mother, her head tilted at a similar angle, lost to me in her concentration as she sewed intricate outfits for Sanjay and myself. Sometimes she would smock dresses for me with colourful cotton, but this was often done by hand, sitting in the living room while she chatted with my father.

Shai is skilled and swift. I ask how long she has known how to sew.

'Since the beginning of time,' she answers after she's cut the thread with her teeth. 'I watched my mother and the other workers, and I simply learned that way.'

'Will you do that work here in England?'

'Maybe, but they pay so little. Padma and me, we went to a factory for a day before you came. The Resettlement Board arranged it. Do you remember Padma? That clothes factory? The pay was not good and they wanted us to be just another machine. You have to put your card in a machine when you arrive, and again when you leave. It was cold and noisy.'

'Was the pay very bad?'

'I went to the bathroom and I talked to a girl there. I

knew she wouldn't tell me how much she was being paid so I tried it a different way. I told her how much the owner was offering us and then I looked at her face. That was all I needed.'

'Why? How was her face?'

'*Ha ha*, it said. *You're an idiot.*'

'So what then?'

'I told the owner we wanted to be paid more than he had offered.'

'He got angry,' Padma added. 'He said beggars couldn't be choosers.'

'And then what?'

'And then nothing. We need a place to live before we know where we can work, and we can't find a place to live until we have money from work. So, we are stuck.'

'Isn't there anywhere?'

'We're on the list.'

'In the queue.'

Padma has helped with cutting the fabric from the newspaper pattern, but it is Shai who holds the passion in her eyes as she pins, tacks, checks and trims until the moment the fabric finally meets the needle. She draws the dress over my head for the first fit. More pinning and tacking and mumbling through lips holding dressmaker's pins. The Singer machine had been stored away for two decades and we were lucky that all it needed was some oil and a new needle, all of which were housed in the bottom compartment.

As Shai is adjusting the fit, I look through the assortment of reels of cotton, odd pins and binding tape. Do these objects still hold my mother? She was the last one to touch them and I touch them now. Is there some connection? There's a little reel of gold thread and I see it's from Japan. The yellowing band of paper that holds the loop together reads *18 Karat Gold, Kyoto, Nishijini*. So hard to believe it's real gold, all the way from Japan. I think of the old woman and the spider's web spun above our heads, as gold as this 18 karat gold. Slotted between some wallets containing needles for the machine is a small photograph. It's of a young black man with an intelligent face and a slight smile on his lips. He's wearing some kind of uniform. It's a studio shot, only passport size. On the back is a stamp: *New Orleans 1942*. That was during the war. Was he going to fight? What did he mean to my mother? How strange that it sits hidden in the bottom of this sewing machine.

The dress is a success and the sisters are thrilled when I finally spin around for them. It's shorter than I'm accustomed to but I'll wear it with my thick tights so it won't be revealing. I wonder what Jack will think when I change for dinner on the Saturday evening.

'Shai, you are a genius,' I cry. 'You must never, never, never do anything else in your life but sew. It is your golden thread!'

She looks at me puzzled, but I can see she is pleased.

CHAPTER 19

Paddington Station consists of huge arches made from steel girders. Passengers walk purposefully in all directions, crisscrossing their routes - down the escalators to the underground, out to the front to hail taxis, lugging suitcases down long platforms. It's not a good place to be if you're not entirely sure where you're going.

Jack guides me to stand in front of a large black display board that clicks and clatters as indistinguishable names of unknown destinations are displayed.

'We need to take the train marked for Bristol and then it will list the other smaller stations that are on the way.'

I watch the board for a while, then look around. Not one food vendor in sight, only two kiosks that sell newspapers, magazines and a few chocolates and sweets. So different to home where there would be noise and colour, talking and laughter. Here's a huge expanse of dirty cold air and loneliness where the pigeons communicate more than the humans.

Once the train sets off, I start to feel a little lift of excitement. I double check that our suitcase is safely lodged in the rack above our heads and mentally sift through its contents in my mind. The new dress that Shai has made me, a pair of soft shoes loaned by Padma and a scarf that Ashika found on another visit to the charity stall. I'm wearing the Biba trouser suit and the pair of patent leather boots. I see the reflection of my hairstyle in the window. A modern woman.

On the journey Jack instructs me in the serious and delicate art of English manners. First, he explains that

English people will ask me how I am, but they don't really want to know, so for goodness' sake, don't tell them of my headache or talk in detail about the problems in Uganda. I must just smile and tell them I'm fine. That keeps them happy. And table manners - these are very important to the English. They will judge you on how you hold your knife. My knife? I ask. When drinking soup (and I must refer to it as drinking, not eating), I should ladle the spoon away from me. I must never shovel peas on my upturned fork or refer to a napkin as a serviette.

How did such a nation create an empire when it spends so much time being caught up in such trivial matters? I turn my attention instead to the English countryside skidding by. The train hurtles past flat fields surrounded by hedges and leafless trees, sometimes with cows or horses; everything tight and contained. I don't see any unfettered space like back home.

It's drizzling slightly when we climb down from the train onto the single platform of the remote station. One other passenger gets off and we follow as he walks purposefully to the gate at the side of the station building. Beyond this there is a grass island with a turning area for cars and a small collection area. No one is waiting for us. Our fellow passenger walks on to the car park and we stand under the awning listening to the rain as it grows stronger. Twilight starts to descend.

Behind us the station building is empty and there are now no cars in the small parking area. Some birds squawk in a nearby tree, but I can't see them in the dimming light.

'Are you sure they're coming to collect us?' I ask Jack.

'Of course,' he assures me, and we continue to wait without speaking further.

Eventually, there's the sound of an engine and a Land Rover hurtles around the corner and almost skids to a halt in front of us. A tall fair-haired woman, dressed in jeans and a green jacket, bounds out of the car and approaches us with her arms splayed out to the sides. I'm not sure if she is going to hug us or beseech her lord and it appears, at first, that she too is unsure.

'Jack,' she says, grasping my husband's hand and shaking it vigorously, 'I'm so sorry, so sorry.' She turns to me. 'And Bulbul, so nice to meet you eventually. I am *so* sorry I'm late. I had problems with one of my mares. Had to get the vet out and he's only just left. I told him I had to meet you at the station, but you can't rush these things, and she's one of my favourites.'

Jack introduces me to Harriet.

'So you prefer to be called Birdie? Sounds very English. Jack and Birdie. I'm usually called Horsie, so between the three of us we're quite a set.'

I don't feel I can call her Horsie as I'm not sure if it refers to her love of horses or the set of her teeth.

We all squeeze in on the front seat as she says the back of the Land Rover is filthy, but she throws our case in without a second thought.

It's hard to believe that these English roads are smoother than those at home, as each time Harriet changes gear we are jerked back into the leather seats. She talks all the time, telling us about her horses and how Buster is getting on, laughing often as she looks over at us in the murky light. She doesn't mention Uganda or our situation, which is refreshing. We laugh along with her while the windscreen wipers scratch and slap their chorus.

Finally, we turn down a long drive and the light from the headlamps bounces off rows of broad tree trunks. Harriet sweeps the land rover into a wide courtyard in front of a solid square brick house with nine large sash windows and a bright red front door. The lights are on inside and a man comes to the door to greet us. He ruffles Jack's damp hair as we walk into the hallway. Still a full head, unlike his own, he jokes.

Buster and Harriet are big people, not only in size but in voice and heart. We're taken through to their sitting room where a fire blazes in the hearth. Two black labradors greet us politely before settling back to lie on the rug in front of the fireplace. Thick red velvet curtains screen us from the rain outside and books and paintings line the walls. Not a tidy room and the high leather chairs that flank the fire appear old and worn, but it's comforting and there is a sweet pungent smell of burning wood in the grate. I remark on the scent and Harriet tells me that the distinctive smell comes from apple wood, an old favourite tree of theirs that was blown down in last year's storm.

Later that evening we eat supper in the kitchen, where a cream coloured range gives out a welcome warmth. I see it's called an Aga and Harriet says she couldn't manage without it. She cooks on it, dries clothes above it, and the lowest oven is even used to warm newly born lambs when they've lost their mothers.

We eat an egg and cheese tart, followed by apple crumble with thick luscious cream.

Buster tells us that two other friends will be joining us the following afternoon, a previous work colleague of Buster's from his time working in London, together with his Italian wife. In the evening they have also invited their neighbours for dinner, so we will be a party of eight.

'I'll show you my horses in the morning, Birdie. Buster's going to take Jack out on a shoot.'

'A shoot?'

'They shoot birds. Pheasants mainly.'

I look at Jack in horror.

'It's fine, Birdie. I won't actually be shooting, I'll be beating.'

'Beating?'

Buster takes control.

'Beating is a way we have of getting the birds moving.

People and dogs walk through the undergrowth and the dogs go sniffing around to find the birds and then any birds that are hiding away from us get startled and fly up into the air. Then that means that we spot the birds and bang! That's how it works.'

'Jack? Are you really going to do that tomorrow?'

Jack looks slightly awkward and blinks a couple of times.

'Yes, why not Birdie? It's not like I'm actually shooting. I'm a terrible shot anyway. I've done it before.'

'Have you?'

'Yes, of course. In my Cambridge days.'

There's a lot I don't know about Jack.

In the morning the rain has stopped and there's a slight mist sitting in the wooded valley that I can see from our large bedroom window. The smell of toast wafts up the stairs and there are sounds of cooking coming from the kitchen. Jack must already be downstairs. Should I join them? What should I wear?

I put on the trousers from my suit with a warm jumper, then follow the smells and clinking sounds coming from the floor below.

'Come in, come in. Sit down. We're lucky this morning. The hens have decided to lay. They can be a bit temperamental at this time of year. Too cold.'

A large mug of tea with milk and sugar is plonked in front of me, followed by toast and a pair of boiled eggs.

Buster's busy filling up a silver flask with some form of liquor which he packs away in his canvas bag.

'Hurry up Jack, no time to dally. You're getting lazy in your old age.' He gives him a jovial slap on his back and Jack smiles sheepishly as he follows his old friend out of the house.

Harriet's stables stand in a neat row with a cobbled yard in front. She introduces me to each of her horses and tells me about their characters and their special traits. I love the sweet scent of hay on their breath as they blow into my face, the softness of their muzzles and slightly prickly noses. I feel I could rest against their warm sides all day, absorbing their kind souls for eternity.

There are five mares and two young foals and she explains that she does some show jumping and dressage, a sort of dancing with horses. The foals that are good she will 'bring on' to their full potential. Some of these she'll then sell and others will be kept for competing, or to continue the line. The breeding is going well.

'Quite ironic really that breeding the horses is a piece of cake, but with Buster and me it isn't quite that simple.'

She doesn't mention their problem again, but neither does she ask me about Moh.

I help her clean the stables, lifting the warm mounds of dung and straw with a hay fork and carrying them to the larger pile steaming in the yard. I think of what Aunt Latika would think of me doing this work, but I find it strangely satisfying. Harriet has lent me a pair of old jeans and a jumper that are too big for me. The planning of my weekend wardrobe didn't include the country exploits of mucking out stables.

Harriet takes me into the small shed to the side of the stables which she tells me is called the Tack Room. Before my eyes adjust to the dim light, my nostrils are overwhelmed by the sweet rich smell of newly cleaned leather. Finally, I see rows of racks protruding from the wall, each one supporting a gleaming saddle. Next to each saddle hangs a bridle on a labelled hook displaying the horses's name. The hide looks supple, and the room is well ordered and clean.

'I usually use a double-jointed snaffle', she says holding up the metal piece connected by the leather, 'More often than not with a drop noseband. Some people say you should use a tougher bit, but I think it all comes down to the rider.

You can use the harshest bit in the world but it's never going to correct inadequate horsemanship.'

'How do you work out how it all connects when you take it apart?'

'Easy. Experience. Come on, we had better get on with preparing tonight's dinner.'

As we leave the shed Harriet spies a black and white bird sitting on the wooden fence. She dons a salute and says, 'Good morning Mr Magpie, how's your wife?'

Catching the look on my face she bursts out laughing.

'Don't you have that superstition in India? Or rather, Uganda?'

She is very amused by me, it seems.

'One for sorrow, two for joy... all that. Oh well, never mind. We're bonkers in this country!'

'Can you explain, please?'

'Well, it's just rather sad if there's only one magpie on his own, it means he doesn't have a mate. Although gipsies, and some other people would say that they're bad luck, so you should be polite to them just in case...'

'Just in case they curse you?'

'Something like that. Come on, we'd better get a move on.'

Harriet seems unconcerned by my inadequacies in the kitchen and turns a blind eye to the amount of time I take peeling the potatoes. Before dusk the two men return to the house with three beautiful dead birds, all hanging by their necks. Two are in various shades of brown and the third one gleams with rich and exotic colours. Apparently, the day's shooting has been a success, and everyone has gone home with good winnings.

Jack has a healthy glow in his cheeks and it seems that he and Buster have slotted back into their old, easy friendship.

The other guests, John and Valeria, arrive later in the afternoon and the hall is full of all of us, being introduced, chatting, laughing, the two black dogs weaving their way between our legs whipping their tails from side to side. The new arrivals are older than us, probably in their mid to late forties, polite and quietly sophisticated. The wife, Valeria, is Italian and has fine features accentuated by dark hair piled up on her head. She wears neatly pressed jeans, court shoes and a cashmere sweater and cardigan, adorned by a row of pearls.

The men go through to the smarter living room, called the drawing room, where they plan to have a drink and catch up on news. Valeria says she needs to put her feet up for half an hour before starting to help.

'I must apologise Harriet. I have a slight headache but I'm sure that two aspirins and half an hour with my feet up will make me, how do you say, as right as rain.'

'Oh, I am sorry you're not feeling well, but there's not much to do now,' says our hostess. 'Mrs Trimble is going to bring a couple of puddings and the cheese has arrived from the cheese shop, so I'm pretty much done. We only need to lay the table and make sure the men have lit the fires. Then we can have a drink and relax.'

I go to the guest room to change for the evening and am greeted by a chill in the air. The ceiling is high with elaborate plasterwork around the edges and the large fireplace seems to be letting in a draft from the chimney. I draw the curtains but I'm not sure if I'm keeping the cold air out or the cold air in. The iron radiator is lukewarm. Maybe it will heat up later. It seems a different world to the warmth and bustle of the kitchen below and a wave of loneliness floods over me. Jack seems to be comfortable with his friends and I've also felt relaxed when I've been with them. But up here, in this room, where the air is still and quiet, I'm aware of how I don't belong. Homesickness overwhelms me, almost more than ever over the past few weeks. For here is a real home, and theirs is a real life. But it's not ours; we are only nibbling at a corner of their existence just for a weekend. And yet how will I feel when I return to the camp? I'll remember this as a dream and we'll go back to our institutionalised life with an unknown future lying ahead.

I take my dress from the wardrobe and lay it on the bed looking at it critically.

So far my choice of clothes for the weekend has been inappropriate as it seems they dress casually in the country, warmth and comfort being the most important consideration. However, I've nothing else to wear this evening, so I'll wear the Biba style dress that Shai and Padma made for me; I'll style my hair and I will stand tall as I join them for drinks later. And that's what I do.

Harriet reprimands Buster for not lighting the fires earlier.

'You've got too involved in your chit chat and neglected your duties, Bee. Now we'll all freeze.'

Buster remains good humoured and assures her that all will be fine, he'll add some coal. He piles a mound of newspaper and kindling in the grate and then manages to suffocate the flame by pouring on the coal too soon.

'Here,' says Jack, 'you get the drinks and ice sorted out. I'll do this.'

'Oh yes, I remember,' laughs Buster. 'That week in the Scottish Highlands - you were the official fire lighter. I doubt you've had much practice since then though.'

Jack smiles wryly at me.

Valeria admires my dress and compliments me on my hairstyle.

'You all must be very stylish in Uganda.'

I smile calmly. If only she knew the trouble I had taken to create this impression. But was it entirely necessary? Although Valeria wears a stylish black dress adorned with chunky jewellery, Harriet appears to have grabbed the nearest items from her closet without any heed to the colour combination or the fact that her blouse would benefit from a press.

I know I look the best that I can under the circumstances. I've styled my hair well and the longer piece of my bob finishes in a smart curl beyond my right cheek, looking shiny and sleek. Thank you, Mr Vidal. I've enhanced my eyes with a modest amount of kohl and have applied some perfume from my treasured bottle of Chanel no 5.

The dinner guests arrive, and the wife confirms my suspicions that fashion is of little importance in the English countryside. The wife is wearing a tweed skirt which falls below the knee line of her thick legs, a flouncy white shirt and flat shoes. Her hair is greying, and she seems to speak through closed teeth. Perhaps she has a form of lock jaw and will have to sip her dinner through a straw. I'm told she and her husband live in the next house which is about a mile away and apparently they have known Horsie and Buster for 'yonks'.

We drink gin and tonics before dinner and leave the drawing room just as the fire has started to give out some warmth. Harriet is relaxed as her daily help, Mrs Trimble, is serving the meal so she can give all her attention to the guests. Buster allocates us our seats, but only after he's tracked down his reading glasses so he can see the plan. I'm sitting opposite the female neighbour, but I can't remember her name. Soon I'll be at the point of no return. Perhaps if I listen carefully, I'll catch someone mention her name, but then Buster calls her 'P' and I realise that I'm lost. How can I possibly call her by her initial?

Mrs P tucks into her prawn cocktail with relish before the thin slices of buttered brown bread have been passed around or Harriet has even started her own. Our guest would have done well to have listened to Jack's little lesson on the train. At least she has no need for a straw.

French Chablis is added to our crystal wine glasses. John and Buster discuss the effect the weather in France over the past few years has had on the wine industry while the rest of us listen and eat quietly. The next course is chicken casserole with creamed potatoes and peas.

The conversation still revolves around wine and John, sitting to my left, turns to me politely.

'Do you drink much wine in Uganda? Is it a drink you produce there?'

I say we rarely drink wine and when we do, it comes from Europe, or sometimes Australia.

'We don't have the right climate for wine growing, or at least, that's what I believe.'

'So what would you say is the native drink in Uganda?' he asks.

'The locals often drink Waragi, but it's terribly strong. It's known as War Gin so it's not good news for us Asians.'

Jack catches my eye.

'Many of us don't drink alcohol but if we do, generally we drink beer or spirits. My father would drink scotch, or whisky as you call it. Every night he would have a scotch and soda on his veranda.'

'That sounds very civilised. I'm sure that it's an extremely pleasant drink to have in the heat.'

Mrs P joins in the conversation.

'And what do you drink in India?'

'In India?'

'If you drink whisky in Uganda, what do you usually drink in India?'

'I'm sorry but I don't know what they drink in India.'

'Really? Are you not familiar with what they drink there?'

'No, I'm sorry but I'm not. I've never been to India in my life.'

'But do you not look on India as your home?'

'No, I don't think any of us do. Our home is...was Uganda.'

'But surely you think of India as home more than England?'

'I'm sorry but I can't answer that as I have never been there. So I can't choose without knowing.'

Mrs P reaches across the table and helps herself to a large dollop of creamed potatoes which she slaps on her plate.

'My mother always looked on India as her real home. It was where she grew up, you see.'

'Really?'

'Yes. She was born in the Punjab. Had a lovely childhood. Polo ponies, servants. She would always make a delicious kedgeree.'

'That's nice.'

Harriet comes to the rescue.

'Birdie and Jack will be settling in the United Kingdom and we are very lucky to have them. Jack has a British passport and a degree from Cambridge University and here is exactly where they are going to stay. Isn't that right Birdie.'

I feel my face growing warm and start to arrange my food. Mrs P's husband, Richard, clears his throat.

'It must be sad for you to leave your country, Mrs Dalal. I suppose one can only thank the Lord that the whole thing was peaceful. In a way, all things being considered, you were very lucky.'

I think of the maimed and mutilated bodies, the women and young girls raped, the wives looking out for their husbands on the hot shimmering horizon.

'Yes,' I say, as I organise my peas. 'We were very lucky.'

I go to take a sip of wine, now a claret, in another crystal glass. I'm on the point of putting my glass down when I catch Jack's eye. He's looking at me in horror. I query his expression with a raise of my eyebrow and he directs his eyes determinedly at my plate.

On the plate below me there is a green mush of peas,

mixed and squashed with the creamed potatoes. Using one of Jack's metaphors you could say that 'the rule book has been thrown out of the window'.

Jack's late coming to bed, rousing me from the silky stream of half sleep.

He's in a jolly mood and walks into a small armchair at the side of the bed, giggling and muttering to himself.

I switch the light on.

'Have you drunk too much?'

'Of course not, why would you say that?'

'Well, you seem a bit inebriated to me!'

'Not a bit of it. I could walk in a straight line if you asked me.'

'You're not used to it, Jack. You should be careful. I'm sure you used to drink a lot in your Cambridge days, but somehow it doesn't suit a grown man.'

'Oh come on my little Birdie, didn't you enjoy the evening? Isn't it nice to feel normal? Here we are having a normal existence with friendly people. Enjoying ourselves. What's wrong with that?'

I can see myself turning sour.

'You're right, Jack, I'm sorry,' and I turn off the light.

I lie still for a few minutes and I can sense that Jack is still awake.

'Why does Buster swear?'

'Does he swear? I can't remember. What did he say?'

'He talked about buggering. I know what *buggering* means.'

Jack snorts.

'That's not swearing! He just said we need to *keep buggering on*.'

'Exactly, that's swearing.'

'No Birdie, you don't understand. He was talking about the economic situation in England at the moment.'

'He was still swearing.'

'He wasn't swearing. All he said was we need to "keep buggering on." That's what Churchill said.'

'Churchill?'

'The great Winston Churchill. He was Prime Minister of Britain and he saved the British in the Second World War.'

'I know who Churchill was. Are you saying the great Churchill swore?'

'No, no, he only said everyone had to keep trying, they had to "keep buggering on".'

'He swore.'

We are silent for a few more minutes and I can see a hint of moonlight creeping in from the edge of the curtains.

'And what was all this talk about cricket? Are you going to be playing cricket? In December?'

'Were we talking about cricket?'

'Yes, don't you remember? You said that Matthews, who used to be in your university cricket team, was now batting for the other side.'

Jack starts to giggle in the dark.

'Oh no, well that's not exactly about cricket.'

'Well, it sounded like that to me.'

'We were talking about Matthews who used to be in our cricket team "batting for the other side". That's just a term.'

'A term for what? What does it mean?'

'Well,' says Jack now in fits of laughter, 'I suppose you could say that Matthews just keeps buggering on!'

I tell my husband to stop acting like a child as I turn over to try to get back to sleep. Eventually Jack's amusement subsides and he's snoring loudly.

When I awake the next morning, the bed beside me is empty and there are sounds of activity downstairs. A dog barks. Jack laughs. I stretch out on the soft mattress and revel in the privacy of this moment, the aloneness, something I have rarely felt since we arrived in England.

Eventually I pull back the chintz curtains and see it is raining lightly but there are patches of blue sky above the valley in the distance. Sheep graze in the field beyond the lawn but there's no fence, only a sharp drop supported by a wall creating a type of ditch. Jack has informed me that this is called a Ha-Ha. At first, I thought he was joking.

'No, seriously Birdie, the idea came from 17th century France. It's a barrier without being as intrusive as a fence.'

'And it's called a Ha-Ha because you don't see it and then fall down and say "Ha-Ha"?'

'Very funny, but in a way, yes. It's supposed to be an amusing surprise. It helps the landscape flow. It's been used for years. The great landscape gardener, Capability Brown, incorporated it in countless landscapes. Don't you like that fact, Birdie? Don't you see? Although we've been uprooted from our home, from so much, here in England we have…' he paused. 'History. Here there are the streets where Chaucer walked, the house where Jane Austen wrote her wonderful books, the buildings where kings and princes were born and beheaded. It's all here, even the Ha-Ha.'

'But it's not our history. We don't belong. That lady last night made it perfectly clear. We don't belong.'

'Well, you could say we don't belong in Uganda either.'

'We certainly don't now.'

'Would you rather we went to India? Do you feel we would belong there more than here?'

We were weary of this well-trodden territory.

I take a bath in the high-ceilinged bathroom that lies at the end of the corridor. After pouring some bubble bath into the tub, the brass taps clank and judder as they pull the water through the ancient pipes. It's a novel experience for me to bathe, having always had showers in Uganda. I feel my limbs relax as I enjoy the feeling of all-encompassing warmth – a rare experience in this cold land.

Breakfast is being served in the dining room and there are various cooked items on the sideboard. I accept the offer of eggs and toast and pour tea from the large silver teapot that sits in the middle of the table.

Buster is loud and jolly despite the gloomy news in the Sunday papers.

'Best not to read the newspaper. Don't want to ruin our day. You think your country has gone to the dogs but what we have here isn't much better. Not the violence, but economically things are a disaster. I would say you're out of the frying pan into the fire!'

I look questioningly at Jack.

'We've fallen out of the sky and got stuck in a date palm,' he explains.

Harriet catches my puzzled expression.

'Did you not know Birdie? Things aren't good in Britain at the moment. High unemployment, heavy taxes and unhappy workers. But I try not to read the papers. I prefer to think about my horses. More toast?'

'Things are not much better in Italy,' contributed Valeria who sat serenely at the end of the table with only a cup of tea. 'Inflation is so high that the smallest change is often given in the form of candy.'

I have a fleeting thought of how Sabu would like Italy. For a moment the room spins. It's a relief when Buster changes the subject.

'We men are thinking of going to visit some old stones that lie around in a village near here. You're most welcome to come but it's raining and I'm not sure it would really be your thing. So the plan is, Birdie, if you don't mind, you stay here with Valeria, we men go off – Harriet's going to do the horses – and then we can all meet for a pub lunch later. How does that sound?'

'Are you going to see Stonehenge? I've heard about those stones.'

'No, Stonehenge is quite far from here, these are some Neolithic stones in a village nearby. We'll take you to see Stonehenge next time you come and stay if you would like to see it.'

I look at the rain outside and agree that it would probably be more pleasant to stay indoors.

While we clear away the breakfast things Buster lights a fire in the sitting room, then the men put on their wet weather clothes and head off with excited dogs at their heels. Harriet excuses herself and Valeria and I are alone in the kitchen. I stand near the Aga and enjoy the heat radiating into my back.

Valeria seems to know the kitchen well and, opening a high cupboard, pulls out an angular metal pot. She then goes to a folded paper bag placed on the kitchen table and unfolds the top, taking out a small silver and red foil bag which she snips open delicately. Putting the bag to her nose she sniffs slowly and steadily, closing her eyes as if in ecstasy.

'Coffee,' she informs me. 'Italian coffee. The best coffee in the world. I always bring it when I come to stay.'

She then proceeds to pour water in the base of the pot, tips the ground coffee carefully in the middle section, patting down gently, screws the pot back together and places it silently on the grey plate of the Aga.

I've seen that look before. It was on the faces of the Buddhist monks I once saw performing a religious ritual in Kampala, it was the light in my Uncle Deepak's eyes when he was intent on getting his outboard motor started.

Valeria then selects an appropriate tray, opens another cupboard and takes out two delicately patterned cups and saucers. The china is so fine it almost looks transparent. She then arranges these on the tray together with small spoons, sugar cubes and cream in a small white jug. I watch her elegant figure as she moves almost silently around the kitchen. Eventually the coffee splutters and spits to a crescendo and my companion appears satisfied that all is in order.

'Come, Birdie, we will go into the sitting room and you will tell me all about yourself.'

I get a fleeting sense that this is planned, that the house has been emptied for this one purpose, that I should sit in front of the fire with this distinguished Italian lady, drinking her native coffee from bone china cups, not merely to pass the time. There is something else.

Before we settle, the ritual must continue. The fire is poked, cushions are plumped, and Valeria pulls the faded curtains back further to allow more light into the room, then unsatisfied, she switches on two table lamps. The coffee is gracefully poured into in our two cups and she sinks back into one of the armchairs beside the fire. I sit opposite her.

A slim gold case is opened, a cigarette removed, tapped down twice on the case and slotted into a tortoiseshell cigarette holder. This is then lit with a bullet-shaped lighter. Valeria pulls gently at the mouthpiece of the holder and inhales slowly and deeply.

All is silent apart from the loud ticking of the grandfather clock and the crackling of the fire. I sip the coffee and say it is good. I would like to reach for some sugar, but I don't dare.

'So tell me Birdie,' she pauses, thoughtfully taking another pull from the cigarette holder. 'Actually, is your name really Birdie? It sounds English to me.'

'My name is Bulbul. It means Nightingale but we have a very good friend, well, you could say he's like a second father to me, he is, was, or is, American. He has always called me Birdie.'

'Because your name means Nightingale?'

'Yes, and also because I've always loved birds. By the

time I was ten I knew the names of all the birds in Uganda, and I could recognise their calls. Dicken taught me that. I love all wildlife really, but particularly birds.'

'How charming.'

'Sometimes he would also call me Popcorn.'

'Really? Why Popcorn?'

'He said I had too many thoughts popping out of my head just like when you heat the corn. And we liked going to the cinema. I would always go with him and we would see nearly every film that came to Jinja. And we would eat popcorn.'

'And you were fond of Dicken?'

I nod and sip some coffee which helps to relieve the lump in my throat.

'And where is Dicken now?'

'I don't know.'

'And the rest of your family?'

'My brother is in America. He's an engineer. He was always mad on engineering. My mother would take him to see the building of the Owen Falls Dam when he was little. I think that started his passion. Every week he wanted to go and see the machines working. Then he went on to study engineering and got a job in California. He was working there before the troubles in Uganda began and now he stays there. My mother died many years ago. And my father,' I take another sip of coffee, 'My father died only recently.'

'I'm sorry to hear that Birdie. That is very sad.'

'Yes, thank you.'

'Was he sick for a long time?'

'No. Well, his heart was not good. For some years his heart was not good. But in the end his heart broke. I think it broke from sorrow. It broke because he didn't want to leave Uganda. He loved Uganda, and his home, and his plantation…'

My voice trails off and I notice that the pattern on the

rug swirls in a never-ending repetition, blue next to green, then on to a rusty orange. Would you call it rust? Yes, I think it is, for it is so close to red that it must be a rust. The fire crackles.

'And you, Birdie? Is your heart broken?'

I look at her and blink. The fire dries my eyes and I need to blink to moisten them.

'I don't know.'

'You don't know if your heart is broken?'

'Sometimes my heart is broken. Sometimes I am cross. I will not let my heart break. If I lie down and let my heart break, what will I give Jack? What will I give our son?'

'Your son? I was not aware you have a son.'

'Yes. But I am not a good mother.'

'No?'

I shake my head slightly.

'Why is that?'

'I know I'm not a good mother. His grandmother, Jack's mother, is better for Moh.'

'How old is your son?'

'He's nearly one year old. Almost walking. He's very strong.' I sound like a proud mother, but I realise I don't have the right.

'But you want the best for Moh, and for Jack?'

'Of course!'

'Well, that is good. Maybe you'll become a better mother. With time.'

I nod and go to sip my coffee. Valeria notices that my cup is empty and gets up to refill it.

'So, what did you do when you were in Uganda, Birdie?'

'Do? Like work?'

'Yes? Or not work? What did you do? What are you good at?

My smile is bleak.

'I didn't do anything really. Nothing important. When I

was younger, I wanted to go to university, but my father would not allow it. I was good at arithmetic at school. I find numbers easy. My teachers said I should go to Makerere University but to do that I would have to lodge at the university as we didn't live close enough for me to go every day. My father would not agree. And I think he didn't want to be lonely.'

'So you stayed with your father?'

'Yes. My father had a tea plantation, and I stayed with him there. I helped him. Slowly, as I started to learn more, we changed the tea production so that the tea was finer, and we got more money for it. My father said that Dicken was right – I did have lots of ideas popping from my head and I was useful. So I stayed home.'

'And were you happy there?'

'I loved my father. I loved the plantation.'

'I see. And then you married?'

'Yes, I married Jack two years ago. I was lucky.'

'Indeed, you were lucky. He is a lovely man.'

'And I was lucky that he would accept me.'

'Why was that? You are lovely as well.'

'That is a kind thing for you to say. But in our culture we are not only ourselves, we are our family, and we are the history of our family. The history of my family is not good. My mother.'

'Your mother who died?'

'Yes, she did not die in a good way. She killed herself. In my culture it is a crime. It makes me… It makes me dirty, in a way. It's hard to explain.'

'That is very sad Birdie. Do you believe that is right?'

I wipe the tears from my face.

'No!' I say, and I realise my voice is almost a shout. 'Why do you ask all these questions?'

'Because I'm interested.'

'Why are you interested in me? I am nothing. Later this

evening I'll return to the camp and this will all seem a dream. These beautiful cups, this fire, you. A dream!'

'Of course you are not "nothing". No one is "nothing". I want to understand. I want to help, and it is only by understanding that I will be able to help.'

I feel ashamed of my outburst and study the carpet further.

'I'm sorry,' I say. 'It's a bad way for me to behave.' I can see Jack's stern disapproval in my mind.

'Tesora, I don't think there can possibly be a correct way for you to behave in such a situation. You have lost everything, and this is a difficult time for you. I understand. That is why I want to help you.'

'That is very kind of you, but how can you help?'

She holds a slender finger up and tilts her head slightly as if contemplating this question.

'First, I need to show you something.'

'What is that?'

'It's not here. I want to show you something in London. I will take you to tea. When we get back. Next week?'

'Thank you, that would be nice,' I reply but my words are empty. I want to be left alone, yet at the same time I'm intrigued. What could she possibly want to show me?

There are sounds of the back door opening and Harriet calls out, then curses as she trips over the boots in the rear hallway. We smile at each other, united in our fondness for this warm and slightly clumsy woman.

The country pub is like an illustration from one of my childhood books. The building is old with small leaded windows and uneven walls painted in a light cream, all topped by a roof of straw. It's called thatch, Harriet informs me as she slams the Land Rover door shut with extreme force.

'Sticky door!' she explains.

Harriet has loaned me an old tweed jacket, having seen me shiver as we were setting out from the house. It's well cut but the lining is torn and there's a hole in one of the pockets. The other pocket appears to contain bits of straw and grain which I idly finger as we climb the steps to the old oak door of the inn. Valeria wears a navy blue woollen coat draped over her shoulders and she walks lightly up the stone steps beside us.

There's a rush of warmth as we open the door, the buzz of people talking, the smell of ale and a wood fire. Jack is sitting with Buster, their backs to us, in deep conversation. John's reading a menu.

'...but I couldn't believe it after so long. Fiona of all people and just when I was about to see you as well. She asked after you of course.'

I don't hear what Jack says in reply.

'No, she's not married. I don't think she's ever really got over you – her first love.'

Harriet pokes Buster in the back and he jolts upright.

'Aha, hello, hello. You've just made it in time.'

'In time for what?' hisses Harriet.

Buster blushes and Jack looks awkward.

Valeria nestles herself into a high armchair next to the fireplace. She has a way of almost folding herself up, tucking herself together to watch the world. She seems to notice everything in her quiet, refined way, but appears to do so without judgement. She merely observes.

I can barely look at Jack throughout the entire meal. Instead I devote myself to asking about Harriet's horses, Buster's new flock of Jacob sheep, John's life as a barrister. My husband is suddenly a different man to me. A man with a private past. It was ignorant of me not to have envisaged any romantic history. Cambridge university was not just for young men but women also. Clever ones, pretty ones. I watch Jack out of the corner of my eye and acknowledge he is an attractive man. He was studying in this country in the 'swinging sixties' - the age of sexual liberation. Didn't Aunt Latika mention an English girl? My mind starts to wander but I slap it down. I don't want to take that trail.

After lunch the weather has cleared and we take a relaxed walk around the village, admiring the duck pond and the stone memorial cross that lists the names of young men from the village who died in the two big wars. So many of them. Young men in their uniforms, closing the door on this cottage, or that square house with the weathervane on the roof, walking down the path for the last time, past the duck pond, not knowing if they would ever return. Or did they know? Did a shadow fall across their spirit? They would have had no choice but to walk on, regardless.

How, given a choice, would they not have preferred to lose all their worldly possessions and remain with their lives? To grow old and enjoy their children and their children's children, even in a foreign land? Would they not have preferred to live?

My husband and Buster stroll ahead of us. They walk easily together in deep conversation, their elbows occasionally bumping as they walk close. I see that there is a part of Jack that already belongs in this country. He's right, there is a history here. At the moment it's Jack's history but in time, maybe it will also become mine, and Moh's and even Ashika's.

It's time for us to catch our train back to London. Harriet and Buster both drive us to the station. Valeria and John have already left to visit some friends in Oxfordshire on their way home to London. Before they climbed into their smart BMW, my new friend hugged me warmly and arranged to collect me from the camp on the afternoon of the following Thursday. Despite me suggesting another meeting point, she was determined to come to the centre and finally I relented. It would only be one further humiliation amongst many. In any case, my curiosity was aroused. What could she possibly want to show me?

Although we only arrived in Wiltshire forty-eight hours earlier, when we return to the station it looks less foreign, almost familiar. I can now picture where it stands in relation to our friends' house and the village where we were this afternoon. The canvas is no longer blank.

On the platform, as we are saying our goodbyes, I realise I'm still wearing Harriet's jacket and I start to take it off.

'No, Birdie, please. Keep it. It's ancient I know, but it's kind of comfortable and it's warm. You keep it. Anyway, you would freeze if you took it off now. There's nothing worse, when you're nice and nestled in.' She smiles and rubs my shoulder and we all say our farewells as the train draws in.

I climb the steps into the carriage with a heavy heart. A whistle sounds and the train starts to chug slowly away from Wiltshire, from our friends, from an oasis in this bleak desert called England.

CHAPTER 20

We are alone in the railway carriage, Jack and I, sitting opposite each other by the blackening window. Hills and trees race by as phantoms in the dusk until they are finally lost and the thick glass acts as a black mirror. Husband and wife as strangers.

Finally, Jack closes the book he is reading.

'You may as well come out with all your questions. Then we can then get them out of the way, and maybe carry on with our lives.'

'Very well. Fiona?'

Jack looks to the heavens.

'It was a shame, a great shame that you heard Buster. He made it out to be more than it was.'

'I heard him say that you were the love of Fiona's life!'

'For goodness sake, I hardly have any control on what she thinks of me. She certainly wasn't the love of *my* life.'

'But you had an affair?'

'Yes, well yes, but no! It was just a phase. We were students, we drank too much, partied, had picnics, punted on the Cam, we enjoyed life.'

'And each other's bodies?'

'I'm not a brahma, I'm a man. Did you expect me to have no past when we married? I was 34 years old!'

'And I suppose she was terribly pretty, with golden hair. An English Rose.'

'No, she was Scottish.'

'All right, Scottish then.'

'Come on Birdie, don't be ridiculous!'

'I suppose you just couldn't help yourself. All that temptation.'

'I never said I was pure. I'm a man. This is a modern world.'

'How strange that there are two modern worlds. Or one modern world, spliced down the middle - one half for men, one half for women.'

'That's not the issue here. You're over-reacting to a tiny piece of information you overheard and blowing it out of all proportion. We're talking about years ago.'

'So you're saying you don't have any feelings for her?'

'No, my life is with you and Moh. What we can make of it.'

'Because that's what you're stuck with.'

'That's not true, it's the life I want. Together. We just need to find work and a home. We're bonded. A family. Will you put this silliness away! No more mention of it. Agreed?'

'Very well,' I reply reluctantly, and I close my eyes. I must stop myself now or bad words will spew out of my mouth like a swarm of bees and I'll never be able to take them back. I must stop, breathe, keep silent. I know I can never give back those words I overheard in the pub, but it slices at my heart that, throughout our argument, Jack never says he loves me.

I'm rocked by the rhythm of the train which sways slightly as it negotiates bends in the track. I think of returning to the camp, of Moh and how I yearn to pick him up and pummel his pudgy hands with my lips, breathe kisses into his neck. But I won't.

Until this weekend the camp has been bearable. It was the only England I knew. Now I have tasted the edge of a comfortable, warm world and my heart is desolate.

My mind starts to wander. I remember a story that Sabu told as we all stood, shaded from the sizzling heat of the African sun. It was about a poor little beggar girl, a happy little beggar girl, who was spotted by a beautiful maharani as she drove by in her carriage of gold.

Now this young girl had very little in her life. She existed on one bowl of rice and lentils a day and any other scraps that she could wrestle from the stray dogs that patrolled the dusty streets of her remote village. The maharani, on the other hand was bedecked with jewels and nestled back in her pillows of damask silk as she was travelled home from the neighbouring province. But, (at this point Sabu held up his forefinger and paused, looking around at his captivated audience) but, despite all the diamonds and emeralds and servants at her beck and call, the Maharani's heart was desolate. She had lost her only one true love - her young daughter who had been merely five years old when she passed away in her mother's arms during the last rainy season. There was something about the little girl, (I think Sabu called her Bhanu) that reminded the maharani of her cherished daughter. Before she could help herself, she had tempted the child into her chariot with the promise of sugared figs and gulab jamun - and who, asked Sabu, with eyes as round as saucers, could resist gulab jamun!

I smile to myself in this dimly lit train carriage. Sabu had always had a sweet tooth.

The story continued.

Now, what the maharani did not know was that, despite the girl's rags and unshod feet, this little beggar girl Bhanu, had a mother who loved her very much, and a baby brother who waited for her in the shadows of their tiny shack on the edge of the village. But Bhanu was destined for greater things and was carried off to the next province where she was dressed in silk clothes, slept on a soft bed and became accustomed to playing in the long marbled halls of the palace.

All was well until - Sabu crouched down slightly at this point and rested his hands on his knees as he looked at each of his audience in turn - until the maharaja returned home, after several months of absence fighting the enemy with his army. He saw Bhanu lying in his adored daughter's bed, wearing her clothes, and he flew into a terrible rage. He shouted, and he bellowed; he stamped and he scowled. At one point he even drew his sword on his wife.

Sabu particularly liked this part as he unsheathed his wooden sword from its scabbard and held it aloft.

He said that he would denounce her as his wife unless she returned the child immediately to the village from whence she came. And he vowed not to look at his wife again until Bhanu was removed from the palace forthwith. Despite the maharani's tears and pleading, her husband would not budge. So, it was with a heavy heart that she took the child in a simple, unadorned carriage and returned her to her mother, to whom she gave five gold coins in compensation for the distress that she may have caused.

Now Bhanu had always been a happy child and had loved her mother and brother, and the simple village where she grew up, but a strange thing was happening to her. As they travelled back over the rough terrain, she felt the colour was seeping out of the landscape. She rubbed her eyes and blinked but it still seemed the sky was less blue and the leaves on the trees were less green. By the time she was nestled in her mother's arms she noticed that her mother's familiar pink sari barely had any colour at all. Everything looked dull and lifeless and no matter how much Bhanu screwed up her eyes it seemed that the rich tones of colour in her life were gone forever.

'Would it not have been better,' said Sabu in a conspiratorial tone, leaning towards his audience, 'would it not have been better if Bhanu had never experienced the riches and luxuries of the maharani's palace? For then she would still have all the colour and light in her poor life. Before she was whisked off to those weeks of luxury, she didn't know any better and was happy. Now she was lost.'

The train judders and the breaks hiss. We are pulling into Paddington station. We are back in our refugee lives.

CHAPTER 21

On the Monday morning, Shai grabs my hand and leads me into a small corridor near the laundry room.

'You wouldn't believe the raucous calamity we've had this weekend. Honestly, as soon as you left, it felt as if the sky had been blown off our heads!'

I can't understand how any excitement has happened in our short time away, when the whole camp lives in a dreary rotation from one day to the next.

'Hana's father has arrived and has brought with him her betrothed. There wasn't room for them – they hadn't been booked in. So then there were huge arguments with the administrator and they called in the Resettlement Board. He said that they had misled him and lied. Then he started treating Hana badly – I saw him slapping her, and not only that, digging his fat fingers right into the base of her neck. Here, you know, where it really hurts.'

I got the message and shook off her hand.

'And why was he being so cruel to his daughter?'

'I think it's something to do with her not wanting to marry the other man. He's ugly and coarse, and not much younger than her own father!'

'That's a great shame because she's so pretty and gentle. She deserves better.'

'Well, there's not any hope of that happening – he'll probably drag her by her hair kicking and screaming. It looks like he's going to force her to marry the brute.'

It's hard to believe that even with our change in circumstances, the control of women in families goes on the same. I bless Pappa in my mind and send him golden flakes of love from my heart.

Shai tells me Hana's father and his companion have now been housed in the back room of Mr Caxton's long shed. At least they will share the same attitude to women, even if their race and religions differ.

'And how is Hana?'

'At first she sobbed, and she screamed, but only in our dormitory, away from the men. Her mother doesn't have any sympathy and just tells her she has to be a dutiful daughter, then she goes back to gossiping with her friends. She's a silly woman.'

'And how is Hana now?'

'Now she's gone silent. There is no light in her eyes, just like when she first arrived. But…'

'But…?'

'But worse. She seems darker in her mood than when she arrived. Like her world has turned black.'

Later in the day I catch sight of the new arrivals. The father is tall and solid with a thick head of hair and a slightly overshot jaw which gives him a stubborn look. The other man is shorter with slanting almond eyes which remind me of Kartik. They're leaning against the side of the main building talking with three men who listen intently. Something tells me they are troublemakers.

Jack's in a gloomy mood when I see him. He's received yet another letter from a university, thanking him for his enquiry, but advising him that there are no vacancies in his field of expertise.

'If you can't get a job in a university, how about looking further afield? How about teaching in a school?'

'That's not so easy. I can't teach in a government school as I don't have the additional qualification required and taking a teacher training course would take a year. That would mean no income for a whole year, which is impossible. Some private schools will employ teachers with degrees but without that extra qualification. It still doesn't get away from the fact that we're right in the middle of the academic year.'

'Well, you never know, maybe there will be some extra help needed. You should start sending independent schools letters, or maybe the Resettlement Board can help you.'

'I suppose so. Perhaps I'll end up being a schoolteacher. I can't suddenly change my career and become an accountant, unfortunately.'

What can I be?

That evening I see Hana across the dining room sitting with her mother, father and betrothed. She sits quietly, looking down as if lost in thought. When addressed, her eyes flick upwards, and she answers lifelessly, before looking down again and playing with her food. Even her mother seems slightly subdued in the presence of these forceful men. The atmosphere has changed.

CHAPTER 22

The telephone is ringing. It rings and rings and I pick it up, half asleep.

I hear the spit and the sobs as Nanda's voice erupts into the earpiece.

'They've killed them! They've killed them all. They cut off Kenzi's arms.' She sobs, the air rasping as it refills her lungs. My stomach lurches and my legs go weak.

'Killed them? Who?'

'Kenzi and his family - all his family. Just because they're Acholis!'

I reach out and try to wipe the window. If only I can wipe the mist off the window, they'll be all right. Kenzi and his family will be fine. Everything will be back to normal.

I wake to my sobbing and see my arm reaching out into the gloom of the dormitory. The women around me seem undisturbed and Moh sleeps on by my side.

Only a dream. But there's a dark tuber of despair gnawing at my stomach.

Think of something else.

Tomorrow I'll see Valeria. I dread the humiliation of her collecting me from the centre. I'll meet her at the gate.

A police siren sounds in the distance. Sleep eludes me.

I'll wear my blue dress tomorrow, a necklace, a spray from the Chanel no 5 that sits in my wash bag. And where is the bag now? Did I bring it back to my cabinet after visiting the washroom this evening? No, I feel sure I left it sitting on the windowsill. No, I remember now that I've left my wash bag in the shower room. Leave it there - it will still be there in the morning. But what if someone helps themselves to the small bottle of perfume that nestles in the bottom? Leave it, it's warm in the bed, it can wait.

Eventually, I put on my dressing gown and softly pad through the dormitory in my bare feet. My path is illuminated by the yellow light from street lamps and additional lighting within the camp grounds. I pass through the toilet area, turn the corner and quietly open the door to the shower room.

As I start to cross the room to the basins, I can make out the sound of running water. Someone's left a shower running. But there's something else. A small sob. A moan. It's coming from the third shower cubicle on the left. I pause. An unknown word, a sob, then the word repeated.

'Hello?' I say.

There's no sound apart from the spray of water.

'Hello? Are you all right?'

Nothing.

How strange to be having a shower in the middle of the night. I nearly walk past, then quickly detour back to the cubicle and tug back the curtain.

At first it's hard to make out the details in the gloom. I see her eyes. They look up at me as a dog about to be beaten. She's crouched like an animal in the corner, her wet nightdress clinging to her body. She holds something in one hand. The water looks dark around her and I can't understand why the water should be muddy. In Uganda, yes, but in London? Strange thoughts.

It's then that I notice her wrist oozing dark liquid and I realise what she's holding in her other hand.

We look at each other for what feels like a full minute. Our eyes searching the depths of a dark void.

'Hana! Up!' I order. 'Get up. Now. Put that down.' I shake her hand and the small razor blade streaks to the floor. I grab her clean wrist and pull her out of the shower cubicle and towards the bench.

'Stupid girl! Stupid girl!' I hear myself say.

She slips in my grasp so I hold on to her wet nightdress. I need to find something to stop the bleeding. I grab a small hand towel by the basins and press it down on the wound.

'Stay, hold your arm up like this. Sit here while I go and get help.'

'No, no, no!' she rasps in anguish. 'You *mustn't* get anyone. My parents, my father! They must not know!' Her beautiful face is distorted with torment and fear.

'Don't be ridiculous. We have to get you to a doctor.'

'No, no. It's a silly cut. See. I haven't done it well. No one must know. No one!'

I hesitate. I can imagine the chain of events. The doctor, the questions, the abusive father, the insipid mother.

'Please, no.'

I look around helplessly.

'Here, hold your arm up, higher, like this. I'll try to find something else.'

I remember I have a couple of sanitary pads in my wash bag and a small pair of nail scissors. I should be able to concoct something to staunch the bleeding. She follows me with her eyes.

I get a sanitary pad, cut a piece of cord from my dressing gown and tie it tightly around the make-shift bandage.

Hana's shivering wildly and her teeth are chattering like a terrified animal.

'Here, take your nightdress off. It's soaking.'

I manage to pull the sodden garment over her head, being careful not to dislodge the dressing. Then I put my dressing gown around her and order her to sit on the bench under the hook and hold on to the cord, so she keeps her hand above her head. This should help to slow down the blood flow. Have I learned this somewhere? I can't remember, but it seems to make sense.

'Stay there. Don't lower your arm.'

I go to inspect the shower and retrieve the razor which I place in my wash bag.

The water's still running in the shower. There are only a few darker puddles left at the bottom and I'm thankful for the yellow light that takes the edge off the scarlet. I push the water around the tray with my foot until the ceramic looks completely white. Then I get the soiled hand towel and dab at dark spots on the floor and rinse it in the shower tray. Finally, I turn off the water.

She sits silently on the bench, dutifully holding onto the cord loop. I return to the bench and inspect the pad. No darkness seeping through yet. We need to wait.

I sit down heavily next to her. Another police siren sounds in the distance.

'It's the only way,' she finally says in a quiet voice.

'The only way?'

'You could not understand.'

'Why is that?'

'You have your husband, a kind man, your child. You have so much.'

'I know, I'm blessed. But that doesn't mean I can't understand.'

Silence.

'I have no choice.'

'There's always a choice, Hana. And sometimes there are other choices that you couldn't even imagine. You just need to imagine.'

'I can't marry him.'

A feeling of revulsion rises in the centre of my chest and my heart goes out to her. But it's no good agreeing with her that she is due to marry a cruel-looking man.

'You may grow to love him,' and my voice is a lie, even to myself.

Again, the weight of silence.

'No, it is not that. It's true that I don't love him. I dislike him very much but…'

'Yes?'

'I cannot marry him because I am unclean.'

'Why? You have loved another?'

'No. Not willingly. I've never loved another. But I'm unclean.'

'Because of a man?'

She nods slightly.

'You have known a man?'

'No!' she snaps, looking at me defiantly. 'He has known me.'

I'm puzzled. Then her voice is barely audible.

'They have known me.'

'Were you taken? Against your will?'

She leans her head back, tears streaming down her face.

I touch her shoulder. There are no words.

'Maybe in time… Maybe in time you'll be able to overcome this memory. You can marry and start a new life. In time it will become an old history.'

'I cannot.'

'Perhaps in time you will.'

'I cannot because I carry it with me.'

'The memory?'

'Not just the memory. I have the history here,' she punches her lower stomach once, then twice.

'A growing baby. A disgusting, growing baby!'

For a moment I feel winded.

'No baby is disgusting.'

'This one is. This is a scorpion that grows in my stomach. It disgusts me. I disgust myself. It's the only way. I want to die!'

My mind darts this way and that, looking for a solution.

'Perhaps if you marry soon, you can pretend to have an early child and your husband will think it's his.'

'That would not work.'

'My girl, it has worked for centuries. Since the beginning of time.'

'No, it won't work.'

'Why are you so sure? Because of the time?'

'Yes.'

We fall quiet.

'And something else.'

'Which is?'

'The colour. The child will be dark. Too dark to be ours. Too dark to be his.'

I can barely hear her voice in the still of the night.

When we first heard that we were to leave Uganda, we couldn't believe it but that is the same for all of us. The shock. It was all so unfair. My father made good money from his shop as well as other business that he did with Rami, who was his partner.

After a few days, we realised that President Amin was serious and then we started to hear stories. Widow Pasha's daughter was taken by soldiers and it was said that they did unspeakable things to her. When she returned to her mother's home two days later, she was unable to walk, and our neighbour said that now she would never be able to bear children. But that didn't matter in the end as she died of infection very soon afterwards.

My father said it was the best thing that could happen to her. No one would want her after her 'soiling' he said. As if she had stood in pigs' shit and smeared it over her face, her body. As if it was her choice.

My mother agreed. 'It's for the best,' she said.

There were more tales like Old Ghalib who had the gas station. They raped his wife, then they cut them both up and left them tied up, to die in the sun.

I don't tell you this to shock you, but I want you to understand how much these stories would ring in our heads. Over and over. Such fear. Every day we lived in fear.

My father told us he was going to come to England early with

Rami, before my mother and I departed from Uganda. That way, he said, he would be able to prepare things so we would not have to go to a camp, so there would be a house to live in when we arrived. He didn't even care that perhaps it would be good for us to have a man with us, to protect us.

So he and Rami went away, then the weeks passed. We didn't hear anything. In the end my mother thought that something must have happened to them and we would have to make our own plans. Time was running out. Things were getting more dangerous for Asian women in our area so my mother bought tickets for us to join her sister, my aunt, in Kampala. From there, we would plan our journey to England or India. We didn't know where we would go in the end.

There were about twenty of us on the bus and our suitcases were piled up on the spare seats around us. I noticed there were two other young women like me travelling. We didn't talk, but we recognised the fear in each other's eyes. We were nearly gone from this vicious country, but this was the most dangerous part for we had heard bad stories of buses being stopped and passengers being robbed. And worse things.

I tried to read a book to take my mind off things, but eventually the bumpy road made me feel sick and I closed my eyes and started to fall asleep.

Through my slumber I felt the bus slowing down and when I opened my eyes, I saw soldiers through the dusty window. They were holding their guns up and waving the driver to stop.

I looked at my mother and she put her hand on my shoulder.

'Don't worry Hana, just do what the soldiers say, and everything will be all right. Give them what they want, and everything will be fine.'

Sometimes I wonder. Did she really know what she was saying? Did she mean everything?

Two soldiers came up into the bus and told us all to get out and bring our cases with us. One man was too frightened and refused to leave the bus, so they hit him twice with the end of their rifle.

We all got off and stood in front of the bus and then they started to split us up. The men they took lower down the slope, away from the bus. They made them kneel down and I was so frightened they were going to shoot them. But the soldiers seemed to think it was funny. I heard them laugh and joke between themselves.

Then a tall soldier came up to the rest of us.

'You! You! You!'

He pointed to the two other girls and finally he pointed to me.

'Come' he said, almost laughing to himself.

'Let's see what jewels you are hiding up your skirts.'

One mother started to shout and cry and held onto the soldier's arm, but he threw her to the ground and pointed his rifle at her bindi and started to laugh.

'You wahindi women are very clever, very clever. You even have a mark to show us where to shoot! You want me to shoot? Shall we shoot all you wahindis right between the eyes? Shall we do some target practice?'

The woman on the ground started to cry. She held onto his ankle and begged him not to shoot her. She begged him to save her daughter. But my mother stayed quiet. She didn't say a word.

Then some more soldiers came and walked us down a slim track, not far, but we couldn't see the bus or the other passengers, and they couldn't see us. We came to a clearing where there was a small shed and there they made us take off our clothes and stand naked while they played some game with stones to see who would have which girl first.

We were lined up as if we were latrines. Their latrines. Their relief.

My mother's words were in my head, echoing in a big empty cave. 'Give them what they want, and they won't hurt you.' Was this what she meant?

Not one of us said anything. I tried to remove myself from my body. I tried to imagine that I was up in the trees above, where I could see the breeze moving the leaves. I tried to believe I could soar away in the sky above. But there was the pain slicing through my body, and the sounds, right here, in my ear. The grunting, the laughing of the others as they watched our shame. I said to myself, 'This is not my body, this does not belong to me. It does not belong here, inside my head.

I am up in the trees where the sunlight is clean.'

After a time, I don't know how long, they zipped up their pants and slapped each other on their shoulders. Then they shared out our gold bangles and left us.

For a few moments we stayed, not moving. Why didn't we go immediately? I suppose we couldn't believe it. We couldn't believe what had happened. We couldn't believe they had just left without killing us.

Then, one girl took some leaves from a tree and wiped the blood and spume from between her legs. She picked some more leaves and passed them to me and the other girl and quietly we tried to wipe away the evidence of our violation. Then we adjusted our clothes and brushed off the dirt that we could. Not once did we speak.

Before we started to make our way back up the path, one of the girls, the tallest, turned around and put her finger to her lips. In turn, we each put our own fingers to our lips, and we understood.

Not one of us ever said a word, not from the time we got off the bus, not even when we finally joined the others who were now sitting back on the bus.

We tried to mount the bus easily, despite the pain, but I couldn't raise my eyes or cool my burning cheeks. I sat down by my mother who squeezed my hand and closed her eyes. She never asked me what happened in that time. She only held my hand and closed her eyes. And still she closes them. Closes them to the truth of my shame.

I hold Hana gently until she stops shaking. I've followed her journey through the trail of her words and I can sense the bleakness in her heart. There are no words, only touch.

After a while, I check Hana's wound again. There's little evidence of fresh blood seeping through the make-shift bandage. How lucky it is that the girl is ignorant of the more vital places to cut.

'You must promise me you won't try to do this again.'

'I don't promise anything.'

'It is a terrible thing to do, Hana. Think of the people who love you. Think of your mother.'

'She doesn't care. She didn't want to know. She didn't want to help. She closed her eyes on it. See, like this,' she said, tilting her beautiful profile back and closing her eyes.

'But you are young Hana, there can be so much good in your life.'

'The end is the same.'

'I don't understand.'

'My father will kill me, or my new husband will kill me when he learns that I bear a child that is not his. A black child.'

'But it's not your fault Hana. Surely they would try to understand.'

'Never.'

'Perhaps you can have an abortion.'

'Abortion is a sin.'

'So is suicide. If you killed yourself, it would have the same result for the child. But it would be two lives instead of one.'

'Abortion is a sin.'

'Don't you understand, Hana. It would still be the same result! We must talk to the administrator tomorrow and see what we can do. There must be a way for us to arrange an operation.'

'No! My father will kill me.'

'But maybe he doesn't have to know.'

'He will have to know. I'm only seventeen. With the laws of this country I'm still a child.'

'Perhaps your mother can help. Without your father knowing.'

'My mother will never help. She's a stupid woman and she's my father's slave.'

'For you, her own daughter? Surely she will help.'

'No. She has closed her eyes. She has closed her mind.'

'Listen, Hana. An old friend of mind used to have a saying. It went "there is a solution to everything in life, except death". Do you trust me to try to find the solution?'

She looks at me questioningly.

'Give me two weeks. I need two weeks. Do you promise?'

Silence. A slight nod.

'Come, I think it's safe for you to return to bed now. Keep your movements gentle and watch your wound carefully. If you notice anything tonight, you must come and wake me. In the morning I'll get some ointment and a bandage and then you'll need to hide your left wrist with a long-sleeved shirt. Soon it will heal.'

I send her ahead of me and her hunched figure shuffles down the shadows of the corridor like an old woman.

CHAPTER 23

Time was running out. We had four weeks left before the cut-off date to leave the country and still many of my countrymen were scrambling for paperwork to be sorted, anxiously awaiting news of where they would go. Most of the world didn't want us. We were too many, a tidal wave of rejected citizens forced to tick boxes and sign papers.

Jack and I were organised. We were to go to Britain with Moh and Ashika but there were many who were not so lucky.

Sabu had no papers and whenever I spoke to him of it, he would brush it aside.

'I'm happy at Rutubasana. I want to stay here and help Okello.'

'But don't you see, Sabu? Things are going to change. Rutubasana will change. We don't even know if they will allow Okello to stay on as manager. We have to get your papers sorted out. You can't put your head in the sand like an ostrich.'

That made Sabu laugh. He liked the vision of the large bird displaying its posterior to the world.

Finally he relented, and Dicken drove us both to Kampala, depositing us outside the British High Commission at dawn. Even at that time the queue was snaking around the side of the building.

So once again, within the space of three weeks, I stood in a slow, seemingly endless queue. The first time, with Jack, Ashika and Moh, we had waited in the hot sun for five long hours but eventually come away with our stamped visas.

This time, with Sabu, I held out little hope. But I knew we had to try.

'Listen Sabu,' I said sternly as we stood in line, 'You're going to have to tell them your real name.'

'Sabu Dastagir!'

'No Sabu, that's the name you've given yourself. You're going to have to give them your grandmother's surname. As your father didn't feature in your life, your mother's name will be the one on the birth certificate.'

'No papers!' he said pulling up his shoulders and showing me his empty hands.

'I know you don't have any papers, but there must be something on record. Tell them your grandmother's name and they'll probably be able to look it up.'

Sabu's mouth drooped comically, and he looked to the heavens.

'You must know your grandmother's name.'

'Yes, of course.'

'Well, then tell them.'

'If I tell them my nani's name they will look at me as a dirty poor boy. If I tell them, they will say I'm not Sabu and they will go STAMP! with their silly bit of rubber and then they will say that I can never be Sabu again and I will have to be a dirty poor boy. That's what their stamp will say.'

'It doesn't matter what they say. You can always be Sabu.'

'Yes, I will always be Sabu,' he agreed and crossed his arms stubbornly across his thin vest.

Despite the turban and exotic trousers having been replaced by a baseball cap and shorts, he was still the same Sabu. Or almost the same Sabu. I noticed he stood closer to me, was more watchful, alert, always with half an eye on the uniformed guards who kept the crowds in order.

The queuing seemed interminable with the sun beating down viciously on our heads. An old man ahead of us groaned.

'You can tell this country will never survive,' he grumbled. 'It's baking hot, and here you have a line of thirsty and hungry people queuing and not a street vendor in sight! Now, if we were in a normal situation, our people would have set up a stand by now selling cold drinks and street food. But do the Ugandans think about it? No they don't! They are too busy complaining, saying that we are taking their trade! They need to use their heads but they don't. This country will be ruined.'

Eventually, after five hours we were ushered into a stuffy office. Two clerics sat at separate desks and we were beckoned towards one occupied by a plump man with thinning blond hair. For a moment I was amused that the name plate sitting on his desk read G C Crane - our national bird, the Grey Crested Crane.

A fan fixed to the high ceiling moved as slowly as a worm, having little effect on the stale air. I could see the clerk was hot and irritated before we even started.

'Name?' he snapped in my direction.

'Mrs Bulbul Dalal,' I responded. 'But I'm not coming about me. It's about Sabu here.'

'Very well. Name?'

'Sabu' he said.

'Full name?'

Sabu wiped the palms of his hands on his trousers and looked me square in the face.

'Sabu Dastagir'

'Date of birth?'

Sabu hesitated.

'The date when you were born?'

I had done my homework. If he wanted to follow through with his story, I would help as best I could.

'Second of December 1963.'

'Papers?'

'Well, this is a bit of a problem. Sabu doesn't have any papers.'

'What, no papers at all?'

'No.'

'No certificate of birth?'

'No'

'Family?'

'Sabu's mother is dead. He doesn't have any other family.'

'No family? So who cares for him?'

'I care for myself,' announced Sabu proudly.

'Boy, you are barely nine years old. How can you care for yourself?'

'I have friends. Lots of friends. And I'm the best story-teller in the whole of Uganda!'

'He had a grandmother, but she's recently died'

The man sighed and slowly put down his pen so that it was aligned with the edge of his papers. In hushed tones, as if he was telling us a very important secret, he explained that without any papers or any family there was nothing, absolutely nothing he could do.

'What if my husband and I adopt Sabu? We have British passports.' It was a crazy suggestion. Jack would never have agreed.

'No time. Even if we had some sort of papers from the outset, the whole process would take months. As you know, we only have weeks.'

'But he must be safe. He needs to come to England with us!'

'Young woman, do you know how many of you Asians there are in this country? Eighty thousand! And a huge number of you want to come to Britain. Can you imagine the amount of work involved in sorting all of you people out? So, sad as it is, one little boy with no papers is not going to be given priority. The boy isn't your family, and he doesn't have any papers. Without documentation he can't get a passport, and without a passport there's no possibility of getting a visa.'

'So, you're saying it's one big circle!'

'I suppose you could put it that way, yes.'

'One big circle of no hope.'

'I'm sorry' he said mopping his brow with a spotted blue handkerchief. 'Unfortunately, I can't see any way that Britain can accept him. You'll have to try other avenues.'

Without even a second glance at Sabu he went back to shuffling papers. Sabu looked up at me questioningly. It was the first time I had ever seen the strange light beneath his heavily lashed eyelids. I could almost imagine it looked like fear.

CHAPTER 24

I only see Hana briefly in the morning after I've armed myself with some thick plaster strip and gauze as well as antiseptic cream. The wound looks clean and it only starts to bleed briefly before I bundle it up. I only hope I'm doing the right thing medically, but she still refuses to see anyone, so it's the best I can do.

She doesn't thank me or promise she won't do it again. She just watches me as I dress her wrist, as if her arm is merely an appendage and of little concern.

Later in the day, precisely at 2.30 pm as promised, Valeria draws up outside the camp in a sleek chauffeur-driven Jaguar. Hana's father and Rami are loitering in the courtyard and watch with cold eyes as I slip through the wrought iron gates and open the car door into another world.

The dark leather seats remind me of Nanda's car back home where Kenzi would sit in the front, solid and comforting, and the sun would beat its heat through the polished windows. Today the weather is dreary with cold damp air, but the interior of the car is warm from the heater and there's a luxurious smell of leather mixed with Valeria's perfume.

I've been asked not to wear trousers so I'm wearing my blue dress and have borrowed Ashika's camelhair coat. Valeria is wearing a simple tweed skirt with her usual cashmere, pearls and a dark wool coat draped over her shoulders.

After we've brushed cheeks and exchanged a few pleasantries, I ask where we are going.

'Julian is going to take us for a bit of a tour of London, aren't you Julian?' she says to the driver.

'I imagine you haven't had much time for sightseeing. Of course, this is not my country, or the city of my birth, but I've grown fond of it. There are many of us here who don't belong. That's the good thing about it.' She pauses. 'That is also the bad thing about it.'

'Meaning?'

'You will see.' She indicates that I should look at the view.

We continue on our way along the side of Kensington Gardens, past the domed Royal Albert Hall, and down wide avenues of large white houses with grand steps and pillared doorways. Some of the doors have circles of green leaves hanging on the front and Valeria says that these are wreaths, decorations for Christmas, later in the month.

The buildings change from houses to clusters of smart shops and restaurants and back to houses. Then we are travelling down the King's Road lined with fashionable boutiques. Long-haired hippies walk past pristine middle-aged ladies wearing high heels and holding shiny handbags.

Next, we are driving past the Houses of Parliament with Big Ben. Valeria explains that here there are two 'houses'. One is for the Members of Parliament who are elected by the people and the other, which is called the House of Lords, is where only the titled members preside. Rather like a higher caste, she explains.

We then swoop alongside the wide river until we turn to drive over a bridge flanked by castle-like towers at each end.

'This is Tower Bridge,' Valeria informs me. 'You've probably seen pictures. It can split in the middle so it can open up for tall ships. Over there, you see that other bridge on our left, it's a new bridge, still being built to replace the old London Bridge. Many people get the bridges confused and think that this is London Bridge, but in fact that one over there is actually the real London Bridge. There's a story that even the American who bought the old one got muddled. But who can tell?'

'Why did he buy it?'

'I suppose he liked the idea. It was taken apart, piece by piece and it is now being rebuilt in Arizona.'

We drive slowly and I barely notice a bump when we cross over the connecting section of the bridge.

London goes on for ever and ever. I look down the river and up the river and the buildings continue for an eternity.

'It's good to have the river,' I say to Valeria. 'Otherwise, how would everyone in London breathe? There's no space.'

'Ah,' she replies. 'It all depends on where you live, whether you have money or no money. The houses we saw earlier, near where you are staying, they're large. They have good gardens at the back. Space. But not all Londoners are so lucky. I'm going to show you a different side now.'

We are on the other side of the river, leaving the waterway and heading down into narrower, darker streets. Here the houses are soot-stained brick with litter in doorways and shabby curtains behind dusty windows. I don't notice any Christmas wreaths on the doors.

'What an odd name,' I say as I point out a road sign.

It reads *Elephant and Castle.*

Valeria smiles. 'There's history to many of the names in London.'

We pass a large railway station and drive slowly down a narrow street that lies nearby.

Along one side of the street stand girls wearing thick makeup and skimpy clothes. Some stand with companions, others on their own, leaning against walls or lamp posts as if they're waiting for something.

'Why are those girls standing here? Aren't they cold?' I ask.

'They're waiting for their clients.'

'Clients?'

'They're prostitutes, Birdie. They sell their bodies.'

I shrink into my seat. My eyes meet those of a red-haired girl who wears thick black lines around her eyes. At first her face is blank, but she catches the expression of shock on my face and gives me a challenging stare. It's a cold, hard look that dares me to judge her, dares me to believe I'm a better person than she is. After a few two seconds she looks away, uninterested, and runs her hand through her hair. Her low top of emerald green and the short leather skirt with high patent leather boots expose cold white flesh. I have a vision of her bare thighs being stroked later, maybe only in an hour. How would she ever feel clean?

I feel a lurch of fear for Hana. Could this be where she will end up if she's rejected by her family? If she lives…

The car continues on. I assume that Valeria has already planned the route with her driver. Isn't he ashamed?

I watch my escort out of the corner of my eye. She's sitting back comfortably with her hands folded on her lap, as if we are taking a leisurely trip to the shops.

Sharp concrete lines rise up ahead of us: a modern complex of angles and tunnels. We draw to a stop alongside what looks like an underpass. There are cardboard boxes and some blankets, a pile of newspapers, some figures in the dim light beyond. Two old men sit on a concrete ledge, sharing a rolled up cigarette. Then one of them turns and I notice that he's not old, probably only in his thirties. His profile is fine and beautiful. Is it the dirt, the rags or the matted hair that diminish him, or is it the resignation in his eyes? We hear tuneless singing and another man approaches the two seated tramps, gesticulating and swearing. A fight ensues.

I look at Valeria questioningly.

'Drive on Julian,' she says quietly.

'Homeless. There are many like them in London. More than you could count.'

No more is said between us as we traverse the Thames again. We drive through grand shopping streets where the shop windows glitter and twinkle in the dusk with their Christmas decorations. Hampers, stylishly piled in artificial snow, spill out glorious jams and biscuit tins. Windows displaying smoking pipes and silver clothes brushes sit next to others presenting fine cotton shirts and ties for the gentlemen of the city.

A large wine merchants is resplendent with piles of luscious grapes interwoven with festive greenery and rows of gleaming wine bottles of all descriptions.

'So much, so much,' rings in my head. 'So little, so little,' echo the chugging, idling, London cabs.

We draw up outside a high, arched arcade which runs in front of a palatial hotel.

'Here,' says Valeria. 'Here we are.'

A uniformed door man steps forward to open the car door and Valeria alights regally as I slide out along the seat behind, following her into the lofty foyer.

The marble floor of the restaurant gleams and tall pillars are wrapped with festive garlands of red and green. A waiter greets us as we enter.

'Good afternoon, Hector. Tea for two please, somewhere quiet.'

The waiter leads us to a corner where the reflections in the mirrored panels make the palm fronds and crystal chandeliers go on forever.

'Full tea please. And two glasses of champagne, I think, don't you tesora?'

She doesn't wait for my answer, then lights a cigarette which makes me feel nauseous. I need to find the bathroom, but this hotel is like a city and the prospect of navigating my way leaves me weak-kneed. Loneliness overwhelms me. I want my Jack and Moh and even Ashika.

‘May I have a glass of water, please?’

‘Of course,’ and she indicates to a waiter who returns swiftly with a jug and two fine glasses.

My eyes burn hot as I drink the cool liquid. I curse myself for my weakness and pinch my thigh under the table.

‘Are you not well, Birdie?’

I can’t speak. She’s a stranger who needs amusement. She’s not a friend.

‘Why?’

‘Why what?’

‘Why do you have to show me all this? All this… grandeur. And all the horrible things with the women and the rough men. Why?’

‘Because I want you to know.’

‘Know what? Don’t you believe that I know that life can be hard? Even in Uganda, before our troubles, there was hardship and sadness. It’s not only in London. So why do you show me?’

I’m gathering strength and I look at her boldly.

She ponders as she draws slowly at her cigarette holder.

‘You need to understand.’

‘Yes, yes, I understand. Can we go back now?’

‘Before tea and champagne? This is the icing on the cake, as they say in England.’

‘I would like to go…’ I pause as I realise I was going to say I forget myself.

She carries on as if she hasn’t heard my plea, stubs out her cigarette, leans forward placing her elbows on the table and folds her hands under her chin.

‘Tell me Birdie, how’s Jack getting on?’

‘Jack? He’s fine. He’s… well, he’s not happy. None of us are, not really. But he’s fine.’

‘And work?’

‘There’s no university work. In Uganda it’s something very special to have a master’s degree from Cambridge, but in England it's normal. He's tried some universities, but it's the wrong time of year.'

'Are there any other avenues for him to follow?'

'There's a possible job in a private boys' boarding school outside London but they want him to live in a flat as he needs to be there for the evenings. But it isn't good because the flat only has one bedroom and we are a family with Moh and Ashika, Jack's mother.'

'I see. But it's good that there's some possibility of employment. When would that start?'

'In January. It seems one of the teachers is ill. He needs some medical treatment. Jack could work there until he recovers, so it's not a solid job.'

The waiter delicately places two splayed glasses of bubbling liquid in front of us.

'Drink, carina. Bubbles always make us a little happier.'

She toasts me with a slight nod, then remains silent until a tower of miniature sandwiches and delicate cakes arrive. There are tiny rectangles of pastry puffed as light as air with layers of cream and topped with intricate sugar patterns, glazed strawberry tarts the size of a shilling piece, cigar shaped pastries crowned with shiny streaks of chocolate.

'The tea is Darjeeling, is it not an Indian tea? Did you grow this tea in Uganda?'

'No, we grew a similar style tea but Darjeeling only comes from India.'

'Is that so?' she responds as she continues to pour the tea and indicates that I should help myself to some of the delicacies.

Is this the best moment? If I don't do it now, the time may pass and be lost forever.

'I wonder…'

'Yes?'

'I have a problem. Well, not my problem exactly but a girl in the camp.'

'Go on.'

'There's a girl. She's very young. She's in trouble.'

Valeria raises an eyebrow.

'Women's trouble?'

It sounds very refined coming from Valeria's lips with her gentle Italian accent surrounded by this splendour. It's a million miles away from the rough earth under the trees, the grunting sounds of men.

'Yes, but… different. She was raped in Uganda by soldiers, about nine weeks ago. She knows she carries the result of that.'

'Has she seen a doctor?'

'She doesn't dare. She's only seventeen and her mother goes everywhere with her. She says her father will kill her if he finds out.'

Valeria makes a gentle tutting noise and nods her head gently as she's thinking.

'It's not easy. Not easy at all. She's a minor.'

I recount the events of the previous night and I can tell she is moved by the girl's desperation.

'And you say that this young girl is betrothed? Already?'

'Yes, although he's not her choice. A horrible man. He was a business partner of her father. There's an agreement.'

'And you want me to help this girl?'

'I don't know how I can help her. I don't know the way.'

'And why should I help this girl?'

'Because she's lost, she's desperate.'

'But as you saw today, there are many people like that.'

I fold the starched napkin on my lap and reform it until it becomes a clump of thick linen.

'Yes, I'm sure there are.'

'Where does one start?'

'Yes. I understand. But do you know someone who will be able to help, even if you won't?'

She sits back and watches me closely, the thumb of her

left hand playing with the rings on her third finger.

'Ah, but I haven't said I won't help.'

'Oh, so you will! Or, you may?'

'Perhaps. But tell me, as a matter of interest, how does one choose? There are so many people who need help. How do you know who to support? Forget about your girl for the moment. How does one choose?'

'I don't know. I can't help anyone, anyway. I'm helpless.'

'But if you could. If you had the means, the money, how would you choose? You can't help everyone. No one can help everyone, not even governments. How do you choose? Think of the people we saw this afternoon. The prostitutes. I saw you catch the eye of one of them, the redhead. Would you help her?'

'I don't know. She looked hard. I'm not sure she would want help.'

Valeria nodded as if satisfied by my answer.

'And the tramps near the underpass. Would you have helped them? Would you have given them money? And if you had given them money, how would you feel if they didn't spend the money on food but went out and bought a large bottle of vodka instead? In their minds that might help them more than food. At least they would forget their problems for a few hours.'

'I can't help the world! I'm only talking about Hana. She's one person.'

'They are all "one person", Birdie.'

Tiredness overwhelms me and the sounds of the restaurant reverberate in my skull.

'I suppose,' I pause, searching for the solution in my head. 'You are only able to help the people who want to be helped, and those who touch you, here.' Valeria watches me place my hand on my breast. 'But sometimes you can't do anything, even if you want to help. Especially if you have no money.'

'And if you did have money? How would you choose?'

The vision of the old lady in the rainforest comes into my head, and we are watching the spider spin her intricate web above our heads.

'I suppose,' I search for the words. 'I suppose you trust that you will be guided to the people who need you. And you don't turn away. That's all you can do.'

She sits back in the damask chair and observes me for several moments.

'I think, Birdie, that you and I are going to get on very well.'

Chapter 25

The fact that my mother died when I was only seven years old meant that I had a large amount of freedom in my youth, certainly more than other Asian girls I knew. Pappa was usually distracted by his work on the plantation and didn't seem terribly concerned about our upbringing. As long as Kuki kept the house running smoothly, my brother and I were well cared for, and we received good reports from school, he was happy to give me the run of the estate. I was also lucky that he didn't marry again, so I didn't have a stepmother to stir up imaginations of unsuitable friendships or improper behaviour. Most of my friends' mothers seemed to live in constant terror of their daughters having relationships with local Ugandan boys so they would not tolerate any socialising with the opposite sex. Luckily, my father didn't seem to consider that my friendship with our farm manager's son could be anything but innocent, so it continued with a natural ease.

While my brother, Sanjay, was tinkering with his mechanical experiments I would be with Okello, practicing long jump in the red dust or climbing mango and papaya trees in a quest to find the most succulent fruit. We would try to race our pet geckos until we became as bored as they appeared, and we would spend hours swinging from a tyre tied to the sturdiest branch of the jackfruit tree.

Okello was only a couple of years older than me and had lived on the farm all his life with his parents and twin sisters in a small bungalow near the sorting sheds. It was the original home of my grandfather, a simple structure surrounded by Acacia trees with a small vegetable plot to the side. He was close to his older sisters, but his mother was short-tempered and would nag him and grumble constantly. A tall woman with beautiful bone structure, she had been afflicted by an inelegant limp for as long as I could remember, and I would often wonder whether this was what made her so cantankerous. Okello's father, Mukisa however, was a sweet natured man who had been our loyal and capable manager until his death two years before Amin's decree. Death crept up on him silently after a small cut on his leg turned septic. I remember at the time thinking how odd it seemed that Okello's mother had walked with a harmless limp for so many years and yet her own husband should eventually die of a trivial cut to the same area. Stranger still, after our manager's death, his widow barely seemed to limp at all.

Mukisa's passing was a huge sadness in all of our lives and Rutubasana bore the constant echo of our trusted manager's memory. But he had trained his son well and Okello followed seamlessly into his father's footsteps. The plantation continued to run smoothly.

When Idi Amin came to power, it became evident that Uganda's new ruler was driven by lust, greed and hatred, especially towards the tribes he believed were still loyal to his predecessor, President Obote. Okello was from one of these tribes.

There were stories of the slaughtering of Acholi and Langi soldiers. Huge numbers had been taken from the Mbarara barracks, herded into trucks where they were taken into the wilderness and gunned down. It was said that even in Jinja, so close to Rutubasana, soldiers from the Acholi and Langi tribes had been summoned to carry out a parade in the grounds, only to be crushed to death by tanks. The numbers of dead were growing, and the rumours continued.

Even after Idi Amin's announcement that we Asians

were to be expelled, and after my father's death, Okello stood firm. I pleaded with him to move to safety and start a new life, but he was resolute.

'This is my home. This is where I was born.'

'But Okello, you know that Amin hates your tribe. He's already killed hundreds of Acholi - thousands! Why should he spare you? Take your family. Go to Acholiland. Take whatever belongings you need from here, from our house. They're useless to us. There's some money, not much - our bank accounts have been closed, but my father put some in other areas. We can't take it. It will help you to make a new start.'

But Okello set the jaw on his handsome face, a look I recognised well. He wouldn't budge.

'Don't you worry about me, Birdie, I'll be fine.'

CHAPTER 26

It's nearly a week since my strange afternoon with Valeria and still I haven't heard any word despite her assurances that she would help Hana. The girl watches my every movement when we are in the dormitory, the dining room, or when we pass in the washroom. I, in turn, watch her.

Her wrist appears to be healing, and she draws her long sleeves down so even the tops of her hands are covered. At least the razor was clean, and luckily, her slim figure gives no sign of the growth of new life - despised new life. I remember how she punched her lower stomach, how I had to hold her hand back, clenching it tight as she sobbed in the dim yellow light.

Time in the camp weighs heavily on me and I've even started to help Shai and Padma's mother, Neha, with her cooking, She's taught me how to make naan and even a passable dahl.

I'm in the cavernous kitchen washing pots when Jack steps through the doorway to tell me that Valeria is sitting in a taxi by the entrance.

'She's asked to steal you for an hour. I said I would find you.'

My hands smell of onions and my clothes reek of frying.

'Did she click her fingers?' I snap at Jack who looks surprised by my reaction.

'I can't see her now. I smell of cooking and I'm not dressed properly.'

'Don't worry about that. She won't mind.'

Is Hana not more important than my personal feelings?

Nevertheless, the saucepan still rings loudly as I stack it on the shelf.

'Tell her I'll be five minutes,' I instruct Jack as I run upstairs to put on a pair of beige trousers and a black jumper – more products from the Donor's Boutique as Padma calls it. I need something warmer so I pull out Harriet's jacket that I still haven't returned. I zip up my patent boots and make my way to the gateway.

Hana's father is loitering as usual in the courtyard with the sneering Rami. He doesn't miss a trick and follows me with his bulging eyes, noting every move.

The taxi ticks and chugs, Valeria sitting sedately on the back seat. She taps the seat beside her.

'Come, get in. I have something to show you.'

She sees my suspicious look and smiles.

'Don't worry, There won't be any more depressing sights of London. I'm hoping you'll like this trip.'

We move off and Valeria and I exchange pleasantries. This is a silly dance, I think to myself. I want to ask about Hana, about arrangements that can save the girl, but I have to take my cue from Valeria. It seems she's not ready. I must bide my time.

After about fifteen minutes, the taxi swerves off a busy road into a side street that opens out onto a large square with a grass lawn in the centre. The sign reads 'Theobald Square' and bony trees and a green hedge surround the fenced central garden. On two sides of the square sit tall white houses with thick pillars facing each other across the expanse. On the other two sides, the houses are slightly smaller and constructed of red brick with white detailing, some with elaborate gables. One line stops short and a modern block of flats stands plain and squat at the end.

We stop outside one of the brick houses that has a solid container of rubble on the road in front, a ladder leaning against the railings, and a thick plank of wood running down the steps from the front door. There's loud music coming from within the building and Valeria and I have to step aside as a workman swoops down the ramp steering a wheelbarrow full of debris. He gives a nod to Valeria and then proceeds to deposit the contents in the skip.

'I've just come to show my friend around,' she informs the workman who then tells her that Max is in the back if she needs to talk to him.

We walk into the dark and dusty interior and towards the rear of the building.

'How's it progressing?' she asks the foreman.

'Getting there, getting there. The second floor should be habitable by the deadline, not sure about the rest. There'll be a bathroom, but the kitchen may take a bit longer. Not much though. I reckon six, seven weeks before we're out of here.'

'Good. This is Mrs Dalal. I'm just showing her around if you don't mind. We won't get in your way. Come Birdie, we'll start at the top.'

She pauses on the landing to show me the large plans pinned to the wall.

'Look here,' she says spreading her slim hands on the paper. 'The house is originally Edwardian, just after Queen Victoria, and it would have been a family home in the beginning. But it was in a terrible state when I bought it – divided into bedsits, small rooms with kitchenettes. Nothing had been done to it for years. That's why I got it at a reduced price and because of Mrs Waterhouse who sits downstairs.'

'There is a lady who sits downstairs?'

'Oh well, it's a legal term. She's called a *sitting tenant*. An old lady who rents the flat on the bottom floor and she must be allowed to stay. So, because of her, and the state of the property, I bought it for a good price. Also, this area is not smart. Despite the lovely houses, there are two busy roads that run either side of the square, so it means the prices are lower than those in the surrounding area. But it will get there. It's a good investment, don't you think?'

I'm sure it will be very nice, I respond.

We walk to the top level and look out over the garden. Two women wearing thick coats are sitting on a wooden bench chatting while a little girl pushes a toy pram along the paths. Moh would enjoy this garden.

'In the summer it looks beautiful. There are flowers and lovely shade when the leaves are out. Only the residents of the actual square can use the garden, provided they pay towards the upkeep. The gardener and plants need to be paid for so people have to contribute a small sum of money each year.'

'See over there,' she points to the modern building which sits diagonally across the square. 'There used to be the same line of houses running all the way down to the main road beyond, but it was bombed in the war, so they put up that block instead. They are council flats where poor people live, who are helped by the government.'

Poor people like us, I think. They would be similar to the flats in Hackney but much better - nearer greenery, and the building is only five stories high. But it would be doubtful there would be any flats available there, I've heard there aren't enough to go around.

'The house has three floors and this attic. The ceiling here isn't really high enough to give a good living space - storage, perhaps. Then, besides Mrs Waterhouse's flat, there are two good floors. Come.'

We work our way through the house. Three bedrooms and a bathroom, then down to the raised ground floor with a large high-ceilinged living room, a smaller sitting room, and an airy room at the back where we had met the foreman earlier. The music has now subsided and the workmen are sitting at the front of the building drinking cups of tea.

'This is going to be the kitchen,' explains Valeria, 'But it's very big so I'm not sure whether to divide it to create a dining room or whether you would prefer it to remain as one large room.'

She seems confused by my expression.

'What do you think? How would you prefer it?'

'I don't know. I suppose it depends if they like cooking, or if they have a family.'

'Yes, well, you have a family, don't you?'

'Yes, I suppose we are a family, but everyone is different. Maybe you should ask your tenants.'

'I am.'

'You are what?'

'Asking my tenant. That is if you're interested.'

'Me?' I feel winded. My mind travels up to the view from the top floor, across the expanse of garden, to where you can see the sky above. A place where I could breathe.

'I... we would never have enough money to rent a house like this!'

'Special terms.'

I shake my head.

'We can't take charity.'

'It's not charity, Bulbul.'

'No, no, no. It's impossible. We would never be able to afford a house like this. I don't know what we'll ever be able to afford. But not this. It's impossible.'

Valeria leads me to the tall french windows that lead onto a yard at the rear. The area is safe and enclosed. I can imagine it with a sandy play pit in the corner.

'This is not charity, it's a business proposition.'

She explains that the first year would be rent free, the second year at a reduced rent and then, following into the third year, if we decide to stay, a low-interest mortgage would be set up so that we could buy the property over a number of years. During that time, the rent for the first two years will be factored into the payments. She'll make money from it. It will be a good investment for her.

It seems a gift from the skies and my heart is racing but I'm sure I appear wooden and ungrateful.

'Jack would never agree. He won't take charity.'

'You leave Jack to me, or I should say, to John. My husband is a barrister after all, he has a way with words. They say he has a silver tongue. That's why he wins so many law cases.'

'I dare not dream, Valeria. It is too wonderful.'

She squeezes my hand.

'You must dare to dream, tesora. If we don't have dreams, what is there? I grew up in comfort, lavish comfort. I had everything I could possibly want and then… Well something happened and everything changed. I couldn't stay. Then I had nothing, nowhere to go, no home. Just like you. That was when I met John. It was John who saved me. We all need someone in our lives to save us, or who can help us to save ourselves. That is why I do what I do.'

'John is very kind.'

'My husband is a wonderful man, but he doesn't fund my ventures. As you may have guessed, I live in a certain degree of comfort, but I now also have a large sum of money at my disposal. I do not look on it as my money, but it is a fund I can use. This wealth came to me several years ago but it has, shall we say, a history. A bad history. At first I didn't want to touch it. Every note is stained with blood, lust, heartbreak…'

A workman tramps in to collect some tools and leaves whistling the tune that was playing earlier on the radio.

'I hated the legacy when it came to me. I was going to refuse it, but then I met someone who opened my eyes. He said it must have come to me for a reason and if I turned my back on it, I would be turning my back on all the people that the money could help. This person also taught me that I should treat wealth like water - that I should never let it trickle out to the sea, dislodging a few pebbles along the way. That is useless. Before long, it is gone. He taught me that I should let it flow like a brook filling a lake, bubbling and bringing happiness on its journey. That is the ultimate prize – that it does good and it never diminishes. And this is the reason I bought this house. I didn't buy it for you as I hadn't even met you at that point. But now I know it's Birdie's house. If you want it – on my terms – and if Jack agrees.'

My cheeks burn. Have I misjudged her? Could I truly contemplate living here? If I dream, will I fall off the precipice? It's far worse to hope, and then to lose, than never to hope at all.

What will Jack say? If I tell him, I know I'll stutter and stumble over the words. I know he'll say no. He'll say it's charity and he'll feel ashamed. Then the book will be closed and my hope will die. I realise that Valeria is right, John should explain to Jack in a cool and calm way. A financial agreement, that is all. Perhaps we could help them financially by occupying the property for a while. I won't ask. I'll let the deed be done in a calm and practical way, in an English way.

I have no words. I take Valeria's hand and hold it to my cheek.

'Let's see, tesora. Let us see what words of magic my husband can weave.'

In the taxi on our way back to the camp, Valeria reveals her plan for helping Hana, but not before quizzing me further.

'So Birdie, if we go ahead with my plan, how much are you prepared to help?'

'I'll help as much as I can.'

'Despite the consequences?'

'What do you mean?'

'Everything we do has an effect. Everything is cause and effect. If we help Hana, we either harm the baby or hurt her parents. Or both.'

'I don't want anyone to be harmed. Or anyone to be hurt.'

'That would be a perfect world, Birdie. We have to deal with the situation as it is now. Are you prepared to help?'

'Yes, I am.'

'Very well, I want to meet your Hana and I want to see how we can help her. But first she must be examined by a doctor who will report on the situation. Then we'll make our decision. Agreed?'

'Yes, of course. Maybe you can think of a better way.'

'A better way?'

'Where no one can be harmed anymore.'

Valeria says I must tell no one, not even Jack. She'll send a taxi to collect us the following Friday and Hana and I are to come to her flat near Regent's Park. There Hana will see the doctor and someone else who isn't named. They'll assess Hana's situation and work out what can be done to help her.

Hana's father and Rami will be away from the centre on the Friday. She won't ask permission. After all, it's merely an excursion to visit the sights of London and perhaps a trip down the river Thames – that's what she'll write on the note. It's wiser to leave without asking in case her outing is refused. Then she would suffer from the hands of her father if she knowingly goes against his wishes. Better not to ask.

I warn Valeria that Hana will most likely be reprimanded by her father anyway as he will disapprove of her enjoying this modern city.

'Well, I can't see what we can do about that. Do you think he'll hurt her? We can't contemplate any violence towards her, especially when she's in a fragile state.'

'I don't know. I think he's a cruel man.'

'Let me think on that one,' she says as she waves away my final thanks and the taxi drives off.

Chapter 27

Occasionally, when Nanda and I were young, we would spend time in Uncle Deepak's office which was situated above an insurance company on Commercial Road in Kampala. I remember these visits were often linked to trips to Drapers store to buy our school uniforms, or sometimes the dentist. At other times, my aunt would be running errands in town and didn't want us around her feet, so she would drop us off at the office under the care of my uncle.

The receptionist, Mrs Rwamirama, would sit upright and regal at the front desk and would beam at us kindly whenever we visited. She had the blackest and smoothest looking skin I had ever seen in my life, and I was fascinated by the way the light gleamed on her high cheekbones as well as the flashes of bright orange from her beautifully manicured fingernails. When she walked, which we did not often witness, she would sway, as if she was listening to a slow beat of music in her head and the jangling bracelets and necklaces that adorned her would keep the rhythm. Slow, swish, swish, slow. This would be accompanied by the sound of her nylon tights rubbing together at the top of her voluptuous thighs as she moved across the room. Nanda and I would often giggle when we heard this sound and would have to pretend that we were laughing about something else.

As Uncle Deepak became more successful, the office expanded, overflowing up into the floor above. The decorators were brought in and no expense was spared on the carpeting, furnishing and office equipment which was to set my uncle's stockbroking firm above any possible competitors in the country.

Of particular interest to us girls was the small room at the rear of the building. This housed the stationery department, with boxes of biros, pencils and paperclips; piles of crisp paper that we would sniff loudly, and my uncle's pride and joy: the Xerox machine. This wonderful mechanism was able to photograph any document or picture placed face down on the glass under the lid. Then, after a good deal of chugging and readjusting itself in the caverns of the enormous cube, an exact copy of the original would shoot out from a slot situated at the base.

We would spend hours in this stationery room cutting sheets of paper, stapling them together to create small books, writing and illustrating stories. Then, when no one was looking, we would place our artwork under the lid of the vast machine, press the button and magically, multiple copies would appear.

It was a shameful afternoon when Mrs Rwamirama caught us in the act. We had finished designing an elaborate poster announcing the forthcoming marriage of Nanda's cherished Chihuahua to the German Shepherd owned by Mr Shah who lived on the eastern side of her compound. We had then progressed to the invitations, when the door opened suddenly.

My uncle's receptionist brought herself up to her full height and this time there was no humorous swishing or jingling, only a rigid and stern expression upon her fine features.

'Girls, girls, girls. Do you have no shame! Do you have any idea of the cost of each of these sheets of paper that you are wasting? Let me see. What do we have here?'

She walked (silently) over to the machine, hovered her finger over the large red Stop button and, looking us both full in our faces, pressed down firmly. The beast chugged and groaned to a halt. One last sheet shot out as a final insult. Mrs Rwamirama leaned over and removed the sheets from the tray.

'Ah, a wedding! What fun! And between two dogs. Now that sounds a very interesting wedding indeed. How many people are you anticipating will attend this very interesting wedding?'

Nanda and I squirmed. My mouth was dry.

'There seem to be sixteen invitations already printed and more were undoubtedly on their way! It appears to be an extremely popular event. Are you going to give me an invitation? I do hope one of them is for me and Mr Rwamirama. We do love weddings. Oh yes, we do.'

'Of course,' announced Nanda. 'Yes, you must come to the wedding.'

'Thank you, Miss Nanda, I will look forward to it. But I do think that you've printed enough invitations for the time being, don't you?'

We nodded in unison and started to relax as Mrs Rwamirama opened the door to the hallway when she paused, turned and held up her long, manicured finger.

'ONE! One more copy. Just one, and I will tell your father, Miss Nanda, your uncle Miss Bulbul, that you have been wasting his money and you *know* how much he hates to have his money wasted. This is your warning, girls. No more copying on the Xerox machine or I will have no choice but to report this to my very superior boss. Understand?'

I do believe that was the last time we used the Xerox machine, until many years later when I crept into the empty stationery room and prayed that its magical powers could turn the course of fate

CHAPTER 28

And so it's raining again today. Do the skies never get dry in this country?

I'm sitting at the small table in our dormitory trying to succeed with my mother's sewing machine. Shai has already given me several lessons but this time I'm determined to conquer it on my own. I now know how to load the bobbin and to thread the needle and Shai has expressed the importance of always using the same type of thread for each material. Cotton for cotton, silk for silk. Today I'm using the navy blue cotton left over from the sewing of my dress and I'm not following the rules, but it seems to be working on the fine silk fabric.

Last Friday I went to the Donor's Boutique and found the most beautiful scarf - a large square of silk displaying an elaborate tangle of leather straps and stirrups, all interwoven with horse's heads and saddles. As soon as I saw it, I thought of Harriet and I knew exactly what I would do. I would repair the jacket she had lent me and then I would send it back to her as a 'thank you'. A thank you for showing me the other side of English life, where lives are not dominated by rotas and regime. I'll send it to her, better than it was before. As if new and unique. It will be my gift of gratitude.

First, I carefully detach the torn green lining from the main body of the garment, leaving the sleeves intact. After that I separate each piece to use as a pattern and then, with a certain amount of juggling, I manage to cut a duplicate of each segment from the colourful scarf - a tricky process as the silk seems to have a mind of its own. Now I need to fit the pieces of the puzzle together and I'm struggling to keep the sections from sliding away from each other. If only I had three hands.

I hear weeping in the corridor and immediately think of Hana. But I'm wrong.

Padma rushes into the dormitory followed by Shai and her mother. The younger girl is soaking wet. She grabs a towel and starts rubbing her boyish hairstyle dry, sobbing as she scrubs.

'I can't believe that you're so old-fashioned! You're completely stuck in the dark ages. I'm only trying to do my best!'

Her mother, Neha, clings onto her arm.

'I know you *think* you are helping my dear. But you can't just go and do these things on your own. You should have asked your father.'

'What for? What would he have said? "Oh no, Padma you must not get a job. Not until we know where we are living." And when will that be? How many months will that be? How can we possibly know where we will end up living? And what are we supposed to do during that time? Just wander around like helpless children stuck in this school?'

'It won't be so long, my dear. Every day we make a bit of progress.'

'Well, I can't see *anything* happening. Nothing at all!' All he does is stand around with his friends grumbling about our situation. Someone has to do something to earn some money for the family. If we don't earn money, we won't be able to rent a house, or a flat or even a *room*!'

'But Knightsbridge! We'll never live anywhere near Knightsbridge. It's where the rich live. We'll live miles away. How could you afford the travel costs?'

'Somehow I'll manage. At least I've got a *job*! Think of

that. A job! That has to be good news. You just turn it around and make it bad news. I can't believe you!'

'But you won't really be earning anything. You'll be a trainee. Whatever you earn will go on transport. How can you afford it?'

Padma shakes off her mother's grasp and sits, dejected, on the metal bed. The springs groan at her slight weight.

'Don't you see? I have to start somewhere. I may be a trainee in the beginning, but it won't be long before I'm earning proper wages. Hairdressers make good money. People's hair will always keep growing.'

I realise what has happened.

'Padma, did you go back to the hairdressers? Where we went?'

'Yes, I did. I walked in the door and asked them straight out. "Are you hiring any new staff? Are you taking on any trainees?" Yes, they said. Just like that! I saw the manager, and I signed the form. He wants to see my papers but, provided everything is in order, I start on Monday. That's good news, don't you agree, Birdie?'

'Talk some sense into her Birdie,' pleaded her mother.

'I can't,' I say. 'I think it is good news. Very good news.'

'How can you say this is good news? We don't know where we will live.'

'I'm sure there will be a way to work it out. But I think it is wonderful news. Padma, you are the first among us to get a job. Now we all have to follow your success.'

Padma gleams with pride and Neha holds her hand to her head, muttering to herself as she returns to the kitchen to continue her work.

Shai goes over to her sister and starts to help her out of her wet clothes.

'Mama will understand soon.'

'One of us has to do something!' responded Padma.

'Don't worry, they'll both come around in the end.'

Shai looks over to the table where the sewing machine sits.

'What are you doing?' she asks.

'Sewing.'

'I can see that. But what are you possibly sewing with that fabric? You've cut it up!'

'Yes, of course. I had to cut it up before I sew with it.'

'But I can't believe you cut this up? Where on earth did you get it?'

'In the Donor's Boutique, as you call it.'

Shai and Padma laugh as they pick up the pieces, inspecting some of the off cuttings that have fallen on the floor. They laugh even more when they find some writing from a corner of the scarf.

'You are amazing, Birdie. You find the most wonderful clothes in the boutique. And then you find this and cut it up!'

'I don't see what is so amazing.'

'See here, see what it says. HERMES!'

'So?'

The girls laugh as if I have told a very funny joke.

'Don't you realise how expensive Hermes scarves are?'

'I've never even heard of Hermes so how should I know how expensive they are?'

'And you cut it up. Into all these pieces!'

I shrug.

'It will give Harriet just the same pleasure on the inside of a jacket as it will draped around her neck. Instead of a Hermes scarf, it will be a Hermes lining.'

CHAPTER 29

It was my last evening in Rutubasana, the last one ever. The following day I was to take any final possessions from the house and Dicken would drive me back to Kampala, to the next stage of my life.

My father dead, my brother uncaring in his new life in California. I had Dicken and Sabu by my side, but not for long. Tomorrow I would have to say goodbye.

We sat out on the veranda, eating a dish of katogo which my beloved Kuki cooked for us, and we listened to the sounds of the animals and birds settling for the night. Dicken recounted the names of some of them for Sabu who soaked up this new information and laughed when his teacher couldn't pronounce the names in Gujarati.

Later, the conversation became more serious and Dicken spoke of his plans to leave Uganda and head for Kenya where the government was more stable.

'I know that country hasn't been kind to you Asians either, but at least it's not ruled by a bloodthirsty madman.'

'My mother grew up in Kenya,' I remarked.

'Yes, your father said, but she lived there when times were good. They became difficult for you lot a while back, but nothing like as bad as here.'

Dicken felt sure he would be able to pick up work. He had spent some time in Kenya before coming to Uganda, and he knew the land well. The wildlife was rich and varied and more American and European tourists were landing in Nairobi now instead of Entebbe.

He said he would be fine. He was a survivor.

When Sabu went to fetch some soda, I asked Dicken quietly.

'And could you take a helper?'

'Now why would I need a helper?'

'Sabu?'

'Oh, come on, Birdie, have you been hatching some sort of plan? You're not expecting me to take him on, like adopt the boy, are you?'

'Well no, not adopt him. But just think, he could be useful to you. Help you arrange things. He's a hard worker, and he's bright.'

'Look Birdie, let's get things straight. I've never been the type of guy who wants to be tied down in any way. Never married, never been interested in having a family. Having a tag-along urchin is the last thing I need.'

'Lawrence of Arabia did. He had two. Do you remember?'

'Yeah, I remember. And they both came to sticky ends.'

'And what about Sabu? What future is he going to have? He says he wants to stay here and Okello is happy to have him, but even Okello doesn't know if he has any future here himself. Amin hates people from his tribe. I've asked him to leave, take whatever he can carry, but he refuses. He says he's the manager and he'll stay as the manager. He won't budge.'

'He'll probably be fine. He's got the knowledge. They'll need someone who knows the ropes. What's the point in getting rid of him?'

'And Sabu?'

'Don't worry about him. They're hardly going to bother about a little boy.'

Sabu came back onto the veranda carrying the tray with the sodas and a bottle of scotch for Dicken which he placed carefully on the table with a cut-glass tumbler.

Our conversation stumbled along for the rest of the evening, awkward and jerky, none of us forgetting that this was the end. The end of our Rutubasana.

That night, lying in bed, I was restless, hot and fidgety with the background noise of the cicadas and the fan purring round and round. Just before dawn, as I drifted off to sleep, I thought I heard the faint song of a nightingale.

CHAPTER 30

Valeria's duplex apartment is situated in a palatial terrace to the south of Regents Park. In front of broad cream pillars and the arched windows of the ground floor sits a slim private garden which I imagine is for the use of the occupants. Beyond a dividing road lies the large expanse of the park and I marvel at the amount of greenery that this hugely populated city contains.

We press the bell at the main door and it immediately buzzes open to allow us into a high-ceilinged hallway with large black and white tiles and a classical sweeping staircase which we ascend as instructed. A maid greets us at the door to the apartment and we enter what appears to be a house within a house as a further set of slimmer stairs continue to a higher floor. Although we get a glimpse of a larger living room with high wide windows overlooking the park, we are shown into a small sitting room to the rear of the building and informed that Mrs Lake won't be long.

The room reflects Valeria's elegance and is painted in a soft light blue. A delicate white fireplace gives focus to the room and is flanked by a pair of embroidered armchairs. Simple silk curtains hang either side of the large sash window and a delicately patterned pastel rug covers most of the floor. Hana flops dejectedly into the deep sofa that faces the hearth. Does she truly appreciate the effort that is being made to help her? Behind the sofa sits a slim mahogany table and I can't help myself from inspecting the various photographs that sit on the polished surface.

There is a young girl, about the same age as Hana,

dressed in skiing clothes, holding up her ski sticks triumphantly as she stands on a snowy slope. She has thick dark hair and bears a resemblance to Valeria. Another photograph shows the same girl, slightly older now, sitting next to John at a dinner table. They sit close, laughing at the camera, an assortment of plates and wine glasses in front of them. I didn't know Valeria had a daughter. She never mentioned her, but then Valeria rarely speaks of herself.

A further silver frame shows an image of a young Valeria. I pick up the frame to check it's not her daughter, but no, it's definitely Valeria in her youth. The picture is black and white and shows a young woman looking beautiful and radiant, so happy, with her arm around a youth who bears a resemblance to her. Her brother perhaps?

The door opens and I jump back guiltily, feeling as if I have been rifling through someone's private drawers.

It's only the maid returning to announce that Valeria is ready to see Hana. She turns to me.

'Mrs Lake says that you are welcome to stay but suggested that, as it's such a beautiful day, you might like to take a walk in the park. It's only across the road, over there.'

I'm surprised that Valeria doesn't greet us personally. Perhaps she's discussing Hana's situation first with the professionals. Whatever the process, I'm relieved that I can distance myself and the prospect of a walk in the open air is appealing.

Outside the sun is shining and there's only the occasional cloud skimming across the blue sky. I skirt around the private gardens, cross the road and walk through a black iron gate situated in the hedge on the edge of the park.

Further down the path I look back towards the tall cream buildings that run around the outer edge. Another place where the rich reside. How must it feel to step out onto the balcony in the morning and survey the park splayed out ahead in all its grandeur. What a luxurious life. And I remember the house in the square where there are also white pillared houses and the space of greenery. The square where my impossible dream lies.

Jack is due to meet John near his chambers this evening for a drink. The proposition of us occupying the flat will then be put to him. It all rests with Jack.

There's a wide lake which, I see from a map on a public board, is called the Boating Lake. A pair of uniformed nannies stand by the side of the water with three children. Two of the toddlers are throwing pieces of bread in for the ducks and they giggle and dance as they see the birds fight over the prize.

'More, more!' they shout, and the nannies dutifully produce clumps of neatly squared white bread.

I'm invisible and it feels good.

My clothes blend in, I'm on my own and I realise it's the first time I've walked in London without a companion. But I feel safe. Am I deceiving myself? Should I be watching for danger? I watch the mothers with children, couples walking in a purposeful manner, tourists who inspect large maps trying to get their bearings. I relax, I amble, I tilt my head to the mild winter sun. Is Hana still seeing the doctor? Is he kind?

I think back to when I too, visited a specialist. It must be three years ago now, before Jack and I were married. Did it resolve anything? I'm not sure it did.

Aunt Latika had assured me that I shouldn't be concerned, but as the wedding date approached, she could sense my mounting distress. One day she suggested I visit a doctor who could put my mind at ease. She had been told that Dr Bergman was the most prominent specialist in the whole of East Africa and felt sure he would be able to help. So, in the spring, we accompanied Uncle Deepak on one of his business trips, and my aunt escorted me to a white building on the outskirts of Nairobi, which housed the doctor's consulting rooms.

Dr Bergman was a small man with an abundance of white hair that appeared reluctant to lay flat on his head, but I doubted the state of his hair was of any concern to him. All his attention would be focused on his patients, as it was on me. I sat nervously in the leather chair. At least, I assured myself, the doctor would not have heard the gossip that ran through our community following my mother's death. He was a clean slate.

'So tell me, young lady, what can I do for you?'

'I want to be sure that I am safe.'

'Safe in what way?'

'I want to know that I will not be like my mother.'

I recounted the story of my mother who had always been loving and patient until the time that her body started to change, her temper becoming shorter, her irritation intense. The night she had left, the search for her body. No note, no goodbye. Not even a kiss when I stood on the steps of the veranda and begged her to take me with her. And then I told him of what I had heard Kuki and Jama discussing as I sat on the bench by the kitchen window while I observed my dusty toes.

'Is it true?'

'That women can experience psychosis when they are pregnant?'

'Yes. Go mad.'

Dr Bergman shrugged and rearranged the ink pot and leather diary that sat by his left hand.

'It has been known. It can happen. Occasionally. But it's very rare.'

'And can it be inherited?'

'I don't believe there is any evidence to verify that.'

'So how do I know? How do I know that I won't go mad if I become pregnant? Kill myself? Or worse, kill my baby when it's born. I've heard horrible stories.'

'You mean you've heard stories of postpartum psychosis?'

'Going mad after having a baby. Is it the same kind of madness?'

'Again, it is exceedingly rare.'

'Yes, but if my mother had it, how do I know I won't inherit it?'

'It's really impossible to say. Do you know of any mental instability that your mother encountered prior to her suicide?'

'I don't talk to my father about it. He never talks about my mother. But my aunt, who is here, outside in the waiting room, she has told me that my mother was always happy. I don't think she had any mental problems. Not until she committed suicide.'

'And how did she do that? I'm sorry to ask.'

'She threw herself in the White Nile.'

'Really? Did they find her body?'

'No, but they found her car, just by a promontory. It was obvious what she had done.'

I think back now to Dr Bergman's questioning expression. He didn't say more on the subject, but the consultation continued by him putting my mind at rest. He assured me that there was nothing to say that I would encounter the mental instability of my mother. But how could I shake off the images and fear that had entered my heart as a young child, just like the black mamba snaking its way through my blood?

When I return to the flat, Valeria and Hana are sitting in the drawing room quietly talking.

'Ah, tesora, did you enjoy your walk?'

'Thank you, yes. Is everything all right?'

'Yes, of course. Everything is fine. Are you happy now, Hana?'

Hana nods, looking trustingly between Valeria and me.

'And you know you can change your mind, don't you Hana?'

'I will *never* change my mind. This is the only choice I have. Thank you.'

Valeria looks at me and sighs.

'We have discussed this matter at length, both the doctor and another specialist in this area. We have reached the conclusion that the best solution is to remove Hana from her father.'

'From my parents! They are *both* bad!' Hana interjects.

'Yes, her parents. She is to go a long way away where she will be looked after. Where she can have the child. She may wish to keep the child and…'

'I will *never, never* keep this child. It is the child of cruelty, of animals. I hate this child!'

Valeria raises an eyebrow.

'In any case,' she continues, 'Hana has agreed to keep the child until it's born, and then, if she wishes, we can help her arrange for it to be adopted. This is the moral way. This is the kind way. We have asked Hana if we can consult with her parents, but she refuses. The main problem we have is that, at present, she's considered a minor as she is still only seventeen. But not for long. So, we have formed a plan and hopefully all will go smoothly. But we will need your help, Birdie. Are you prepared to help?'

I nod.

'Yes, of course I will help. Just tell me what I need to do.'

CHAPTER 31

The wooden domed case was covered in dust when Dicken brought it down from the attic. I ran my fingers across the surface revealing an elaborate crest with 'S' in gold on a background of rich wood. The catches were stiff but inside, the machine looked pristine with the intricate flowers and decoration on the black enamel body. Written across the top were the words 'The Singer Manufacturing' and the memories flooded back.

Mama sitting at the machine, clackety, clackety as she wound the wheel in her right hand, the slim fingers of her other hand guiding the fabric under the needle. Sometimes she would hum, but always in rhythm with the fall of the needle as the machine pounded on. Clackety, clackety.

'Take it,' he said.

'Why? I don't know how to sew.'

'You learned at school, didn't you?'

'Only basic sewing.'

'Your mother knew how to sew.'

'It's not inherited, you know. It's not in my blood.'

'Maybe it is. Maybe you could learn to be very good.'

'I doubt it.'

'The fact is Birdie, it's a beautiful machine, your mother's. And who knows, it could come in useful. You could make clothes for Moh, or yourself. Take it.'

My mood was black, my heart heavy. The rooms echoed with the memory of my father, the silence unbearable.

Dicken had given strict instructions that we were to leave before dusk. We should be back in Kampala before nightfall. The roads weren't safe.

I set myself to gathering the limited number of possessions we would be allowed to take to England. How to encapsulate a whole life of memories in one suitcase?

My father's study remained as if he had merely stepped out to fetch a glass of water, two small piles of papers on the surface of his dark mahogany desk. I scooped them up and put them in a large cardboard box. I should also look for documents that might relate to Sanjay's claim on the land in the future, if that time were ever to come.

Two old photograph albums containing various loose envelopes, newspaper cuttings and folded papers, some of them yellowed with age, were crammed into one of the lower cupboards. I didn't have time to go through them so I shoved them in the box together with any official-looking documents I could find. In a lower drawer of my father's desk lay a framed picture of my mother, young, looking shyly at the person holding the camera. Her lips were full and sensual, her thick wavy hair gleaming in the sunlight. I looked closely, searching for any resemblance, but I could only see a likeness to my brother. I had not inherited her looks but perhaps something worse, something within. A cool draft carried through from the terrace and I added the picture to the box, as well as a few other photographs removed from their frames.

I continued through into the living room where my father's old gramophone stood in the corner and I began shuffling through some records stacked in the shelves to the side. Cruising Down the River, Mona Lisa by Nat King Cole, Frankie Laine playing Jezebel. I remembered the evenings when I was very young, before my father became a recluse, before my mother's death. These songs would be playing from our living room and my parents would laugh with their friends as they drank elegant cocktails and spilled out onto the terrace. Memories engulfed me as I slipped the vinyl disc out of a sleeve displaying a well coiffured lady on the cover. The needle crackled with dust and static. 'Jambalaya' it called, and the cheery tones filled the room.

The music and words were sunny and told of having fun on the Bayou, eating cold fish pie and feeling happy and gay. I remember dancing to this song with my mother shortly before she died. She would hold my hands and we would dance as one. Over and over she would play it, and we would spin around, faster and faster. There was a twisting ache in my chest, but the streams of gaiety were infectious and I started to dance. I was only wearing shorts and an old tee shirt but I pattered around on the parquet floor with my bare feet. The song played over and over again, my body moving freely, the sound filling my head, my whole being. I played it until my dance was a frenzy of memories and sadness and happiness and laughter. My mother, my mother. I remember her. I really do remember her.

Suddenly Kuki rushed into the room.

'Miss Bulbul, come quickly. Get Mr USA. There are men down at the yard.'

'What men?'

'Soldiers. They want trouble. Quick, quick.'

Chapter 32

I imagine that for most Christians it would be seen as a blessing for a birth to take place on Christmas Day. Perhaps the infant is perceived as being closer to God - more like the baby doll who nestles in the crib in the corner of the dining room.

This special date doesn't mean much to Hana as she's not of the Christian faith. But it does mean one important thing: Hana is to turn eighteen on the 25th December and this, in England, is when she'll legally become an adult. It's the time when citizens can vote and when they're no longer legally controlled by their parents. Hannah and I watch the calendar every day. We almost hold our breath, so anxious are we that her father may try to force her into a marriage with Rami in the days before Christmas. So far there's been no sign of such a move.

'Can't you ring Valeria?' Hana asks gingerly. 'Just to find out what's happening.'

She winces when I touch her and I pull the edge of her scarf down slightly revealing her neck which is mottled and bruised. As suspected, Parvat has wreaked his revenge for her supposed trip down the river Thames. In reality, she was not floating down the waterways but was planning her escape from his cruelty. How appropriate. Hopefully, this would be the last time he could torment her.

I wonder how Parvat has managed to harm Hana when there are so many people around throughout the centre. Surely somebody would have seen it happen. Wouldn't they have stopped him?

I ask if the blows had fallen on her lower body, on her stomach. Was all well?

'All is fine,' she assures me. 'He was more careful this time. Usually he hits my face. He says my face is evidence of my wickedness.'

'Because of your beauty?'

She shrugs, as if this flaw is something she is used to enduring.

The English helpers in the camp are starting to decorate for Christmas and encourage the children to join in. They create loops made from different coloured paper strips, then string these together and hang swags of the paper chains from the ceiling. They cut out circles of crepe paper and make pompoms of bright red that the girls hold under each other's chins, laughing as they tickle each other, and the boys kick across the room like footballs. I think of Diwali and how it barely existed for us this year. How and where will we hold our own celebrations next year?

Hana is becoming agitated. We still haven't heard again from Valeria.

'How do we know that she will do what she said? She hasn't sent us any details.'

I call Valeria from a nearby phone box that smells of cigarette butts and car fumes.

'Don't worry Birdie, I'm just putting the plans in place, they're nearly sorted. We have no choice but to wait until her actual birthday. If we move before then she'll have no legal rights. Her father could get her back and we could be accused of coercing a junior. Even now we're in murky waters with what we're doing. Technically, she's still underage. Just keep calm and act naturally. I'm going to send you a Christmas card next week and in it there will be a sheet with all the information, tickets and some money. Don't let Jack see the contents. The fewer people who know about this, the better. Be patient. She'll be in safety soon.'

I put the phone down and push open the heavy glazed door, grateful for the cold London air.

In the meantime, a Christmas card arrives from Harriet and Buster. On the front is a picture of a sleigh being pulled along a snowy lane by a beautiful horse. There are little bits of silver glitter applied to the snow, so it twinkles when I angle the card against the light. Little flakes of silver fall off when I brush it lightly with my finger, but the card keeps on twinkling regardless.

Harriet has added a postscript in her large round handwriting.

'Thank you, dearest Birdie. Absolutely LOVE the jacket. Beautiful! You are a star! All my friends think it's amazing and are thoroughly jealous. I think you may be getting some orders for more!'

So the Hermes scarf wasn't wasted after all.

CHAPTER 33

Kuki was anxiously rocking from foot to foot.

'A boy run up to warn you. The soldiers, they are in the yard.'

'Sabu?'

'No, a worker. You must go.'

'Where's Dicken?' I remembered he was checking the outhouse for anything we might need in our future lives. I hastily put on some shoes and rushed to the back of the house.

'Dicken, Dicken! Kuki says there are soldiers down at the yard. We have to go and see that Sabu and Okello are safe!'

His tall frame stepped out into the sunlight and he dusted down his trousers and shirt.

'And how do you propose we do that?'

'We head down there and show that we're around. Make sure they don't hurt them.'

'Look Birdie, it's like this. We're here packing up and it's the last day you're going to be on the plantation. Soon you'll be gone. What's the point in us going down there and stirring up trouble? It's all going to come anyway.'

'All right. But I'm not gone. Yet! I'm here. Now! Right now it's still my plantation and they're not going to trespass and they're not going to hurt anyone. Where's your rifle?'

'Are you crazy! We go down there with a gun and we're setting the scene for real trouble.'

'Okay then, I'll go without a gun. Are you coming?'

He hesitated slightly, so I turned and started walking down the side of the house where the red earth path snaked down to the yard some hundred yards away. Dicken caught up with me and took hold of my arm.

'Slowly,' he warned. 'We may be able to see them before they see us. Gauge the temperature a bit.'

We stayed under cover of the thick vegetation and mango trees. As we got closer, we could hear voices which became clearer as we progressed.

Crouching down, we pushed through the undergrowth until we could see figures about twenty feet ahead. A couple of soldiers stood near the drying trays and to the left of them, two other uniformed Ugandans were questioning Okello. One, who seemed to be in command, held a large rifle in his hands and stood with his legs askance. At his side stood another man holding a clipboard.

The officer barked something about the number of workers. Those were the only words I managed to catch.

Okello answered and then continued, responding to the various questions that were fired at him.

It seemed the plantation was being assessed, ready for the authorities to move in and take control.

Sabu was nowhere to be seen, and I felt relieved. He had probably scampered off somewhere to hide. After what seemed like ten minutes of sitting on my haunches, my legs began to ache and I shifted position. This opened up a different line of vision and I caught a movement out of the corner of my eye. Standing at the side were two further soldiers, one of them with a bony hand on the shoulder of a young boy.

Sabu stood rigid and pale.

I recognised the soldier and my stomach sank.

The interrogating officer had now come up close and threatening to Okello, the barrel of his rifle forcing my friend's head back to an unnatural angle. I could see the distinct 'V' of the jawline and his vulnerable throat. The tempo had changed, and the leader was playing to his audience. His men stood behind him, laughing appropriately whenever he shouted out comments in a jocular fashion. This, in turn, seemed to drive him on.

All of a sudden, he took two steps back and Okello swayed unsteadily.

A word was barked out. I couldn't make it out. Again, repeated, and Okello knelt.

A rifle was cocked, then another and close by I heard the repetitive cry of a Turaco bird in the trees.

As I lurched forward, I felt Dicken's hand reach out to stop me but he was too late. Within ten steps I was standing in the clearing, suddenly aware of my vulnerability.

'What's going on here? What do you want with my manager?'

I could feel Dicken standing behind me. He didn't have his rifle.

'Ah, so what do we have here? A wahindi. Lady wahindi with Mr USA.'

'I'm Mrs Dalal and you're on my land. This plantation belongs to me and you're trespassing.'

'Oh really? Belongs to a wahindi? I don't think so. No, no, no. That cannot be true.'

'It most certainly is true. You can call me all the names you want but Rutubasana is *still* my property and you are trespassing.'

The condescending smile did not reach his cold dark eyes.

'In a few days this property will be gone,' he clicked his fingers. 'You will be gone and this property, this property will be *ours*.'

'You mean you will have stolen our property!'

Dicken's hand touched my arm in warning. Okello was still kneeling, looking from one face to the other as we spoke.

'Come, Okello, stand up. Here, come.'

The rifle was raised again.

'Do you realise how important my manager is to you? Don't you understand how difficult it is to know all the secrets of how to harvest tea? Do you know how to pick the right leaves, tend to the plants? Do you know how to dry the leaves, to sort them?'

The soldier stood rigid, his face expressionless.

'And if you harm Okello here, what will your superior say? Don't you think he'll be angry with you? This farm will no longer make money. And it will be your fault.' I raised my voice and spoke out to all the soldiers. 'If my manager is harmed you will all be blamed for cutting off the good money that this land will bring your leader. What do you think will happen? You will be blamed. You will be punished.'

No one spoke and the only sound was the repetitive call of the native bird.

'Come Okello, here.' I reached for his shoulder and held his hand as he stood up. I could feel him shaking but I held his moist hand tight.

'Now you can go. This will all be yours in a few weeks but your leader, whoever he is, will want the farm to be in good order and my manager here, is part of that. Now go.'

The soldier took a step closer and I could feel his breath on my forehead.

'We will go, for now. Only for a short time. We will go, but we do not go empty-handed. We will take our entertainment.'

He swung his rifle on his shoulder and indicated for his men to follow him.

The two soldiers, standing on the edge, moved forward dragging Sabu with them. The boy's legs were rigid, skidding on the dry dust.

'Wait! You're not taking Sabu.'

'He's our entertainment.'

'No, you can't. He belongs here.'

'And what does he do here? Is he important? I don't think so. Is he your son? No, no, definitely not. We all know this boy. He is a beggar boy, but he tells good stories. The nights are long and dull in the camp. This boy can keep us amused,' and he laughed at his own wit. 'Yes, indeed he will keep us very amused.'

Fear consumed Sabu's handsome features as he tried to wriggle free from the grasp of his captors.

'Miss Bulbul, Miss Bulbul, don't let them take me. Please, Miss Bulbul. They are wicked men, wicked!'

'You cannot take him. I forbid you. I absolutely forbid you.'

Another grin and a spit in the dry earth.

'You! You cannot forbid anything. You have no power. All you wahindis have no power now. For many years you have called us shenzis and treated us like dogs. Now it is *our* turn to treat *you* like dogs. We are kicking you from your beds. Kick, kick. Out you go you dirty wahindis. You call us golas and you think we are stupid but now all of us golas are kicking you out.'

'Yes, I know, we are going, but please leave Sabu here. He's only a child.'

'Ok lady, I give you a choice,' he said, crossing his arms across his chest.

'What choice?'

'An easy choice. Your manager or Sabu.'

'I don't understand.'

'Very simple. Your manager or Sabu.'

My legs felt like liquid.

'Listen Lady Wahindi my soldiers are very bored, very, very bored. They need entertainment. You have a choice. First, we can have some entertainment with your manager, an Acholi I think. Am I right? Yes, I am right. Or we take the boy. You can choose.'

'You want to take Okello?'

'Does he tell good stories?'

'I don't understand.'

Dicken pulled my arm.

'Let it go, Birdie. Don't you see what the man's saying? It's Okello's life or they take Sabu. He wants you to choose.'

'How can I choose that? It's barbaric!'

'Mr USA has understood very well. Good man. Clever man,' and the soldier clapped slowly.

'You see lady, here we have a choice. Like a set of scales in the market.' He held his large hands out, cupped, as if weighing two bloodied hearts. 'In this hand, your manager is very useful, very good for the plantation, the tea, yes, I know, I know. But then, in this other hand,' he feigned a look of mournful regret. 'In this hand, the man is Acholi. So, let us think about it. Will my chief be cross because I kill the manager, or will he be happy because I kill an Acholi? Difficult.' He continued balancing his large hands in the air. 'What do you think?'

There were no words, no choice, no solution.

'Please,' I said meekly, but it was a small and solitary word in a dark, wide continent.

Sabu's pleas tore at my heart, clawed at my very soul. I was mute and frozen as they loaded him in the back of the truck and the canvas roof obscured his small frame. The vehicle skidded around to head up the track when I finally sprang into action and raced after the truck.

'Sabu, Sabu,' I cried. 'Can you hear me Sabu?'

'Yes, Miss Bulbul, I can hear you.'

'Remember the Tale of the Arabian Nights. Remember Scheherazade! You are Scheherazade! Remember Sabu, remember!'

I didn't say I would rescue him. I had no idea how. I was lost.

CHAPTER 34

We are told it's Christmas Eve and the administrators and helpers in the camp put their fingers to their lips when they talk to the children, as if some great secret is soon to be revealed.

The dining room sparkles with swags of silver and gold tinsel. When we go into dinner in the evening all the lights are turned off. The room is lit only by candles lined along the trestle tables and arranged above the serving counter. Our fellow residents gasp and say that it reminds them of Diwali. Are we surprised that the English can also enjoy the ethereal light and symbolism of candles?

We don't seem so sallow in this candlelight, not like under the harsh strip lighting that's normally in place. We almost look as if we're at home.

There's a smell of cinnamon and cloves coming from a hot drink that's being served - spiced apple juice which is sweet and warming. Even the children can have some, provided some cold water is added, so they won't burn themselves.

During the meal Hana catches my eye and I nod slightly to indicate that all is well. It is actually a lie, as so far I haven't achieved anything. Time is running out.

Our instructions from Valeria are clear. Hana is to be collected by a taxi at 11.15 pm on the corner of Holland Street and she will then be taken to Kings Cross station, where she'll board the 23.58 train to Edinburgh. Her ticket is for a sleeper berth on her own so she won't be seen by many passengers. When she arrives, she'll be met by Mr and Mrs Roxborough who'll take her into their home in the country. Here they will treat her as one of their own until the birth of her child. She'll receive support afterwards, but at this stage there is no way of saying what form this help will take. So much will depend on Hana's feelings and the decision she finally makes. Valeria says it's best that neither of us know the address at this stage, just in case the information falls into the wrong hands.

Hana will be leaving London two minutes before her eighteenth birthday but first she needs her documents which are locked in the secretary's office. All the documents of the residents are stored in the files in the office but until now, it has been impossible to find the opportunity to retrieve them. I'm hoping that the distractions of the celebrations will help me with my task. Hana will need these papers to start her life afresh. Her birth certificate, passport and entry visa.

After dinner there's a carol service for the residents. This has been organised by the Women's Voluntary Service and takes place in the main common room, where the chairs have been set in rows in front of the small stage. A group of about twelve singers gather around the piano which is played by a large woman, precariously perched on a delicate stool.

Hana sits with her parents near the front and appears absorbed by the singing. Now is my moment. I slip out through the side door and make my way towards the kitchens.

The small metal cabinet that houses the various keys for the centre hangs on the wall outside the pantry. I've seen that, in turn, the key to this chest is kept on a ledge behind the radiator.

The hall is gloomy, but I don't yet dare take out the small torch that I've hidden in my handbag. I'll save it for when

I'm safely in the office. In the distance I can hear the piano and the singing. How many carols will be sung, and how long do I have before the residents will start leaving to go to their dormitories?

I reach down tentatively behind the radiator and my fingers find the warm metal of the cabinet key. It opens the small door easily. The keys hang neatly on the labelled hooks and I quickly use the torch to select the one I need.

Locking the cabinet again, I make my way down the side hallway to the secretary's office. I give thanks that there's no glass above the doorway so my torch light won't be seen, but I know I need to be swift in case anyone sees the light from outside. Luckily I've observed Mrs Harvey, the secretary, filing the residents' papers so I know where to look. Within a couple of minutes I've located Hana's file and extracted her passport and other official documents that will be required. Her papers sit in the same file as that of her parents, nestled like a family. She is now extracted. Should I feel guilty at being involved in this conspiracy? There's no choice.

After locking the office door, I retrace my steps and return the key to the cabinet and take out two more, one a modern Yale key another, larger and heavier this time – a spare key to the front gate which is always locked at night. I slip the keys into my bag along with Hana's documents and my small torch and head back along the dark corridor towards the music. As I turn left at the final corner I'm stopped abruptly by the jolt of walking into the large belly of a solid figure.

Mr Caxton.

'Hello, hello. What have we here? Not interested in the Christmas carols?'

'I just had to go to the bathroom.'

'Really? Now how long have you been staying here as our guest, eh? Don't you know they're that way?' he asked, his fat finger pointing down the opposite corridor.

'Yes, of course. I just got confused on my way back.'

'Really? Is that so? You haven't been snooping, have you?'

'Snooping?'

'Looking around in places you shouldn't be looking around in?'

'No. Why would I do that?'

'Something tells me, my little Paki, that you have a very inquisitive mind. And if you don't know what that means in English, it means nosey!' he says, tapping the side of his bulbous nose.

His eyes seem to drill into my head, but I hold his gaze and tell him, in a steady voice, that I must return to the concert.

There's a rendition of *We wish you a Merry Christmas* being sung when I return to the communal room and Jack asks me quietly where I've been. I touch my stomach and he nods his understanding, telling me that Ashika has taken Moh up to bed as he was getting overtired.

Finally, the singers are bowing to the applauding audience then, after some lingering to chat with our neighbours, we filter off to our various rooms. Hana and I don't make eye contact.

It seems an age before everyone settles down in the dormitory. Shai and Padma are feeling lively, giggling and singing *We wish you a Merry Christmas* even though, to my knowledge, none of us in the dormitory are Christians. But the celebratory mood is infectious. It's Christmas Eve and the dawning of a new freedom for my young friend.

To my relief, by 11 pm the dormitory is quiet and everyone appears to be sleeping. Hana shakes me quietly and together we pad quietly out of the dormitory holding our shoes. Hana carries a small bag with her few belongings. Before we open the front door, I pass her all the documents together with her train ticket, money and the contact telephone number of her new hosts. I shine the torch so she can check the details. We don't speak. We've been through the plan several times.

The streetlights give enough illumination for our journey across the courtyard and I easily open the main gate with the chunky key. Beyond the residence, as arranged, the taxi is waiting on the adjoining street and we pause on the pavement beside it.

'Promise me Birdie. Promise me you won't tell my parents anything. You won't tell *anybody anything*.'

'I promise.'

'Swear!'

'Sorry?'

'Swear it.'

'Don't be silly. Of course I won't tell anyone.'

'Swear it!'

'All right. I swear.'

'Swear on something you hold dear.'

'What do you mean?'

'I have to be sure you will never ever tell *anyone*.'

'You can be sure. I swear it.'

'Then prove to me that you really mean it. Swear an oath on the thing you hold most dear.'

'I swear it Hana. I swear I won't tell anyone.'

'No. That's not enough. Swear on your son's head that you won't.'

'Sorry Hana, I can't do that. I promise, I swear that I won't tell anyone. But I won't swear on Moh's head.'

'Then how do I know that you won't tell anyone?'

'Because I've promised you. I've sworn. That should be enough. Now come on, you must go. Now. Quickly or you'll miss your train.'

'I won't go until you swear on your son's head that you won't tell anyone.'

'No, I can't swear on Moh's head.'

'Then I don't believe you. If you really mean you won't tell anyone you would swear on Moh's head. I don't believe you!'

'You can believe me. You must go. It's getting late.'

'Swear it, Birdie.'

'Come on Hana, go!'

'Swear it!'

'All right, all right, I swear it.'

'On your son's head.'

'Very well, yes, on my son's head. I swear I won't tell anyone.'

She releases the claw like grip that she has on my wrist and I step away from her quickly.

'Goodbye Birdie. Thank you.'

She climbs into the back of the taxi and leans out to me.

'Beware of my parents.'

'You mean your father?'

'Both of them.'

The door slams and I catch the expression on her face. The taxi drives off leaving me ice cold on the pavement.

As I turn to head back to the centre, I see a pub further along the street. The sign reads *The Elephant and Castle*. Such strange names. Such a strange land.

Chapter 35

I was kneeling in the dirt and could feel the hot sun on the back of my head. Everything was quiet in the yard apart from the bird who was still calling, oblivious to the cruelty of man.

'So who the hell is Scheherazade!' asked Dicken finally.

I took a long time answering. What was the point? What was the point in anything?

I stood up weakly and slowly brushed the dust from my knees.

'Scheherazade? She's from The One Thousand and One Nights. Haven't you ever read the Arabian Nights?'

'Do I seem like the kind of guy who would read the Arabian Nights?'

Despite myself, I chuckled. It was a quivering in the base of my stomach that started creeping up through my body until I was overcome with shaking, howling laughter. My legs gave way, and I sat down in the earth again, rocking as the tears of mirth ran down my face.

'No, Dicken, no. You definitely are *not* the kind of guy who would read the Arabian Nights!'

I rocked myself and clutched at my tee shirt. My tears ran hotter and my guffaws turned to racking sobs. I sat there rocking, in the dirt, while Okello, Dicken, and a few farm hands stood and watched as I wept over a low caste beggar boy.

Finally I got up, brushed my legs down once again and explained to Dicken and Okello that Scheherazade was from the book, The One Thousand and One Nights, which was made into a film The Arabian Nights starring the actor Sabu.

'And what's so great about Scheherazade?'

'She told wonderful stories, just like Sabu. And just like our Sabu, her life was hanging on a thread. The only power she had was her ability to tell stories, and so she did. Every night she would tell a story and stop before the end, saying it was getting too late and she would finish the following night. That way her life would be spared until the next night when she was due to finish it. And so she would finish the tale and would start another which, again, she wouldn't finish. And so it went on.'

'And then what happened?' asked Okello.

'This went on for one thousand and one nights.'

'And then what happened?'

'Then the king fell in love with her and made her his queen.'

'Hah!' snorted Okello. 'Fairy tales. You always did love your fairy tale books and your films Birdie.'

Dicken waved our chat aside.

'A thousand and one nights is nearly three years. I think we've got to be realistic here.'

'Of course, we don't need three years!'

'We don't?'

'No, we need two weeks.' I reply.

'Why two weeks?'

'Well, we leave in two weeks and we're going to have to rescue him before then.'

'There's no "we" about it Birdie and you're crazy if you think there's anything you can do. Anything at all!'

'There must be something we can do. Something!'

All the energy seemed to have left the marrow of my bones. Dicken and Okello were quiet and subdued. The three of us trod slowly back up the track to the house and Kuki brought us some ice cold nimbu pani which we drank on the terrace.

'You should leave, Okello. Take my father's jeep, it's yours. And any money there is.'

'No Birdie, I'll stay. I'll look after the farm until you return.'

'But we're not coming back. You know how things are. Once we're gone you don't honestly think they're going to keep you on as the manager, do you?'

'I know about the estate. I understand the tea. They won't kill me when I'm the one who can help them make money.'

'They nearly killed you just now! What makes you think they won't next time.'

He shrugged and a small, unconvincing smile reached the corners of his mouth.

'Maybe your words have done the trick. Now they won't dare.'

A flash of a memory entered my head, a group of dark heads surrounding a burning circle. A scorpion in the middle, or were there two?

'What are they doing Mama?'

'Don't look Bulbul, Sanjay, come here. Don't look!'

But Sanjay, who must have been about eight at the time, was fascinated and peered closer over the dark heads.

Someone was pushing the sides of the burning cotton wool with a stick, so the circle was getting tighter. The spectators were getting more excited. Money was changing hands. A rhythmic chant started slowly and grew louder and louder, and faster and faster, as the circle was prodded more, the diameter getting smaller.

Suddenly a cheer, fists in the air, slaps on backs and thighs as some climax had been reached.

'What happened Mama?'

'Come on Bulbul, come here.'

'What happened Sanjay?'

My brother shook my hand away. There was a small glint of something at the back of his eyes, something I couldn't quite place. I slapped his arm.

'Tell me!'

'The scorpion stung himself,' Sanjay declared.

That vision has often entered my thoughts over the years. The suicide of the scorpion, the cruelty of the men. My mother wanting to protect me from the harshness of the world. Did she? No, not in the end.

'I tell you Okello – go! Take your mother and sisters and any possessions you want from here and go north to Acholiland. Make a new start. Please.'

Okello pulled a face and gave a sarcastic laugh.

'Only problem with Acholiland - it's full of us Acholis.'

Then he downed his drink, scraping the chair legs on the teak decking as he stood up to leave.

I thought he was going without saying anything further, but he turned back when he reached the steps.

'Remember the Pearl of Africa. It will always be here for you. Goodbye Birdie.'

That afternoon the world felt empty and as dry as tinder. Dicken and I barely spoke. Kuki was subdued as she worked quietly in the kitchen. The frustration boiled up in me.

'What are you doing, Kuki! Why are you always working, working? What for?'

She looked at me bewildered.

'What's it all for Kuki?'

'I work Bulbul, I always work.'

'But we're going Kuki? Soon you'll be left all on your own. What are you going to do? Why don't you leave?'

Our old maid looked into my eyes as if searching for an answer. I saw how her eyelids had drooped over the years and how her hair was now steel grey.

'I go to my sister. She live in Masaka. When you leave, I go and live with her.'

'Well, go tomorrow Kuki. Soon the soldiers will come back. If you don't go soon, they'll stop you from leaving and you'll be like their slave.'

I hugged her tightly.

Dicken and I packed my few belongings in the rear of the jeep. I saw Sabu had left his baseball cap on the back seat and my stomach somersaulted with fear. I had already walked through the empty house one last time saying goodbye to each room and the spirit of beloved Pappa. I had looked out of every window to the view beyond etching it in my mind for eternity. I had felt the familiar crunch of soil beneath my feet as I walked towards the jeep. Dicken started the engine, and we swooped out of the drive.

'Stop!' I cried as we came around the corner of the highest point of the plantation where beyond lay the gentle hills that faded to a grey blue in the distance. The sun was still hot, but the day was tipping into late afternoon and the smell of the dry earth and lush bushes filled my senses. In my head was a drumming and I realised it was the sound of the blood in my ears and I tasted despair as the tears ran down my face. This was the end, the end.

Jack barely looked up from the papers strewn over his desk when I returned that evening.

'All sorted? Did you get what you needed?'

'Yes,' I affirmed. I didn't tell him about Sabu, or the soldiers, or Okello's hunched shoulders as he knelt in the dirt.

There were smells of cooking emanating from the kitchen as Mirembe prepared the evening meal. Ashika tiptoed out into the hallway, closing Moh's bedroom door gently behind her. She advised me that her grandson had just dropped off to sleep and it would better not to disturb him.

Had I ever felt so lonely and desolate? One by one, I collected the sewing machine and the three cardboard boxes that I had left inside the front door when Dicken dropped me off. One by one, I deposited the boxed memories of my life on the bedroom floor. I couldn't face going through the papers, so I picked up an old carved box that rested on the top of the pile and meandered through into the living room where Jack still sat absorbed by his papers.

I wandered over to the drinks tray where our soda syphon stood in dark red resplendence next to the silver bucket of fresh ice, filled as usual by our maid. The whisky on the polished tray was the same brand my father would drink. I dropped three cubes of ice into a cut-glass tumbler, a good two inches of the amber liquid and topped it up with a gurgling spray of soda. It reminded me of when I served drinks to Pappa and Dicken on the veranda. A comforting action, a connection to my past.

Flopping down on the sofa, I placed my glass on the low lacquered table by my side and started playing a solo game of Mancala. There was something soothing and earthy about the dry beans rolling into the worn cups, hollowed out of the solid wood. The shallow, single layer of thought that the game required – rather like skidding along on the earth's crust ignoring the bodies below.

Out of the corner of my eye I could see Jack sit back in his chair and watch me.

'Are you now turning to drink?'

I toasted him with the glass and the ice clinked.

'Should I have asked you?'

He shrugged.

'Should I have asked your permission?'

'Of course not. I've just never seen you help yourself to a drink before. You hardly drink at all.'

'Well Jack, the way I see it is that I'm a modern woman so, I thought to myself just now, if I can't help myself to a drink in my own house on the most miserable day of my life, then when can I?'

'Is it?'

'What?'

'The most miserable day of your life?'

I nodded as I raised the glass to my lips.

'I thought the day your father died was the most miserable day of your life.'

'Today my father died again. Today everything died.'

I still didn't tell Jack about Sabu. After all, what would he say? Would he care? Not much, I imagined. He would say I had other things to think about. Sometimes he was a stranger to me.

CHAPTER 36

I'm surprised I've slept at all. The last thing I remember was lying in my bed staring at the ceiling as the hours ticked by. But it must be morning now and the sounds of excited chatter filter through the sandy layers of my slumber. I hear Padma's husky voice exclaim in excitement.

'And look, a bottle of shampoo. It's as if they remember I'm going to work as a hairdresser!'

Ashika shakes my shoulder gently.

'Bulbul, Bulbul, look! Moh has received a Christmas stocking as well. Come. We can help him open it.'

I sit up and look around, trying not to focus on Hana's empty bed.

'Maybe we should wait for Jack. He'll want to see Moh's excitement. Wait while I get dressed and we can go downstairs.' I'm relieved to leave the dormitory before Sudha questions me about her daughter's absence.

I pull on my blue dress, thick tights and boots before descending the stairs with Moh and Ashika. In the hall the large Christmas tree glitters and twinkles and I recognise Bing Crosby's voice singing of sleigh bells in the snow. But it doesn't seem as if it will snow today; it's not even raining for a change.

Jack isn't downstairs yet so we wait in the common room which still has some chairs set in rows, left over from the carol concert last night.

We are sitting on the large sofa by the window, entertaining Moh with wooden bricks, when Hana's mother approaches. This is what I've been dreading. She's still wearing her nightclothes and her hair is loose and unbrushed.

'Birdie, Ashika, have you seen Hana? I can't find her anywhere.'

I try not to blush but the more I think of my involvement the more I can feel my face growing hot.

'No,' I say, turning to Ashika. 'Have you seen Hana?'

My mother-in-law shakes her head.

'No. Maybe she's in the washroom?'

'She isn't. I've looked there. I've looked everywhere.'

Sudha is wringing her hands in despair and her nose looks pinched and white.

I try to concentrate on building a tower for Moh out of coloured wooden blocks. I barely glance up.

'Have you looked in the kitchen? Perhaps she's helping with the Christmas meal.'

She looks relieved and heads off in the direction of the kitchen, muttering to herself that of course, that must be where she is.

My heart is pounding and I think I'm going to faint. I flop against the back of the sofa and am fearful that Ashika will hear the thumping sound, like a jungle drum warning of danger.

The welcome sight of Jack's upright figure walking into the room helps to calm my racing heart. He looks concerned.

'Are you not well?'

'Me? No, I'm fine.'

'You look a bit ill. I just thought, after last night, maybe you have an upset stomach.'

I grab at the excuse he has offered.

'Only slightly. Not too bad, thank you. Look, Moh's received a stocking. I thought you would want to see him open it.'

We help Moh to take his presents out of the large sock.

A wooden train, a small spinning top, a ball and a small windmill. If you blow on the blue folds of cardboard, the windmill spins round and round. This is Moh's favourite toy, but I'm fearful he may harm himself with the stick as he waves his arm about. Out of the corner of my eye I see Sudha heading away from the kitchens, along the hallway and towards the stairs as she continues her hunt for Hana.

We're in the dining room for breakfast and I go to collect a bowl from the sideboard. Hana's father approaches me, leaning close and crowding my space.

'Where is my daughter?'

'Hana?'

'I only have one daughter. Hana. Where is she?'

'Why should I know where Hana is?'

'Because you and Hana keep some secret. I can see it. I watch you and I can see.'

'Of course we don't. I hardly know Hana.'

'You girls. You have secrets.'

'That's not true. Did you look in the kitchens?'

'We look everywhere, *everywhere*!'

'Well, I'm sorry I haven't any idea where she is.'

'The two of you are friends. You take her on the river. Is this something you do?'

'No, why would I do anything? I'm here, aren't I? And it's Christmas Day. Why would I want to do anything on Christmas Day?'

'Because it's her birthday.'

'Oh really, on Christmas Day? We should have a party.'

'She's not here for the party.'

'She must be around somewhere.'

'No, she is gone. Someone takes her.'

'How could someone take her? She sleeps in the dormitory with all of us. That's impossible.'

'Or she goes away. You have made plans with Hana.'

'Why would I do that? How could I do that?'

'You have ways, you have friends in England. I watch you.'

'Just because I have three friends in England does not mean I would plan anything. I only know three people in the whole of England. One, two, three.' I count them off on my fingers and realise I've forgotten Valeria's husband, John, although he's not exactly a friend. Only four. I almost find myself lying to myself.

Hana's father holds his fat forefinger in my face.

'You!' he exclaims. 'You plan this. You!'

I shake my head.

'No, no. You're wrong.'

'I know. You! It is you!'

I see him follow in the footsteps of his wife as he searches for his daughter. As he leaves, I raise my hand to my cheek. My face is burning hot.

CHAPTER 37

The next morning Jack left early for the university so, while Ashika cared for Moh, I started to sort through the three boxes I had brought back from Rutubasana. It would be impossible to take all these papers to England. In any case, there was a wad of unopened letters which would need to be tackled. Any activity at the moment was welcome as it would take my mind off Sabu and leaving my childhood home.

I started to make various piles in front of me on my bedroom floor and sat cross-legged as I sorted through the reams of paperwork.

I took most of the photographs out of frames to reduce the weight of our luggage, although I kept intact the one of my mother standing near the jacaranda tree. Some pictures I had never seen before. My parents when they were younger; would that have been their honeymoon? Didn't they go to Egypt to see the pyramids? There were a few pictures of my brother and me as children, always wearing our best clothes, although I seldom remember wearing anything other than shorts. A photograph of Sanjay with his new bicycle and one with him standing proudly next to two men in front of a large bulldozer and a high mound of earth. Possibly the building of the Owen Falls Dam that my brother loved visiting so much? One of the men was tall and white, probably in his fifties, the other man looked like a native Ugandan and smiled warmly at the camera. An engineer possibly, as he had his arm resting on some kind of surveying equipment and a pen tucked behind his ear.

The bills I put in another pile; they were of little importance as we would be leaving everything behind us - bills and wealth, wealth and bills. It now meant nothing.

Stuck in the middle of the bundle of letters sat an official looking envelope with the Ugandan crest on it - an antelope and a crested crane flanking a carved shield. It was addressed to my father, as was all the correspondence, unopened for weeks. I had been remiss; with Sanjay away in the States it should have fallen on my shoulders to take over the paperwork, or I should at least have passed this duty on to Okello. I tried to excuse myself by thinking there had seemed little point when we would be leaving so soon.

I slit the envelope open with the miniature sword my father had always used so efficiently in his study. The red leather handle was worn and smooth through the years of wear and I felt a comforting connection.

The letter bore the same crest at the top and the address of President's Office, P.O. Box 7168, Kampala. No palace? No dancing girls?

It stated that the lands known as Rutubasana in the region of Jinja, laid to the production of tea, would be reclaimed by the Ugandan government and that all farm equipment and items pertaining to the growing and processing of tea were to remain on the premises. Any act to sell or sabotage said items would be illegal and would incur disciplinary action. The letter was then signed by General Idi Amin Dada, President of the Republic of Uganda, with copies to the Minister of Public Service and Cabinet of Affairs.

I must have held the letter in my hand for a full five minutes, acrid acid running through my heart. Finally, a wild idea flashed through my mind and I laid the letter carefully aside.

After two hours the piles were neat and ordered. I would send the bills back to Okello for him to pass on to the new owner. The photographs I would pack, my only link to my past life in Uganda. The official documents should be sent to Sanjay, but I didn't dare post them; if they got lost my brother will never have a chance to claim his land in the future. I would have to ask my Uncle Deepak if he would send them from Nairobi, a far safer prospect than the mail from Kampala. It reminded me that I should contact my aunt to find out how their plans were progressing.

I looked at my watch and walked through to the living room to make a call to Aunt Latika.

'My dear child, I'm so glad you phoned. I'm absolutely strung up in a tangle of nerves and worry. It seems like we've been packing up boxes for months now. There are piles of crates everywhere and only a few chairs and a table for our use. Can you hear it when I talk? It echoes!'

'Yes Auntie, I can. What are your plans?'

'The lorries are coming in two days to collect our belongings and we'll be taking everything to Nairobi. Deepak is there at the moment. He's managed to find us a small house on the outskirts of the city, although ultimately our aim is to move to the United States.'

'How are you able to enter Kenya? I thought they weren't letting any of us in.'

'You know your Uncle Deepak. He always finds a way. He has friends, and we're taking some guards with us, just in case. But tell me, how is Rutubasana?'

'I left it for the last time yesterday. The last time ever,' I add quietly.

'My poor girl. We will all miss it. Sometimes I get so upset I think I am going to explode. Deepak says it's not good for my blood pressure and so I take a tablet.'

I make the appropriate sympathetic noises as she goes on to explain her medical woes.

'And Nanda?'

'Nanda's fine. In fact, I think she's being very strong.

Especially when you think her life is being ripped apart.'

'All our lives are being ripped apart.'

'But yes, darling, you know what I mean. But I think she's being especially strong.'

'I'm sure she'll enjoy life in Nairobi.'

'Yes, and no. Do you know what she's now saying? She wants to go to university! She says she wants to get a degree so that she's in control of her life.'

A flash of envy ran through me.

'That's a very good idea. What does she want to study?'

'She's talking about medicine. She says she wants to be a doctor.'

'I thought she didn't like the sight of blood.'

'I know, but she says she'll get used to it. Who knows? We've told her that she doesn't need to worry about money. Deepak has been very clever and we're perfectly fine, but Nanda won't listen. She says all this business with Amin has shown her that she needs to be able to look after herself. Her father is pleased. At least he says he is. Will we see you before we leave?'

'Yes auntie, I'll come and visit you. Tomorrow? I also have a favour to ask.'

I arranged to visit her the next morning. She would send Kenzi to collect me and she would get her cook to make some kulfi ice cream. We could sit on the terrace near the damask roses. She would have to leave them behind.

Jack came home early from the university that afternoon. I found him pacing up and down in the living room.

'Why are you back so early? Weren't you giving a lecture this afternoon?'

'Things have changed, Birdie. We're going to have to leave sooner than planned.'

'Really? Why? How much sooner?'

'We leave tomorrow night.'

'How can we do that? Our flight leaves in two weeks!'

'I've made arrangements with the airline. They've managed to change our tickets. We won't all be able to sit together on the plane, but at least they can get us on an earlier flight. A huge relief.'

'How can we possibly pack up so quickly? What's changed?'

'It's just not safe. Frank Kalimuzo's disappearance last week. They say it was the Public Safety Unit that came and there's been no sign of him for six days. We all know what that means. Several of the academic staff, me included, have refused to keep quiet. We've been making enquiries and it seems it has roused Amin's anger. A member of the Muslim council came to warn us this morning. He told us to hide or get out if we value our lives.'

'Can it really be that serious? Maybe Kalimuzo will come back. Perhaps the man who warned you this morning is mistaken.'

'Look Birdie, this is serious. The last report we had about Frank was him being taken into the C Block?'

'C Block?'

'Also known as the House of Death.'

I had heard stories of the things Amin's henchmen did and went cold at the thought of Jack's friend, the university's vice chancellor, being tortured or even murdered. A further slice of razor-sharp fear hit the pit of my stomach when I realised how close it all was now to our own lives. Recently I had heard intangible rumours, but now it all seemed deadly real.

'Very well. Then we have no choice. I just need to phone Dicken. I want to see if he's back from his tour.'

'What for?'

'I need to say goodbye.'

'You shouldn't say goodbye to anyone, Birdie. We have to slip away.'

'But Dicken's like a second father to me. I must see him

before we go. I have to say goodbye!'

Jack reached out and grabbed me by my wrist and pulled me towards him.

'Look Birdie,' he said, pushing my dishevelled hair away from my face, 'This is serious. This isn't one of your books or your films. This is real life. All of our lives are in danger. We need to act quickly and quietly. You can't say goodbye to Dicken. It's too risky.'

'I have to, Jack.'

'No. You must promise me, Birdie. Promise.' I had never seen Jack so anxious.

'Very well. I promise. But I really have to see Aunt Latika. I need to pass over the papers for Rutubasana. Uncle Deepak is going to mail them to Sanjay from Nairobi.'

'Can't Kenzi pick them up?'

'I need to take them myself, and in any case she's expecting me. I arranged it this afternoon. You don't need to worry - it's not like they live in the centre of Kampala. Nothing happens on their compound. Kenzi's coming to pick me up.'

'It's not a good idea Birdie.'

'I won't say anything. I won't even tell her we're leaving early. I'll just keep everything as normal. No one will know.'

Jack took a lot of convincing but eventually agreed, provided I didn't mention anything about Kalimuzo or our early departure. And provided I didn't go into central Kampala or try to find Dicken.

Everything as normal, whatever normal was.

CHAPTER 38

It's three o'clock in the afternoon and we're feeling replete after our Christmas meal of roast turkey with numerous vegetables and dark gravy. I'm proud of my contribution to the cooking - sage and onion stuffing, which I prepared in the kitchen yesterday under the guidance of the head cook, Elsie. Following her instructions, I chopped a mountain of onions, crying and snivelling as I went, then gently fried the onions in butter as my eyes finally cleared of tears. Afterwards I added chopped sage, an earthy herb I've never seen before, then tipped in a huge pile of grated breadcrumbs and this was all brought together with more butter, some lemon zest, beaten egg and milk. I then patted the mixture down in a flat tray to chill in the fridge before it was to be stuffed into the cavity of the large bird.

'Perfect,' Elsie had said. 'Absolutely perfect!'

Despite my nerves throughout the Christmas meal, I manage to enjoy the food and point out to Jack the stuffing I had prepared. Jack laughs.

'Perhaps there's hope for you yet, Birdie. When we move into our new home in Theobald Square, you'll be able to take over the cooking.'

I'm not sure whether Ashika purses her lips about my cooking or the prospect of our new house which won't be close to any of her friends. Valeria was right - her husband really does have a silver tongue and we're due to move at the end of January.

We try to get Moh interested in the bright red crackers on the table but he just looks surprised at the sudden popping sounds and smell of gunpowder.

Now, after the meal, everyone has dispersed to various locations. Some have stayed in the common room, as we have, others have returned to their dormitories. Life will now go on as normal - a life of waiting and hoping.

Now I see uniformed policemen talking to the administrator in the hallway. Hana's parents join them and they are agitated and gesticulating. Perhaps Hana misjudged her father and mother. Perhaps they truly loved her after all. Everyone loves their children, don't they? I look at Moh who has fallen asleep in Jack's arms. The side of his cheek is creased, and he sleeps with the deep rhythm that only comes to children.

There must be six or seven people gathered in the hallway outside the common room and I notice a police-woman with scraped back blonde hair, looking in my direction. In a couple of minutes she and a policeman walk towards our family group.

'Mrs Dalal?'

'Yes?'

'I wonder if we could ask you a few questions.'

'Me?'

'Yes. Nothing to worry about but we just think you may be able to throw a bit of light on a situation we have in this camp at the moment.'

'Of course,' I reply feeling my cheeks starting to burn again.

'Would you mind coming into the dining room, please?'

'Yes, if you like. Just me or would you like to talk to all of us?'

'No, just you, Mrs Dalal, if you wouldn't mind.'

Again, the thumping heart pounding in my ears.

The dining room is now cleared and empty, but the smell of the Christmas meal lingers in the air.

'Take a seat,' the policeman indicates, and he and his

female companion sit opposite me.

I sit on a solid wooden bench and notice a stickiness by my hand as a grab the edge.

'Now,' said the policeman opening his note pad. 'I understand you know Hana Husain?'

'Yes, I do.'

'And are you aware that this young lady has gone missing?'

'I only know that Hana's parents haven't been able to find her. It's been very busy here today.' I can't believe my stupidity! I shouldn't elaborate. Keep it simple.

'Yes, of course, of course, being Christmas and all. Now I'm not sure what sort of friendship you had with this girl, but for some reason her parents think that you may have something to do with her disappearance.'

'Do they? I can't think why!'

'Neither can we but perhaps you could say what has led them to believe that?'

'It could be because of our visit to the river, the Thames. One day Hana and me, we decided to go and see the River Thames. We took a trip on a boat. Hana's father was very cross. He was very cross with me.'

'Right. And was he cross with Hana?'

'Yes he was. He beat her.'

'He beat her? How do you know that?'

'I saw the bruises.'

'Was the administrator aware of that?'

'I'm not sure.'

'Didn't you report it to the administrator?'

'No. I didn't want to cause trouble.'

The policeman gave a slight nod.

'And why exactly do you think he beat her?'

'Because she didn't ask his permission.'

'And?'

'And nothing. Except, he doesn't like her to do things.

Not unless he says.'

'You mean he's controlling?'

I have to stop myself from saying more. I must feign ignorance and make it seem that I know nothing about their situation. I must step back altogether.

'I don't know. Perhaps. I don't really know Hana. She just sleeps in the same dormitory as me. We went for a trip on the River Thames, that's all.'

'And you don't know where she might be or why she might have left the community?'

'No, I'm sorry but I don't. I don't know anything.'

'Very well, that's fine. I'm sure you can understand that we need to investigate any accusations that are made.'

'Accusations?'

'Sorry, no, I mean suspicions, her parents' suspicions. They're probably just grasping at straws. Want to see their daughter back safely. Understandable.'

They stand up and I feel my heart skip a beat and start to slow down, the noise calms down in my ears.

'If you think of anything that might help, will you please inform the administrator. He has our telephone number.'

'Yes, if I think of anything. But I don't think I will. I don't know anything.'

As I follow the police officers out of the dining room, I pass Hana's parents and her father casts me a venomous look.

CHAPTER 39

Aunt Latika looked small and lost in her vast empty living room, a room that had always looked immaculate. There were scuff marks on the dark parquet floor and patches on the walls where their shelves and fine pictures had recently hung.

'You know, Bulbul, you get to a point where tears just don't make it any better. At first you think they do. You weep and you weep but then you finally realise that it really doesn't make any difference. You could weep enough tears to fill the Nile, but it wouldn't change anything. We still have to leave.'

I thought how, if Sabu were here, he could make up a wonderful tale of the lady who wept enough tears to fill a river. Where was he now? What horrific things were they doing to him? Would the entertainment he was to provide really stop at the mere telling of stories?

My aunt was so intent on recounting her woes that she barely paid any attention to the pile of documents I gave her.

'Please Auntie, you will make sure that Uncle Deepak gets these papers, won't you? He needs to send them to Sanjay in America. But he must send them from Kenya, not from here. They're very important documents and I don't trust the post here.'

My aunt assured me she would look after them and placed them next to her handbag in the living room.

'I also have another favour to ask you, Auntie.'

'Which is?'

I asked if I could visit my uncle's office.

'I can't imagine why you would want to do that Bulbul. It's empty. The phones have been cut off.'

'And the electricity?'

'I have no idea.'

'And the furniture and equipment?'

'Oh goodness, we have enough to do with packing up our own personal belongings without having to sort out the office as well. Where would we put it all?'

I was relieved that the contents might remain intact, but my plan would come to nothing if the electricity had been switched off.

Nanda's bedroom was a sea of clothes with piles on the floor and a mountain on her bed.

'There's no point in packing it up all up too early. Everything will only end up getting really creased,' she explained, a certain tighter, more determined set to her lips.

I asked her if it was true that she wanted to continue her studies and she told me that first she would need to take a top-up course in the States. This would be in a private college. Then, if she passed, she would apply for medical school. She would try for one in New York as that's where her parents planned to live due to her father's business.

'But I never knew you were interested in medicine, Nanda!'

'Did you ever ask?'

'No. But you always seem to like a fun life - clothes, parties, music.'

'Well, yes, but not all doctors are boring. I'm not saying I don't still love clothes, but I need something else. All this, with Idi Amin, losing our home, everything - it makes me feel vulnerable. I never want to feel like this again. And I'm going to do something about it.'

I didn't stay long that morning, our usual relaxed chatter being peppered with chasms of awkward silence. Our farewell lurked like a shadowy figure by the doorway. Eventually I hugged Nanda tightly and promised to visit them in New York one day. Later, when we were finally established in London. When would that be, I wondered?

Kenzi, in his usual relaxed way, was amenable to stopping by at my uncle's office on the way back to the university compound.

I stifled my feelings of guilt as the car drew up by the curb.

'I'll only be about twenty minutes,' I told Kenzi. 'Why don't you park down the side of the building, there, to the right. That way, the car won't easily be seen.'

I had promised Jack that I would only visit my aunt and then come straight back, but it was a false promise. I'd known that this was my plan. I had lied.

The main door to the building already looked unpolished and neglected, but it opened easily with the key my aunt had given me. I quietly climbed the stairs to the first floor. There was a smell of stale concrete and I noticed that dust had started to accumulate in the outer corner of the stair treads. Uncle Deepak would never have tolerated dust.

So far it didn't appear that the authorities had taken steps to take over the business. When would that be? Would they try? Requisitioning a stockbroking company that had offices in other countries was like trying to grab hold of a nebulous cloud - it wasn't the same as seizing a piece of land that actually produced something. Not like taking over Rutubasana.

The curved teak reception desk lay neat and empty with Mrs Rwamirama's bright red telephone sitting solidly on the surface. Most of the velux blinds were drawn halfway down the windows and all the office chairs were tucked tidily under the row of desks.

Tentatively I reached for the light switch and breathed a

sigh of relief when the long strip lighting started to flicker on. I checked the time, then walked quickly to the rear of the building, the thick carpet absorbing any sounds from my footsteps.

The large Xerox machine from my childhood had now been replaced by a superior, but equally cumbersome, photocopier and I prayed it would be simple to use.

I placed the official letter from the President's Office face down on the glass plate with a blank piece of paper carefully covering the original typing. The copy paper was easy enough to load, and I managed to select the correct command and set it into action. The familiar smell of dry ink reminded me of earlier days and the great machine clanked and whirred as the first test sheet shot out into the lower tray. Not a success. It was distinctly noticeable that there was a dark line indicating where the plain paper had overlapped the original letter. I would need to mask this somehow, possibly glue.

I rummaged around in the stationary cupboard and found some brand new bottles of C-Fluid liquid paper. How Nanda and I would have loved these! Carefully I pasted the edges of the covering sheet to camouflage the join. Once it had dried, I delicately laid the conjoined sheets on the glass pane and ordered one copy. It worked! No dark line. Perfect. I copied a further three sheets, just in case they were needed.

Making sure everything was turned off in the Xerox room, I made my way to the main part of the office where I found a typewriter and inserted a photocopied sheet. I started to type.

To the Commanding Officer

It has come to my attention that you are holding a young Asian boy by the name of Sabu Dastagir. This boy must not be harmed.

I have a special request from Her Majesty's Government of Great

Britain that this boy must be delivered to Mr G C Crane at the British High Commission in Kampala forthwith.

I have given my personal assurance that this request will be met and the boy will be delivered to the British High Commission within the next twenty four hours. These instructions are to be carried out immediately. Failure to comply with my wishes will meet with severe reprisals.

I then attempted to forge Amin's signature, copied from the original document. It was a passable replica and, at first glance, should look authentic. I would ask Kenzi to pass these to a messenger to deliver as I didn't want to endanger him in any way. Kenzi was almost a member of our family.

It was a hopeless move - as childish and ineffectual as printing invitations to a marriage between two dogs. A pathetic shot in the dark. The letter would probably end up in the bin. In any case, Sabu may well be dead already.

I typed one further letter, scribbled a note and I put these in a further envelope. Then I tidied the desk and put the cover back on the typewriter.

My hand on the door, I turned and paused. Everything was neat, waiting to be discovered. By whom? Would more dust settle? Would anyone come? One thing was certain: no one would remember the two little Asian girls who had whiled away hours cutting and stapling their works of creation in the back room. We were merely a puff of smoke from Aladdin's lamp.

Fatigue overwhelmed me as I switched off the light and the door clicked closed quietly.

Chapter 40

My mind is thick treacle, heavy and slow. Weighed down by the guilt of what I have done and lack of sleep. I cannot bear to see the anguish of Hana's mother and I must constantly remind myself of Parvat's cruelty to the young girl. But what if Hana had lied? What if her father really loved her?

But you saw the bruises.

But what if she had never been raped? What if it was all a lie?

Valeria had the doctor verify the pregnancy himself. You were there. Not in the room, but you saw the doctor arrive. And Valeria was insistent that everything was correct and all the facts were true.

But what if it wasn't rape? What if she had merely had a dalliance with a young lad?

You saw the blood from her slashed wrist. You saw her anguish.

And her mother? Surely her mother loves her?

Beware my parents, Hana said. 'My mother is my father's slave, she will do his bidding. He's an evil man. She is his kathputli - his puppet.'

Did he not just want the best for his child, his beautiful only daughter?

You heard what Hana said. Her father thought death was preferable to living a life after rape. And you saw the bruises. You saw the fear in her eyes.

But his own daughter? Wouldn't he feel different if it was his own daughter?

Remember her face, remember her fear. Remember, remember.

The thoughts echo around my head as if they are

bouncing off the walls of a stone cavern. Round and round they go until I feel I'm going mad.

I must sleep. This will only get worse. But I can't sleep. I daren't sleep. I see how Parvat watches me in the dining room and Sudha watches me in the dormitory. I need to be vigilant. I need to be there for Moh.

I feel my cheeks. They are as hot as when I spun my lies to Hana's parents. I feel my forehead and it burns like an ember. My head pounds and my mouth is dry. The water that I drink from the glass beside my bed tastes metallic, tainted by the lies that lurk in the corners of my mouth.

My eyelids are heavy but I must not sleep, I cannot sleep. I must watch.

CHAPTER 41

What Jack hadn't explained was that, although we were to leave the house the following night, our actual flight was on the Wednesday morning.

'It won't take us nine hours to get to the airport,' I said when he announced the midnight deadline.

'That's right, but we need to detour. We can't take the direct road to the airport from Kampala. They could be looking out for us. Dembe, from the Science department, has a cousin who lives on the edge of the lake's inlet, opposite Entebbe. We'll take the back roads northwest and then through Mpigi and down to Lulongo on the Kasanje road. We'll have to hope that we don't come across any soldiers at that time. In any case, they'll mainly be watching the Kampala road to Entebbe. The moon will still be quite full so we'll try to drive without our headlights. If we can do that, we'll nearly be invisible.'

A momentary vision. A family of singers driving across the alps in war-torn Europe - quietly sombre in the moonlight. But we weren't in The Sound of Music and thinking about our favourite things wasn't going to make anything better. Dicken would scold me. This was real life.

'Then what?'

'We'll stay in the cousin's house until early morning. We'll leave the car there and he'll take us across to Entebbe in his boat. Then a friend of his will meet us on the other side and drive us to the gates of the airport. It's not far.'

'Do you think it will work?'

'It will have to work. We just take it one step at a time

and everything should be fine.'

It was only then that I noticed how quietly Jack was talking. Was he worried that Mirembe would hear? Would Mirembe report us? I found it hard to believe.

We had seven hours before we were to leave. Another farewell to another home.

I laid my clothes out on our large double bed and looked at them critically. Everything was lightweight and cool - cotton shorts and tee shirts, linen trousers, two shalwar kameez outfits in silk and an embroidered sari. Also, lying near the top of the bed, on my pillows, lay my father's silk kurta from his wedding to my mother. It was made from fine golden silk with a slight herringbone design. I knew that I couldn't leave it behind. I held it up to my cheek and sniffed the fabric. There was no remnant of my father's aftershave or his cigars, only a gentle aroma of camphor from the chest where the jacket had been stored. I knew that in time, even this smell would fade, as would our memories.

By one o'clock in the morning we were ready, and Jack started loading our belongings in the car.

'Why are you bringing this sewing machine? You don't even sew,' Jack said.

'Dicken said I should bring it. In any case, it was my mother's and I would like to keep it. I want to take something to remember her by - her sewing machine and my father's wedding coat.'

Jack loaded the Singer in the boot of the car, muttering that we might not even be allowed to take it on the plane.

My mother-in-law looked ashen faced as she rocked Moh gently in her arms. He had been sleeping soundly and only woke briefly when Jack lifted him from his cot. Now he was resting his chin on Ashika's shoulder, a stubborn looking pout on his slumbering face.

I walked through the house one last time, as I had done at Rutubasana. Was there anything else we could take with us? I knew we would have to leave it all behind - the French linen sheets on our bed, the Chinese prints on the living room walls, the silver ice bucket that Mirembe would fill each evening. Everything.

Jack was standing impatiently by the front door when I had finished my last tour.

'Come on. We have to get going. Maata and Moh are already in the car.'

'What about Mirembe. We should say goodbye.'

'She's sleeping in the annexe. We shouldn't wake her. We don't want to incriminate her.'

'But how can we leave without saying goodbye? She's been wonderful to us. She's like family.'

'She's a servant, Birdie. And her brother's a soldier in Amin's personal guard. We can't risk it.'

'Then I should leave a note.'

'No Birdie, nothing. The longer she's ignorant of our movements, the more time we will have to get to the airport in safety. Come.'

We both hesitated at the door. Should we lock it and take the key? For what purpose? We would never need the key again. Should we leave the door unlocked and the key on the console table in the hallway? Would that not be gifting Amin our house and belongings?

In the end Jack clicked the door quietly behind us and pocketed the key before getting into our laden car.

CHAPTER 42

My dreams have been like layers of black sheeting - wild dreams where I run disorientated through mazes and tunnels. Where strange voices whisper words in my head. Am I going mad? When I wake, my skin is hot. When I sleep, I fall into chasms of confusion and despair.

Voices, over and over again.

Everything has a price. Everything has a price.

Is that drumming that I hear, or the thumping of my heart that sears the blood through my ears? No, it's rain. It sounds like rain. English rain. Cold rain. The sheet is rough against my skin as I stretch out and dip back into fitful sleep.

Someone is shaking me harshly, calling my name. I hear Jack's voice.

'Birdie, wake up, wake up.'

'Jack, what are you doing here?' Jack has never been into the women's quarters before.

'Wake up, Birdie. It's Moh. We have to go. Quick, put some clothes on.'

'What do you mean, it's Moh? Where is he?' I look at his cot and see it's empty.

Where's he gone? Why was I sleeping? I was supposed to be watching.

My fingers won't move properly. I'm befuddled by the heavy sleep that hangs over me like a fog.

'What do you mean?'

'Moh's in the hospital. We have to go.'

'The hospital? Jack? Why the hospital?'

Jack helps me put on my boots and my jacket and starts

guiding me towards the stairs.

I stop.

'Jack, will you please explain? What do you mean, Moh's in the hospital? Why? What's happened?'

'I'm sorry Birdie, but it's true. He's been hurt. An accident. A taxi. We need to go. Then we'll find out. Come on. I don't have all the answers.'

My legs feel weak and won't obey the signals I try to send them. I cling onto the wooden bannister as we descend the stairs. I won't hold Jack's arm. I don't want him to touch me. I need to think. I need to know. I need to help Moh.

We sit in silence in the back of the taxi and the rain thunders on the roof and runs in streams down the side windows. Ahead of us the windscreen wipers slap and clank, slap and clank, slap and clank. The noise will drive me mad.

Why?

Jack tells me that I've been lying in a fever for two days now. Probably some virus, the doctor said. They had left me to sleep and he and Ashika had been caring for Moh. This morning Ashika tried to cheer up Sudha by suggesting a trip to Knightsbridge to see the Christmas windows in the smart shops. Soon the decorations will be taken down, and she thought it might distract her friend, with the absence of Hana. As the weather was fine they decided to walk, and took Moh in a pushchair borrowed from Mr Caxton's office. It was only on their way back that the skies opened and the rain came down in torrents. The accident happened when they stopped at a pedestrian crossing waiting for the traffic lights to change. There were crowds of people, pushing, waiting. Possibly a faulty break. Moh's pushchair rolled forward under the wheels of a passing taxi.

My stomach lurches and I see large dark spots before my eyes. I lean back and gulp stale air into my lungs. I need to stay conscious for Moh. I must stay calm.

It seems like an eternity before we finally pull up outside a tall red brick building. The corridors are like a labyrinth and smell of astringent antiseptic and floor polish. Jack steers our course by checking the building plan and guides me gently through wide swinging doors, past ward upon ward until he hesitates outside the one we're seeking. For a moment we halt and look at each other. Is it a silent acknowledgement that from this point our lives may never be the same?

A young nurse sits quietly at the desk with a reading lamp angling light down onto her paperwork. She looks up enquiringly.

'Oh yes, the little boy. I believe his name is Mohin Dalal. Is that right? Are you his parents? His grandmother and aunt are in the waiting room to the left, if you would like to join them. I'll just go and get Matron so she can have a word with you.'

We don't go to join Ashika and Sudha - what right does she have to call herself Moh's aunt? We stand quietly by the desk, my ears alert for every single sound that emanates from the various rooms and wards lying beyond. Something dropping on the floor, a laugh, the sound of gentle clanking of china and the roll of trolley wheels on the linoleum flooring. Footsteps.

'Mr and Mrs Dalal?'

We affirm.

'Would you come this way into my office, please.'

The few steps down the corridor towards the scuffed white door seem to take an age and cold icicles of fear are running through my heart.

'Please take a seat.'

We sit on the wooden chairs placed in front of her desk.

'Now,' she says, settling herself down and adjusting her white cap. 'It seems that your wee son has had a bit of a run-in with a London cab. Not the best of situations, but we're doing everything we can.'

'What are his injuries? Will he be all right?' asks Jack.

'He's with the doctors now. At first, it didn't seem too bad. What appeared to be a broken leg and grazing to his face. It was lucky he was wearing a thick jacket which gave him a bit of extra padding.'

'You said at first?'

'It seems we've run into a bit of a complication. The doctors are just slightly concerned that there may be some internal bleeding, so they are just investigating that right now.'

'What do you mean, internal bleeding? Where?'

'Now, I don't want to cause you any alarm. We don't know exactly yet but the doctors believe there may be some pressure on the brain which could indicate that something is going on.'

'Bleeding in the brain?'

'Possibly, yes.'

I feel as if I'm on a boat that's capsizing at a sharp angle. I grab at the edge of the matron's desk.

'Jack!'

Jack takes over.

'Can we see him?'

'I'm afraid he's in the operating theatre at the moment.'

'They're operating on him? On his leg, or on his head?'

'They'll be trying to ease the pressure, I believe. However, I'm afraid that's all I can say for the time being. A doctor will be out after the procedure to have a word with you. Shall I ask a nurse to bring you a cup of tea?'

Tea again? As if tea would ease this agony.

She rings the bell on her desk and we hear footsteps approaching.

'I'm sorry I can't be of more help at this point in time, Mr and Mrs Dalal. I can only assure you that Mohin is in the best of hands. We'll update you as soon as possible. Now if you wouldn't mind accompanying Nurse Rogers to the waiting room, a doctor will come and find you as soon as he has a moment.'

A tall, dark haired nurse smiles at us warmly and leads us several doors down to a small room where Ashika and Sudha sit dejectedly.

Ashika bursts into tears the moment she sees us and Sudha stands quietly in the corner of the room, wringing her hands. Jack comforts his mother but I can't look at Sudha. Ever since her daughter's disappearance she has watched me suspiciously and, when she thinks I'm not looking, I'll catch her staring, her mouth in a position as if she's just tasted bitter melon. Would she hurt a small child? Would she try to harm Moh in retaliation for Hana's disappearance? Surely not. But then Jack mentioned something about a faulty break on the pushchair. Didn't Mr Caxton refer to a faulty pushchair when I first went to his office? Perhaps Sudha or Ashika mistakenly took the faulty pushchair? But then Mr Caxton and Parvat seem close, now that he and Rami live in the back of his wooden shed. What if Hana's father had persuaded Mr Caxton to give out the faulty pushchair as payment for my suspected involvement in Hana's disappearance?

My head is throbbing and I sit down sharply. I can't tolerate Ashika's wailing and pleas for forgiveness. There is nothing to forgive. We only want Moh to be safe, to be well again.

Eventually, as the dark rain clouds turn into a night sky, a grey-haired doctor enters the waiting room. Once he is sure we are all family, he starts to talk directly to Jack and me, running briefly over the details.

'We've done what we can to relieve the pressure on your son's brain and we're fairly confident that the bleeding has now stopped. He's in a stable position but I'm afraid we just have to wait and see how he gets on.'

'Will he be all right?'

'I'm pretty sure his leg will mend well. Once the swelling has gone down, we'll be able to put it in a caste and it should repair in about six weeks, all being well. A bit longer to be fully recovered, but I'm quite confident he'll be able to walk normally in the future.'

'And his head injuries?'

'Well…'

'He'll be… normal, won't he?'

'I'm afraid it's always hard to say with the brain. I think we caught it in time and the pressure is now relieved, so it shouldn't get any worse. But of course we don't know yet quite what extent of damage has been done. Always tricky with the brain. But the body has enormous powers of recovery. We can only hope and pray.'

'Isn't there anything more you can do?'

'We've done everything we can. Now we just have to wait and pray.'

I feel empty, as if any life force has been sucked out of me.

'Can we see him?' asks Jack.

'He's just in the recovery room at the moment. If you wait half an hour or so, he'll be moved into a separate room. It will be on the next floor up and the nurse will take you through when we're ready. Be patient. Be hopeful. The brain is an amazing organ. It constantly surprises me.'

CHAPTER 43

One day, many months ago, before Jack and I were engaged, before President Idi Amin Dada came to power, before I learned of true sorrow, Jack took me for a picnic on the banks of Lake Victoria.

At first, when he collected me from my aunt's house in Kampala, it had seemed an impulsive invitation. I later realised that he had planned the packing of the picnic hamper, the cooling of the drinks, and had even brought neatly creased white linen napkins that lay carefully under the woven wicker lid.

It was the first time we were to be alone together for any period of time and this realisation made me nervous. What would we talk about? How would we fill awkward silences? Until now we had always had a relaxed way between us and conversation had come easily, but that was when the conversation was diluted by other people around. Now, for the entire afternoon, we would be obliged to make conversation and that thought was like putting a stopper in a bottle. I sat, stiff and uncomfortable in the passenger seat with my hands clasped on my lap in front of me, acutely aware of how stiff and uncomfortable I must look. Why could I not lounge like my cousin Nanda, who undoubtedly would have draped an arm over the back of the seat and acted as if she was sitting in her armchair at home.

Jack was quiet in the car as he drove us towards the lake's shore and seemed oblivious to any concerns that the mute passenger by his side might have. I sneaked a look at his profile. I watched his strong hands, relaxed on the wheel. A fear mounted in me that something would happen on this picnic. Until now we had not kissed, merely touched hands, but now we were alone. The idea of being close to him terrified and excited me at the same time.

He leaned across me to get his sunglasses out the glove compartment and I caught the slight scent of lime and musk aftershave mixed with a hint of manly sweat. My breathing was shallow and the palms of my hands felt damp, but all the time Jack seemed unaware of my anxieties as he guided the car along the lakeside road. Eventually he pulled into a dusty car park by the edge of the beach.

After unpacking the car and dumping a large picnic rug into my arms for me to carry, he led me to a spot where he indicated we were to sit. Then, without a word, he proceeded to walk towards two locals working on a fishing boat by the shore and momentarily his receding figure was a silhouette against the sapphire blue water. The three men talked for a while, laughing, Jack clapping one on the back, then chatting with arms crossed, gently kicking distractedly at the sandy earth. What were they talking about? He had brought me on a date and then left me while he talked to two strangers, oblivious to the fact that I was still standing clutching the picnic rug in my arms.

I cursed myself for being so passive, so unlike the person I was at home. The girl with ideas, action, volition - that was my true self. Here I was being reduced to a meek and needy woman whose hands go clammy when she's near a man.

I forcefully shook out the rug, put large stones at the corners and flopped back to lie under the African sun.

'Look!' said Jack.

Jack's head had a halo of sunlight and I couldn't see what he was holding. Sitting up, I saw a large fish lay on his outstretched hands.

'Freshly caught. We're going to barbecue it.'

'With what?'

'Musoke and his friend have got it all sorted, haven't you Musoke?'

My eyes adjusted to an ebony face with a large smile and the whitest teeth imaginable. Musoke and his companion then dug a small pit in the earth and filled it with dry wood which they lit before returning to the water's edge with the fish. After several minutes they returned with a plate holding two fillets of the fish and a grill which they put over the fire.

'Leave for fifteen minutes before you start to cook, about, more or less,' Musoke said, gently rocking his hand. He then gave a final big smile and cast a cheeky wink in Jack's direction.

Jack opened a bottle of beer for himself and some 7-Up for me, remembering my loathing of ales. He had brought salt and limes and a tamarind sauce that his mother had made. The plates were china, which he lined with parathas to soak up the juices. Afterwards we ate laddus and succulent mangoes.

It was a meal made in paradise. We licked our fingers with relish and barely used the neatly ironed linen napkins. After the meal, we left our picnic rug and the fire still smouldering on the beach and walked along the lakeside with no awkward pauses in our conversation, paddling in the water as the sun turned orange.

I remember the warmth of the soil beneath my feet, the low sun blinding me at times, the way Jack's hair curled out at the nape of his neck. And I remember the feeling of his strong hand in mine and the exhilaration in my heart as we walked along the shore.

He never did kiss me that day. That came later.

Chapter 44

The rain lashes angrily at the large pane windows. It's the only sound in the room apart from the regular bleeps coming from the machinery hooked onto our son.

Jack and I are silent. We've been given a few minutes to be with Moh and I stand next to him holding his tiny hand. In addition to the casing on his leg, one side of his face has a patch of medical dressing and the crown of his head is bandaged after the surgery. Over his nose and mouth is an oxygen mask that obscures most of his face - a harsh foreign object butting up to the corners of his thick eyelashes. A flexible tube leads to a needle inserted into his strapped arm.

My breathing is laboured but I don't cry. There are no tears. I think of my Aunt Latika and how she said that in the end, you realise that tears just don't make things any better. Sometimes life's tragedy is just too big for such an indulgence.

Jack stands on the other side of the bed. He doesn't touch Moh and looks down at our child with a cold, angry expression. It's a look I've never seen before.

'Jack?'

He looks up at me and his eyes are ice.

'You don't even cry.'

'What do you mean?'

'Are you a normal mother? You don't even cry!'

'Do you think it would make it better? Do you think my weeping would help Moh?'

'Of course not. But any mother would weep seeing her

son like this.'

'Maybe I'm not a normal mother.'

Jack grunts and I feel a vice tighten around my chest.

'Maybe you believe I don't love him. Is that it?'

'Your words, not mine.'

'So that's it? You think I don't love Moh enough?'

'Not like a normal mother loves her son.'

'You mean not like your mother loves you?'

'If you like, yes.'

'Not like your mother loves Moh?'

'At least she looks after him more than you. She cuddles him more than you.'

'She loves caring for him. Sometimes I feel like I'm redundant.'

'Because you've always held back.'

'So you think I haven't loved Moh enough, is that it? You think that if I had loved him more then this would never have happened? You blame me for Moh lying here, like this?'

'Of course not! That's not what I'm saying.'

'Then what are you saying Jack?'

'It's just there's something, something I can't work out. You're not really *there* when you're with Moh.'

I bite my lip and gently squeeze my son's tiny hand. Jack's accusations slice into my heart. He wouldn't understand. I don't think I even understand myself.

I do know one thing with every ounce of my being. I would gladly be lying on this hospital bed instead of my lovely boy. I would willingly give my life. Is that what mothers do?

Once, Jack said that I paid more attention to Sabu than I did to Moh and, at the time, he was right. But why?

Fear. Fear. Fear.

It echoes in my head. If I had loved Moh more, this would never have happened. Surely, in some way things would have been different if I had loved him fully. Perhaps, when they came to take him for a walk, I would have had him in the bed with me. *No*, I would have said *No, he must stay here with me, with his mother who loves him beyond anything or anyone else in her life.*

A nurse comes into the room and puts a hand gently on my shoulder.

'I'm sorry, but I have to ask you to leave now. All being well, we'll move Mohin into another small ward tomorrow but I'm afraid visitors, even parents, aren't really supposed to come in here.'

'We understand,' says Jack and kisses Moh's hand gently. 'We'll be outside, in the corridor.'

I kiss the small exposed triangle of Moh's soft cheek. I want to breathe his sweet breath, but the plastic mask claims him, clasps him to this medical process - a frontier between health and sickness, life and death.

Maybe Jack is right. I never really did love him enough.

CHAPTER 45

Valeria touches me. She touches my forearm gently as she talks. She rests her hand on my shoulder as she guides me to the canteen to be presented with a cup of tea. Her hand comforts me - a connection with another being, saving me from the heart wrenching loneliness of grief.

Why do the English not touch each other? It's so rare to see one reach out to another. They shake hands, but that's not a true touch. Did I not hear, years ago, that the gesture was to show you came in peace and were not holding a weapon? Merely a clarification. And then of course, there's the sex. I understand there's a lot of that in England. They say the girls are loose and 'ready' but maybe it's just their way of asking to be touched, to be held, to be loved. Or perhaps they just want to get warm.

'You need to talk to someone, Birdie.'

My eyes are fixed on the light green teacup sitting on the light green saucer in front of me. There's a slight ridge just below the lip of the cup and I wonder if it's there to catch any drips that may continue their way down to the saucer. Or maybe it's there merely for decoration. Who designed this cup? Perhaps he or she argued for the cause of that little ridge just below the lip at the top. Or maybe not. Perhaps it was an inspirational addition at the last minute before the prototype was made - a swish of the paintbrush and there you have it. An indelible ridge on the rim of the teacup.

'Birdie. Did you hear me? You really should talk to someone.'

I pull my gaze away from the table and look into the dark

brown eyes of Valeria. Italian eyes. I've never once seen her without her swoop of eyeliner on the top lid or the mascara stylishly thick on her lashes. Always elegant and composed.

We must look an incongruous pair sitting in the canteen. If we were flowers, she would be a rose - one of Aunt Latika's damask roses, and I would be a thistle. A dried husk of a thistle.

'I talk to you, Valeria.'

'Yes. But not really. You don't *really* talk to me. You need to talk to someone who will help you feel better.'

'Nothing will make me feel better.'

'You think that, Birdie, but there's still hope. The doctors have said there's still hope. We just have to wait and see. But we should wait with hope, with faith, whatever you want to call it. We have to wait and we have to pray.'

'I can't pray. I have no faith. I have no religion. You are the same. You told me once, in Wiltshire.'

'Just because I said I am no longer a Catholic doesn't mean I don't believe in hope and love and *something*, something that will help Moh pull through.'

'I wish I could believe that.'

'That's why I want you to see someone.'

'Who? A psychiatrist or a priest?'

'Well…'

'Yes, well?' Her eyes don't lie. 'Don't tell me! You want me to see a priest!'

'He's a little bit of both, I suppose. A very wise man, the wisest man I know. I think he can help you.'

'Really? I find that very hard to believe. What will help me now is Moh waking up, Moh being normal, Moh having a life ahead of him. But I can't imagine it, up here, the picture is black. And it's all my fault.'

'You are so wrong, Birdie. You've done nothing wrong.'

'I have, I have. Everything I do seems to turn sour, Moh, Sabu. Jack blames me. I know he does.'

'He doesn't blame you, Birdie, truly. Everyone grieves in different ways. Please.'

She slides a small white card across the table to me and it rests in front of the sugar bowl.

'My car's outside. Please let me drop you off at the place where you can meet him. Birdie.'

'I must watch over Moh. I can't leave him.'

'Jack's here. He'll watch him. You won't be long.'

I hesitate and Valeria sees a shift in my resolve.

'You need to help yourself, Birdie. Only in that way will you be able to help Moh. Do it for Moh.'

Darkness is descending as we walk down the hospital steps into the cold air. Our breath puffs out ahead of us. Valeria's dark car is waiting in a parking bay at the side of the building and slides quietly to the main entrance to scoop us up. We purr off through the London traffic. Somehow everything feels different - not the normal congestion for the city. I remark on this to Valeria.

'New Year's Day,' she replies. 'Everyone's on holiday.'

So that's why it feels different. A day of celebration. A new start. How ironic.

Most of the large London houses are still decorated for Christmas although the feeling is not quite so exuberant as before. Some buildings are in darkness and I envisage the owners visiting their families and friends in the countryside, or skiing on alpine slopes.

The car glides to a stop outside the front of a small church set back from the road.

Valeria checks I have the card in my hand and points to the writing in the dim light.

'You see his name? There. He knows you're coming. Now go.'

She leans across me and opens the car door.

'Go,' she says, pushing my shoulder gently.

'How will I get back?'

'Julian will return with the car in half an hour. He'll wait and take you back to the hospital when you're ready. I would stay if I could but I'm afraid I'm entertaining friends this evening and need to get back. Spend as much time as you like. Go.'

I slip along the leather seat and hesitate before stepping onto the pavement.

'Go, go,' she motions with her hand, almost impatiently.

In a minute I'm alone, standing in front of an arched portico. The door looks black and heavily carved in the gloom and as I open it there's a waft of unfamiliar incense. If the smell were music it would be slow, low and heavy.

Four large chandeliers hang from the lofty ceiling and the interior is surprisingly warm. There's a janitor cleaning the floor to the left of the raised area where a large cross sits. Two people sit separately near the front, facing the alter. I hear the door click closed behind me and the sound echoes slightly against the hard surfaces, as do my footsteps as I walk down the aisle.

Where should I wait? Will he come to me? I sit on one of the benches and look up at the stained glass windows and the pillars that then morph into curved stone struts that support the vaulted ceiling. I'm not sure where I should find Valeria's friend, so I wait and absorb the quiet, the scent, the peace. I rest my arm against the pew in front of me and lay my head against the back of my cool hand, feeling the knobbly ridges of my bones through my skin. It's a soothing movement, my hand massaging my forehead, pulling and kneading. I think of Moh and I try to pray, but my thoughts are like wisps of vapour, lacking substance and faith.

After a while, I become aware of a presence near me. The janitor I noticed earlier is now sitting a few seats away to my left. He wears a blue boiler suit and has a thick mop of greying hair. I'm about to turn away, to return to pummelling my forehead on the back of my hand.

'Well?' he says.

He laughs at my expression.

'Were you not expecting a man in a boiler suit?'

'No. I was expecting a priest.'

'Well, that will teach you not to judge a person by appearances, won't it now?'

He has a soft lilting voice and some sort of accent but I'm not sure where from.

'Are you the priest?'

'I'm many things.'

'But I was told I was meeting a priest.'

'Come on, I very much doubt you were told that. You may have been told that you were meeting Finley, who happens to be a priest, but you were not told you were meeting me *as* a priest. You were just meeting Finley. Now am I right or am a right?'

I'm too weary for games with words.

'Would it surprise you to learn, young lady, I was once a policeman?'

I look at him askance.

'And would it surprise you to know that I was once a jailbird?'

'A *jail bird?*'

'A prisoner, in a jail. In a prison.'

He notices my small start and chuckles as he draws his hand through his thick hair.

'The fact is Birdie... do you mind me calling you Birdie? The fact is that people are many things, all rolled into one and you can't take the policeman out of me, or the convicted prisoner, or even the small boy who grew up in the Irish bog. All of those people are me, rolled up into what I happen to be at the moment - a priest. Now take you for instance, what are you? Who are you?'

I'm too tired to answer his questions. His words form a riddle. Sanjay used to play riddles with me. I'm so tired. Hot tears well up in my eyes.

'Now girl, please don't get upset. I didn't mean to make you cry.'

I shake my head.

'No you didn't, it's not you. It's just… everything. Everything.'

He nods as if he understands and he moves a couple of seats towards me until there are only two or three feet between us. He doesn't talk, only looks ahead at the alter and lets me cry quietly.

After several moments of silence, he clears his throat and speaks.

'So, Valeria tells me you're going through a tough time at the moment, very tough. I'm sorry to hear that. And she's also told me that your babby is in the hospital. Now that is something I wouldn't wish on my worst enemy. Your poor little mite linked up with tubes.'

I see Moh's small hand in my mind's eye, his little wrist still bearing the creases from his chubby babyhood, softening slightly now. From time to time his hand will twitch, not much, but a definite movement. Everything else still but his little thumb and a finger twitching slightly and me watching, always needing the reassurance of that tiny movement.

'There's nothing you can do about it so I don't really know why I'm here.'

'Because Valeria said so. I imagine that's why?'

'Well, yes.'

'Valeria has that way about her. You should see how she manages all of us.'

'All of you?'

'You haven't met the others?'

'Others?' I sound like an echo.

He waves the matter aside with his hand.

'Now young lady, let us look at the facts. Valeria tells me your son's in hospital, but she says the doctors seem happy enough with his progress. But she's worried about you.'

'I don't know why she should be worried about *me*.'

'Are you saying you really don't know? Do you want me to tell you?'

I nod slightly.

'Firstly, you're this poor little lad's mother and there'll be no one here on earth who he's more linked to than his own mammy. He's made from your own flesh and blood. It's the strongest bond there is on this earth, mother and child. Look at our Lord Jesus and mother Mary over there. It can never be broken. He needs you.'

'I'm there for him. I sit by him, day and night.'

'But how do you sit there, Birdie?'

'I sit and I hope.'

'And?'

'And what? I sit and hope.'

'And what's your primary feeling then as you sit and hope.'

His eyes are a piercing blue and I notice deep creases around the outer edges.

'I can't pray to your God if that's what you mean. I hope. That's all I can do.'

'What other feelings do you have in your heart as you sit and hope?'

'I suppose I feel guilt.'

'Really. Now why would a loving mammy, sitting by the bedside of her darlin' tot feel guilt?'

'Because it's my fault.'

'In what way is it your fault? Did you push him under the taxi?'

'No.'

'Were you even there when the accident happened?'

'No.'

'In that case, how in the name of the Lord, can you believe this is all your fault?'

'It's my punishment. I never loved him enough.'

'Ah, so that's what it is then? You think somehow you should have protected him from this? Don't you know how many mothers feel the same as you? All mothers think that their love should create this impregnable shield around their children, so they'll never be hurt. Sadly, that's not the case. You can't blame yourself because the force of your love hasn't protected Moh. It's just a fact of life.'

'No!' I stamp my foot on the flagstone floor. 'You don't understand. Everything I touch turns bad. Moh, Sabu, Hana. I should never have had a child. Now, see how I've harmed him - just as I always feared.'

'I very much doubt you've done anything to harm your son, Birdie.'

'But I have, I *have*. Don't you understand? This is the price. Everything has a price. That's what it said in my dream. Over and over.'

'And why are you paying this price, Birdie?'

'Because of what I am. Because of who I am.'

Finley looks puzzled, rests his elbows on his strong legs and looks down at the ground. He asks me to explain what I mean, and it all gushes out. My mother's suicide, the conversation I overheard in the kitchen at Rutubasana. The fear all my life that I would have the black mamba slithering through my veins, that one day I would harm my child like the wife of the man who took his cattle to market.

'But you say you went to a doctor, to a specialist.'

'Yes, but how did he know? He couldn't see inside me, inside my blood.'

'But he reassured you that you shouldn't worry.'

'That was when I was a grown woman. I've been fearful since the age of seven. It's very hard to rub out a fear that you've lived with for so long.'

He nods in understanding.

'Very well Birdie, let's look at it from another angle here. You say you love your child.'

'Yes, I do. I only understand now how much I love him.'

'But feeling guilt is not helping Moh. It's a great big boulder standing in the way.'

'A boulder?'

'A whacking great stone. We have some huge stones like that in Ireland. Monolithic they are. Been there since the beginning of time. So let's say, for example, you close your eyes and you're walking along a path. Let's say, for the sake of argument, that this path is in Ireland, running along the side of a mountain. So you're in this dream and you're walking along, come around the corner and what do you see? A whacking great big boulder! So, now here's you, here's the boulder right bang in the middle of the path and there, on the other side of the boulder - can't see him, mind you - on the other side is Moh. Now you need to get to Moh. But remember, you're in a dream. What do you do?'

'I can't go around the rock?'

'No. Sheer drop one side, cliff side of mountain on the other. What do you do?'

'I climb over the stone.'

'Is that what you want to do? Haven't you been climbing over this wretched boulder for years? Wouldn't you like to get rid of the blooming thing?'

'How do I do that?'

'Now remember this is in our mind, like a dream. Have you ever done anything super-human in your dreams?'

'Yes.'

'Right. That goes to show you that in your dreams you

can do anything you want. So here we are, in your dream, and there's a whacking great rock right in front of you. What do you do?'

'I suppose, if I have the strength. Like you say, a magical strength in my dream, I could push it off the side of the mountain.'

'Just like that?'

'Yes. I'm in a dream, aren't I?'

'Exactly.'

Finley folds his arms across his chest and just looks at me.

'That's it?'

'Of course it is. You've just tipped that boulder over the edge of the mountain.'

'But that's only pretend.'

'No my girl, it's not. You need to see that boulder as encompassing everything - your fear, your guilt about what you've done, Lord knows what that is. Every time you see this rock here, in your head,' he points his finger to his temple, 'Every time you see it, you just chuck it over the side of the mountain. Only then can you clear your path to Moh. Only then can you learn to forgive yourself.'

'I can't see that it will help.'

'Never say can't. It's a terrible word. A feeble word. Will you try?'

I nod slightly.

'The power of your mind is incredible. You have no idea how strong it is. And the power of love is healing. But it needs to be pure. Now I'm not predicting that your darlin' son will pull through. I can't say that. Only the heavens know the outcome. But what I do know is, if you want to open your heart totally to loving Moh, you'll have to chuck that boulder of guilt over the side of the mountain. Forget about what you think you've done wrong. Forget about the fear you held when you were a young lassie. Just feel the purity of your love. Can you do it for me? Can you do it for Moh?'

'Yes,' I reply firmly and an image flashes in my mind. A fast running stream with clear water cascading over small pebbles. Maybe it's near that mountain in Ireland.

CHAPTER 46

After six days, Moh opens his eyes. A small slit at first, a momentary movement before he sinks back into sleep. A short while later, he stirs again and looks directly up at me for more than a minute. A full unquestioning look, a long deep sigh and then he sleeps again.

I'm alone in the room as Jack has returned to the accommodation to shower and change his clothes. When he returns, I recount Moh's brief spell of consciousness. Although we share our constant vigil, we barely talk these days and I realise my life really is full of boulders and obstacles. Moh may forgive me, but will Jack? And can I ever forgive myself?

By the next day, Moh is fully awake and becoming fractious, attempting to pull the tube out of his arm.

'Now that's a good sign,' says the nurse with a satisfied nod.

At dusk the doctor is doing his rounds of the wards and leads us into the corridor.

'Well, Mr and Mrs Dalal, it seems that Mohin is turning the corner. It's looking positive.'

'Is he in pain?' I ask.

'He shouldn't be. We're still keeping him on pain killers, but soon we'll be able to phase these out.'

'And his brain? Is there any damage?' says Jack.

'Hard to say with a child, especially when so young. With an adult, you would be able to gauge pretty soon. Things like their level of speech and whether they can remember people and events from their lives. With a child as young as Mohin we can't quite use those benchmarks.'

'How will we ever know?'

'Time. Over time, as he develops, you'll be able to tell if he's keeping in line with other children his age. I imagine you'll start to pick up on clues, tune into whether everything feels right. It's often the best way. Parents usually have an inbuilt sense of this.'

He tells us they'll monitor him for another twenty-four hours and then will consider a transfer.

'A transfer? Why?'

'I'm afraid we're short of beds and this is more of an emergency hospital. We're not so geared up for convalescence. Mohin would probably fare better in a special children's hospital. There's one literally ten minutes away, completely dedicated to children. They'll be able to chart his progress while his leg heals. In any case, he'll be happier there with other children. Believe it or not, it's a happy place.'

'What's it called?'

'It's known by our doctors as GOSH'

'What does that mean?'

'Great Ormond Street Hospital for Children.'

Two days later we walk down yet another labyrinthine corridor, trying to find the ward where Moh now resides. I travelled with him in the ambulance when he was first transferred, but I hadn't noted my return trail and now I'm relying on Jack to find the way.

The smell of antiseptic is the same as in the first hospital, but there are brightly coloured pictures on the walls, seemingly drawn by children. My eyes alight on one that clearly depicts a little boy flying in the air. He's dressed in green and wears a pointed cap on his head. Haven't I seen something like that before? The next picture shows a little fairy with wings, also dressed in green. Another, and another, all similar with fairies and the boy flying in the air.

'Jack! What are these pictures?'

Jack stops and returns to where I'm standing.

'That's Peter Pan. And there, that's Tinkerbell. Don't you remember, we saw them in the park?'

'Peter Pan? The statue?'

'That's right.'

'Why here?'

'I suppose because this hospital is all about Peter Pan.'

Jack sees my puzzled expression.

'The author of Peter Pan, J M Barrie, has given an enormous amount of money to the hospital. Still does.'

'How? Isn't he dead?'

'Yes, long ago. But all the funds that come from the book go to the hospital. They say that he was asked to be on a committee to raise money for an extension, but he didn't like committees, so he did something else. He just said "Here, you can take all the money that is made from the book," and he simply handed it over.'

'When he was alive?'

'Yes. And when he died. The money keeps coming in. Like from the Disney film. You never saw the film, did you?'

'No, I didn't'

'Well, it still raises money. And the books.'

'What a kind thing to do.' The writer's enormous compassion lights an ember in my heart. Such goodness, such grace.

'When Moh's older, we'll read him the book,' Jack says. 'Together,' and he reaches for my hand.

Chapter 47

I spend nearly every waking moment in the hospital with Moh, and Ashika stays with me. The ward is painted in bright colours and the doctor was right. In its way, Great Ormond Street Hospital is a happy place. I've seen some very sick children in the corridors accompanied by anxious parents whose eyes look like those of animals caught in headlamps. But the nurses and doctors are upbeat and warm-hearted, caring not only for their young patients, but their families as well.

Jack doesn't come very often now. He's had no choice but to start his job as a teacher in the boys' school. He doesn't finish his duties until after the sports lessons on a Saturday morning when he always comes straight to the hospital. Every week he's encouraged by Moh's improvement and every Sunday night he has to return to Surrey.

I make friends with a large woman called Edna, who says she comes from the East End of London. Sometimes I find it hard to understand her accent, but I enjoy her warmth and candour. She laughs when I say that she doesn't seem very English to me.

'Cor Blimey, you couldn't get much more English than me, or my skipper, Fred.'

'Your husband?'

'Yeah. I call him my skipper coz he thinks he can steer me in any direction he wants. But I tell him he can keep his hand off my rudder and leave me in peace. Five kids we've got. Five! Don't want any more. They cost a fortune to feed and it now looks like Fred's business is going tits-up. This country's in a mess. Lord knows how we'll survive if he's out of work.'

Edna's son, Alfie, is four years old and was hit by a car when he ran across the road. He wears a plaster cast that seems to cover most of his body, and his right arm is immobilised as well. Moh's leg is still in traction but the bandages have been removed from his head. He's healing well.

At the weekend Edna's family fill the corridor. Her mother brings tupperware containers full of cream cakes and biscuits and they all take it in turns to visit Alfie's bedside, returning to sit in a long line and munch their way through the grandmother's baking.

It's the only time I see the nurses get mildly irritated as they try to weave their way through the abundance of bodies, jostling and fidgeting outside the ward. Sometimes three family members try to creep in to see Alfie.

'No, no, no. How many times do we have to tell you,' admonishes the nurse. 'Visitors are limited to two at a time. No more than two.'

Edna's mother tries to do calculations in her head, and on her fingers, as to how many minutes each of the siblings, aunts and cousins can spend with Alfie before they need to be nudged out.

One day Sudha comes to see Moh in the hospital and starts to weep by his bedside. I leave her and go to sit in the corridor. I don't want her tears. I don't want my guilt.

I can see her through the open door as she talks to Ashika. My mother-in-law nods her head from time to time as if she is being told something very important. Has Sudha heard from Hana? Does she know of my conspiracy?

The woman leaves the ward and briefly takes my hand.

'I wish you well and I wish your son a long and happy life.'

'Are you going away?'

'Yes, the Resettlement Board has found us a house. We leave tomorrow.'

'That's good. Where are you going?'

'Birmingham. I know nothing about the city, but we go. We go.'

I'm relieved she isn't staying in London.

She hands me a small piece of folded paper.

'Here,' she says.

'What's this?'

'My address. For Hana. If she contacts you.'

'Why should she contact me?'

Sudha closes my hand around the scrap of paper.

'For Hana. You tell her. For Hana.'

Her eyes bore into my soul.

CHAPTER 48

Sometimes, when I'm lying in bed at the end of the day, when I've returned from the hospital and sleep won't come, I think of Sabu.

There are two images that flash into my mind. One, his smiling face and lively inquisitive eyes, his laugh and the happy pirouettes he would perform with his lithe, young body. Then, there is the look of terror that engulfed his features as he was dragged towards the army truck.

Guilt. Why do I feel it?

'Tip the boulder over the cliff,' Finley had said. 'That is your guilt.' But it's not so easy.

So why should I feel guilty? Was I to blame for his capture? Or is it because I feel as any mother would feel - that somehow my love should create a protective wall around him?

And I think back to our trip to the rainforest.

If we hadn't had the flat tyre, we wouldn't have passed the old woman at precisely the same time and place where the youths were tormenting her. She would have merely been an old lady we drove past on the road.

But we did stop, and she came with us. And so we took her to the station where the soldiers saw Sabu and recognised the distinctive truck of Mr USA.

If they hadn't seen us, would they have come to Rutubasana anyway? Would they have known that Sabu was there?

Can I ever forgive myself?

Everything has a price, even an act of charity can have reverberations that we can't foretell.

And I think back to the old lady as we watched the spider spin the web above us in the forest.

We all have a golden thread in our lives.

Am I following mine? Did I follow it then, when we first picked her up? When I met Sabu and formed such a close bond? Did I have a choice?

Despite the consequences, would I have turned my back on Hana? Was Moh's accident a result of my actions or was it just chance?

My head goes round and round. Whirling with questions.

But at the core of it all, despite trying to 'throw the boulder over the cliff,' I will always feel the weight of guilt when I think of Sabu. That I couldn't help him. That somehow, somehow I should have found a way.

After all, isn't that what I should do? Always find a way to help? Isn't that what the old lady said? Isn't that my dharma?

CHAPTER 49

It's Spring now in London and new leaves on the urban trees are unfurling into a hundred shades of green. Every morning, when I open our thick curtains, I drink in the vision of the pink fluffy cherry blossom and the expanse of verdant grass that lies in the communal gardens below our new home. Compared to Rutubasana, the view is small and meagre but I'm happy now with moderate pleasures and I find I'm slipping into an easy contentment.

I bless Valeria in my heart for saving us from a closed, grey life inhabiting a high-rise apartment in some nameless red brick tower block. The vision of the free bird and the stained orange sofa on our visit to Hackney haunts me, and I count myself one of the lucky ones.

Little Moh is walking well. Every day, when the weather allows, Ashika and I take him to play in the garden. Finley has given him a bright red plastic lawn mower which he likes to push around the paths, gathering speed until he inevitably trips over his feet and tumbles onto the ground. But he rarely cries. He just picks himself up, clasps the handles with his chubby hands and continues on his mission, only to repeat the whole process again.

Sometimes I think I detect a limp in Moh's gait but it's momentary and the doctors aren't concerned. The incredible reparative talents of the young body, one doctor said.

At times I see Jack watching as I play with Moh and I feel self-conscious. Is he assessing my love for our son? I don't want to be judged. I want to let this newly opened channel flow naturally. I need to love without thinking, without regrets, without fear. So in a way, I'm glad Jack stays away for most of the week as he teaches in the boys' school in the suburbs. This leaves me to bond naturally with our son whilst Ashika and I try to re-adjust our roles in Moh's life.

Luckily, I don't only exist with Ashika and Moh for company during the week as I believe I would find my mother-in-law suffocating. Most probably I would lose patience. As it is, I have the relief of Padma's company for some nights during the week. Sometimes Shai will join us as well, when she has occasional work in the centre of London. Their parents have finally moved to Hounslow, but they share their house with another family and life is crowded and noisy.

Padma's training in the hairdresser salon in Knightsbridge is going well, and she enjoys it. As the salon is only half an hour's walk from our home, and travel is expensive from Hounslow, it makes sense for her to stay with us several nights a week. On the nights she is due to stay, I look forward to the click of the front door as she lets herself in. Her lively company always brightens my evenings.

Shai doesn't yet have any permanent employment, but she gets the odd job, usually closer to where we live than her own home. When both the girls come to stay, we laugh until my sides ache and Ashika will take herself to bed early with a cup of camomile tea, a few mutterings on her tongue about our childish behaviour.

The sisters sleep in the large low attic at the top of the building where I've placed my mother's sewing machine under the roof light. Shai continues to teach me dressmaking skills which I practice when Moh sleeps in the afternoon. Every time she visits, she inspects my work and advises me how I can improve. I now know the basics of most techniques and recently completed a little sailor's outfit for Moh, with French seams and applied navy blue binding. Dicken was right after all. I would end up making outfits for our young son.

A few weeks ago, Valeria and John took us to The Royal Opera House to see the ballet. It was the appreciation of these arts that first nurtured the love between our two friends and Valeria wanted me to experience the wonder of my first ballet at Covent Garden. Anthony Dowell and Antoinette Sibly were to perform in The Sleeping Beauty. A rare occasion, she said, and she was pleased that she had managed to secure tickets in the private box that John's company holds.

'You must only see the best,' she said. 'There's nothing worse than your first experience of ballet being tainted by awkward dancers thumping around the stage. It will put you off for life. It must be like the first taste of nectar. Clear and perfect.'

I had not heard of the stars she mentioned, nor had I ever seen a ballet but, from the moment we stepped out of the taxi and walked into the palatial building I was awestruck by the lavish opulence of the theatre. We were in another world. Deep pile carpets and intricate plasterwork covered in gold leaf. Perfumed ladies wearing evening gowns, draped with fur coats; these, in turn, being handed over to the scrawny cloakroom attendant who seemed to be drowning in fluff and hair.

Valeria had warned me that I should wear evening dress for the occasion, but my wardrobe is meagre, and we have no spare money to waste on an outfit I may never wear again. I knew I could wear my sari, but something made me falter. Was I ashamed of who I was? Was I ashamed of where I was from? I knew in my heart that this was not the case. But I also knew that I want to break free. I want to be part of this life, here, now.

I cast my mind back to the black lady I witnessed in the perfume department of the store, when we first arrived in London. Her control of the situation, her energy, her confidence. She was a woman of today. The way she dressed, her hairstyle, the sense of her owning the space around her. I wanted to be like that lady, the one who never even noticed the newly arrived refugees passing silently behind her back.

So I took out my father's silk wedding jacket and went up the stairs to the attic and sat at my mother's sewing machine. And there, under the pale London daylight, I proceeded to expand on my new tailoring skills. Once the sleeves were shortened, the shoulders narrowed, and the waist nipped in, the jacket looked tailored and sleek. I bought some black velvet and, with Shai's help, made a pair of slim trousers to wear beneath the golden silk kurta. The outfit was then finished off with some high black shoes that I borrowed from Padma and a black feather boa from Kensington Market.

Jack gave me a quizzical look as I joined him in our hallway at the start of the evening.

'A new style?' he said.

'My own,' I replied as I clicked my purse shut.

I had sprayed the last of my Channel no 5 perfume behind my ears and my hair was glossy and sharp. I really did feel like a modern woman.

Valeria was right. Ballet dancers are rare and wonderful creatures - like 'chir batti' or 'will-o'-the-wisp' they say in English. They are more spirit than body and appear to float on the music as their fluid movements express every detail of the story. The orchestra, the lights, the colour and costumes made me feel as if I was flying on the wind with the dancers themselves. Finally, I could understand that special glint in Valeria's eyes when she spoke of ballet.

The performance was long, until the point where Princess Aurora found the spinning wheel and pricked her finger on the poisoned needle. As she fell into a deep sleep, the safety curtain descended, and the lights came on. Valeria led us to the bar where she had arranged for drinks to be waiting our arrival. A wise plan, as other members of the audience stood three deep at the counter attempting to be served.

We were discussing the process of ballerinas learning to stand on points, when a well-dressed lady standing to our right caught my eye.

'I do absolutely love your outfit. So original.'

'Thank you.' I answered, flattered by the compliment coming from someone so elegantly dressed.

She was about to say something further when she noticed Valeria at my side and a look of recognition crossed her face.

'Mrs Lake? Valeria Lake isn't it?'

Valeria nodded serenely.

'Do you remember me? We were on the Dr Barnardo's committee together a few years ago.'

'Yes, of course, Mrs…?'

'Osborne. Margaret Osborne. I seem to remember you were very good at keeping us focused. Too much chit chat, you said. You were definitely right. We needed to keep our minds on the job. William!' she called to a rotund man who was approaching us, a glass in each hand.

'William, do you remember Mrs Lake? We were on the orphanage charity together, a while ago. Do you remember?'

'Yes I do, indeed I do. A pleasure to see you after so long. And you are? He asked, looking me up and down.

Valeria stepped in to make the introductions, and pleasantries were passed until a further acquaintance of Mrs Osborne joined us, together with her partner. Soon, our swelling group had started to obstruct one of the doors leading to the lower balcony.

'Did I hear you saying you were from Africa?' asked a dark-haired lady with a hairstyle similar to Padma's.

'Yes,' I answered. 'Uganda.'

'How very exotic! Do you have some good wildlife in Uganda?'

'Yes, we do.'

'How wonderful. Actually, wait a moment, I think a friend of ours has been to Uganda.'

'Really?'

'Hang on. Joseph!' she called across to a tall man on the other side of our group. 'Jo, where was it that the Simpsons went for their safari recently? Was it Uganda?'

'Uganda? That doesn't sound familiar. No, I don't think it was.'

A loud bell rang and Valeria touched my shoulder.

'That means it's the end of the interval and we should be getting back to our seats.'

'Wait, I know,' I heard the same voice again.

'I remember now. It wasn't Uganda. It was Kenya. They went on a private safari. Had some American guide. Very good apparently, knowledgeable. Had a little boy as an assistant.'

'Really? Kenya?'

'That's right.'

'And the boy? Was he his son?'

'Don't think so. A little Indian boy. Told wonderful stories apparently.'

Why was my hearing dimming as I heard the blood coursing through my veins?

'Lovely meeting you…' the wife was saying, but I didn't hear any more.

Dark spots were growing in my eyes, getting larger and merging with further black circles that would greet and overlap each other. I swayed and grabbed hold of Valeria's arm.

'Are you all right Birdie? You look like you're about to

faint. Here, sit on this chair. Take in some deep breaths. It will pass. The feeling will pass,' I heard her faint voice say.

And I remembered another seat, a long time ago, in another life. A small hand that reached out to guide me. A hand of kindness and love that taught me many things.

All these months I had mourned Sabu. All this time I had been unable to forgive myself for failing him. I felt sure he had been killed, and I had tried to turn away from gory imaginings of his end. I had surrendered to despair and hopelessness.

But Sabu was made of stronger stuff. He was a survivor. Now, somehow, he was with Dicken in Kenya. I felt certain that this was true.

And the realisation alighted on me, as soft as a downy feather. I had got it all so wrong. I always felt that I should have saved Sabu, but now I realised that, in fact, he had saved me.

For was it not Sabu who taught me how to love as a mother could love a son? Without the fear, without the conscience. Was it not Sabu who brought joy into my life, even if only briefly? I knew I should rejoice in that.

And, as I sat on the velvet chair in the lavish Royal Opera House in this city of London, it became crystal clear to me.

The thread that draws out from the spool of our lives is not merely a solitary strand. It is interwoven with the gossamer filaments from all the people who enter our existence. Some fibres will weaken us, others will help us flourish. Some will teach us fundamental lessons, such as love and strength. So it was with Sabu.

And I think of the old woman in the rainforest and her words as we watched the spider spin the web above our heads. I wanted to know the answers, but her words were riddles, now muffled in my memory. Apart from one thing she said, which I now know to be true.

'You just have to listen to the feel.'

Note from the Author

I do hope you have enjoyed this book and I would be very grateful for any reviews either on Amazon or Goodreads.

Even a small sentence would be really appreciated.

Please visit my website and sign up for the newsletter if you would like to be notified when my next book, involving Birdie, her family and friends, is being published.

www.claireduende.com

ACKNOWLEDGEMENTS

Firstly, I would like to thank my family and friends for their patience and tolerance during the writing of this book. To Di and Ron Aldridge, and Hilary Rogers for their constructive appraisals, and to my lovely beta readers - any mistakes are my own. Thanks also to my reading group, The Albion Book Club. We've had enormous fun over the past twenty years and all the books, whether enjoyed or not, have helped to inspire me. Thanks to Mahmood Mamdani for his book From Citizen to Refugee which told of his placement in a resettlement centre in Kensington Church Street, London. To Yasmin Alibhai-Brown whose book No Place Like Home helped give me an insight into her life as an Asian in Uganda and England. To an unknown journalist in some newspaper archive (I can't remember where) who wrote of a little Asian boy who didn't seem to belong to anybody - my inspiration for Sabu, and to Urmila Patel for her book Out of Uganda in 90 days. And finally, to all the displaced Ugandan Asians – this is for you.

Printed in Great Britain
by Amazon

72634034R00170